Penelope's Song

A Seventeenth Century Tale for a Twenty-First Century World

To a very dear and extraordinary friend, Linda Gunn

With gratitude, Carol 2019

Carol J. DeMars

ISBN 978-1-64559-180-1 (Paperback)
ISBN 978-1-64559-181-8 (Digital)

With permission
Song of a female Eskimo shaman from *Touch the Earth:*
A Self-Portrait of Indian Existence
Outerbridge & Dienstfrey, 1971, NYC. Copyright T.C. McLuhan
"Trip a trop a troenje" from THE MATCHLOCK GUN by
Walter D. Edmonds, copyright 1941 by Walter D. Edmonds,
text. Copyright © renewed 1969 by Walter D. Edmonds. Used by
permission of G. P. Putnam's Sons Books for Young Readers, an
imprint of Penguin Young Readers Group, a division of Penguin
Random House LLC.

Art credit
Front cover design by Donald DeMars and permission for use with
Vermeer, Johannes (1632-1675). *Girl Reading a Letter by an Open
Window,* Ca. 1659. Oil on canvas. Inv. 1336.
Photo Credit: bpk Bildagentur / Gemaeldegalerie Alte Meister,
Staatliche Kunstammmlungen, Dresden, Germany /
Herbert Boswank / Art Resource, N.Y.

The characters and events have been fictionalized based on history.

Covenant Books, Inc.
11661 Hwy 707
Murrells Inlet, SC 29576
www.covenantbooks.com

To the healers, the dreamers, the lovers, believers

and with gratitude to
my loving husband, Donald, constant companion and
inspirational support, who died prior to publication of
Penelope's Song

and
our beautiful daughters, Genevieve and Fabienne.
Their endearing qualities guided my portrayals of
Sarah Elizabeth Kent, Penelope, and Lady Deborah Moody.

REFORMATION BEGINS

Path to Liberty of Conscience in Penelope's Song and Our Twenty-First Century World

1517 Wittenberg, Germany
Martin Luther issues his ninety-five theses against indulgences and other papal offenses. The Protestant Reformation begins.

1579 Utrecht, Holland—The Union of Utrecht signed by the United Provinces of Holland, Zeeland, Utrecht, Gelderland, Friesland, and Groningen—Article XIII
"Each person shall remain free, especially in his religion, and that no one shall be persecuted or investigated because of their religion, as is provided in the Pacification of Ghent."

1642 Siena, Italy
Galileo Galilei, first great scientist of the modern age, died under house arrest. Nine years earlier, accused of heresy by the Office of the Inquisitor in Rome, he was forced to renounce his proof and writings that Copernicus was right that the earth revolved around the sun and was not the center of the universe.

1642–1646 England—The First English Civil War
King Charles I raised his standard at Nottingham, the official beginning of the Civil War. Puritan leaning Parliamentarians of Essex, Suffolk, Norfolk, Cambridgeshire, and Hertfordshire counties, region of many Puritans, banded together against the Church of England and Royalists of Charles I in 1642 escalating the conflict.

1644—London, England
Roger Williams secured a charter from the English *Parliamentary Commissioners for Plantations* that officially created the first English colony founded on the principle of soul liberty comprised of Warwick, Portsmouth, Newport, and Providence in Narragansett Bay, New England.

1646 London, England—Westminster Confession of Faith Adopted— Chapter 20, Part II
"God alone is Lord of the conscience, and hath left it free from doctrines and commandments of men which are in anything contrary to his word, or beside it, in matters of faith or worship. So that to believe such doctrines, or to obey such commandments out of conscience, is to betray true liberty of conscience; and the requiring of an implicit faith and an absolute and blind obedience, is to destroy liberty of conscience, and reason also."

1648—North Western Germany—Treaty of Westphalia
This treaty ended the Thirty Years War between Roman Catholicism and Protestants and countries against countries— Austrian Habsburgs and Spain, Bohemia, German Princes, France, Sweden, Poland, Denmark, Russia, Switzerland and the Netherlands— and redrew the religious and political map of Europe no longer controlled by the Roman Catholic Church. Separate German princes gained their sovereignty while Holland and Switzerland their full independence from Catholic Spain.

1649—Maryland Toleration Act—An Act Concerning Religion

"And whereas the inforceing of the conscience in matters of Religion hath frequently fallen out to be of dangerous consequence…that noe person or persons whatsoever in this Province…professing to believe in Jesus Christ shall henceforth bee in any waiess troubled, molested or discountenanced for or in respect of his or her religion nor in the free exercise thereof within this province…nor in any way compelled to the belief or exercise of any other religion against his or her consent…"

1657—Vlissingen (Flushing), Lange Eylandt, Nieuw Nederland—The Flushing Remonstrance

In response to Governor Stuyvesant's persecution of Quakers, the Remonstrance in part states, "The law of love, peace, and liberty in the states extending to Jews, Turks and Egyptians, as they are considered sons of Adam, which is the glory of the outward state of Holland, soe love, peace and liberty, extending to all in Christ Jesus, condemns hatred, war, and bondage…in whatsoever form, name or title he appears in, whether Presbyterian, Independent, Baptist or Quaker, but shall be glad to see anything of God in them, desiring to doe unto all men as we desire all men should doe unto us…for our Saviour sayeth this is the law and the prophets."

1663—London—Rhode Island and Providence Plantations Charter of King Charles II

"That no person within the said colony, at any time hereafter shall be in any wise molested, punished, disquieted, or called in question for any differences in matters of religion, but that at all times hereafter, freely and fully have and enjoy his and their own judgments and consciences, in matters of religious concernments…and not using this liberty to licentiousness and profaneness, nor to the civil injury or outward disturbance of others, any law, statute, or clause therein contained, or to be contained, usage or custom of this realm."

1664—New York (including New Jersey), English Colony—Monmouth Patent

English Governor Colonel Richard Nicolls by authority of the Duke of York proclaimed, "In all Territories of his Royal Highness liberty of conscience is allowed, provided such liberty is not converted to licentiousness, or the disturbance of others in the exercise of the protestant religion". Such was granted to the twelve men of the 1665 Monmouth Patent at Sandy Hook Bay, East Jersey, and their heirs.

1776—Williamsburg, Virginia—The Virginia Declaration of Rights—Article 16

"That religion, or the duty which we owe to our Creator, and the manner of discharging it, can be directed only by reason and conviction, not by force or violence; and therefore all men are equally entitled to the free exercise of religion, according to the dictates of conscience."

1787—Philadelphia—Second Continental Congress—The Northwest Ordinance

"No person, demeaning himself in a peaceable and orderly manner, shall ever be molested on account of his mode of worship or religious sentiments, in the said territory."

1788—Philadelphia—Second Continental Congress Ratified Article VI of the Constitution

"No religious test shall ever be required as a qualification to any office or public trust under the United States."

1791—Philadelphia—Constitution of the United States of America—Amendment I

"Congress shall make no law respecting an establishment of religion, or of prohibiting the free exercise thereof."

1978—Washington, D.C.—Public Law 95-341, American Indian Religious Freedom Act

President Jimmy Carter signed into law "That henceforth it shall be the policy of the United States to protect and preserve for American Indians their inherent right of freedom to believe, express, and exercise the traditional religions of the American Indian, Eskimo, Aleut, and Native Hawaiians, including but not limited to access to sites, use, and possession of sacred objects, and the freedom to worship through ceremonials and traditional rites."

1992—The Vatican, Rome

Pope John Paul II formally acknowledges the Church's condemnation of Galileo in 1633 that the historic clash of reason and dogma, science and faith was in error.

2016—Evangelical Lutheran Church in America to the Muslim American Community

Reverend Elizabeth A. Eaton, Presiding Bishop, "Together with you, we are committed to building a stronger society based on the dignity of each human being, the value of diversity, the holiness of creation and the common good."

2017—Worldwide—500th Anniversary of the Protestant Reformation

Penelope's Song

PART 1

Amsterdam, Holland, United Provinces of the Netherlands, 1643

The Laws of a country are necessarily connected
with everything belonging to the
people of it; so that a thorough knowledge of
them, and of their progress, would
inform us of everything that was most useful
to be known about them; and one
of the greatest imperfections of historians in general, is owing to their
ignorance of the law.

—Priestley's *Lecture on History*
and General Policy, 1788

CHAPTER 1

Reverend Dr. James Kent's Study

Sarah Elizabeth poked her head out the window of her uncle's spacious four-story gabled town house. The pot of tulips Aunt Alice left on the *stoep* of her father's much smaller dwelling early that morning signaled it was time to visit the grave of Sarah's mother, Mary. Long awaited crocuses, hyacinths and daffodils—the first regal harbingers of spring in Amsterdam—had already thrust their amethyst gems, brilliant sapphire scepters, and golden crowns through the ice-crusted ground and then all too soon faded. In turn, Holland's beloved tulips—their crown jewels—burst into full bloom. The Lowlanders's floral love affair reawakened as vibrant yellows and romantic reds, passionate pinks and innocent whites courted attention. It was their time, and it was Sarah's time to feel exquisitely alive.

When the first winter arrived chilling the ground after her mother's death, Sarah asked her father for a warm blanket to cover her grave. "She will be so cold, Papa, and we must do something." Reverend Dr. James Kent nestled the little girl in his arms, gently wiping her tears and caressing her soft curly locks.

"Your mother is like the beautiful flowers we all love so much when spring arrives. God, in his wonderful wisdom, gives us amazing surprises, Sarah Elizabeth. He always knows exactly what his creation needs. The crocus corms and daffodil, hyacinth and tulip bulbs need the cold ground where they sleep during the winter months and where we can't see them, just like your mother. We do not see the quiet change that gives them the strength and vitality to come out of hiding and makes the sap to wake up the trees when the days grow longer and the world starts to warm up again.

"Do you remember when you asked what happened to the leaves last fall when they all dried up, fell to the ground, and Amsterdam began to grow cold with our first frost?"

"Yes, Papa, I do remember."

"And I said that the bright, warm sun of spring and summer follow even the coldest winter?"

"Yes, Papa, I do remember."

"The brittle, fallen leaves die and enrich the soil so that new shiny green ones and cherry blossoms can take their place to dress up the bare trees in elegant new clothes when it's spring again after the cold passes."

"Yes, Papa."

"Winter always was a time of quiet, hidden thoughts for your mother too, but when spring finally arrived, she also blossomed with fresh exuberance more alive and beautiful every year. That's what you need to remember, my precious daughter. Your mother will be that lovely person again, like the tulips we love so much, in God's good time in his good place." Sarah's love affair with flowers and trees and other plants began that day filling her with the happy thoughts about life she needed to cope with her mother's absence. Her father always said just the right words. Wisdom never failed him.

Sidewalks and stoeps were already swept and scrubbed clean when Sarah closed the door behind her and stepped into the chaos and cacophony of children's play—chatter and giggles, hobbyhorses and hoops, drums and bugles—always familiar and predictable. She wend her way through the little ones and their toys and across the busy cobblestone street and footbridge over the canal to her father's simple, narrow town house, yet every moment in that space made grand by the large spirit of the man who lived there. The young woman, scarcely more than a girl, briefly reflected, "It's a good day, a very good day—a bright, cheery kind of day."

Dirck seemed to be in a hurry to leave Dr. James Kent's study after his lessons and avoided looking directly at Sarah when she brought in her father's noonday meal and beer as she did every day.

Humph, she thought, he didn't even say "Hello".

"What is going on with Dirck, Papa? He isn't himself today, all in a rush and a huff to get out of here, and a little red between the ears if I do say so."

"Sarah, we need to talk," her father replied. "I will not be able to tutor Dirck much longer."

"So that is why he is flustered?"

"Well, yes, and not exactly."

"But you just said that he cannot continue his studies with you much longer."

"My dear, precious daughter, we need to talk about your future. We all come to a crossroads in our lives at just about the right time—according to God's good time."

"I just don't get what you are talking about, Father. What crossroads? I certainly have no plans to cross any road other than the one I always do between our two homes. I'm quite happy where we are, and what does Dirck have to do with all this anyway?"

"Sarah, you know that Dirck is the fourth generation of very proud Dutch cabinetmakers and now some of the most sought-after finish carpentry specialists in the shipping industry. You also know that when his father married an English woman who came from an educated family, not unlike your aunt's situation, she made use of the Dutch custom of prenuptial agreements to include funds for their future children's instruction in English.

"Of all their children, however, Dirck showed special promise in his academic studies. Apparently, he was quite miserable and out of place in his father's shop after he completed his public school education. When that did not sort itself out with time, his mother, quite an endearing and persuasive woman, finally secured her husband's reluctant permission for Dirck's advanced study with me for three years. She wanted her brilliant son to further pursue Latin, the classics, philosophy, and theology in hope that he might earn a place at the University of Leyden and do well. Dirck's father gave his consent but with the stipulation he still had to continue his apprenticeship in the family trade twenty hours a week."

"Yes, I do know that, Papa. You've always taken an interest in all your students, but it was obvious you thought he was exceptional, and I think there is a bond between the two of you that may be absent between Dirck and his own father. It was only when Dirck was here that you allowed me to join you both while you studied the world trade maps that Aunt Alice's husband gave to you for your students. I especially love the beautifully illustrated one of the *wilden* rowing their peculiar little boats alongside our Dutch ships in the harbor of *Nieuw Amsterdam* and the one with the exquisite drawings of those faraway plants and animals.

"Much too often such images dance around in my head bumping up against what I should be thinking about. Sometimes I fall asleep wondering about the strange people who live in those places and your insistence that for them and for us, it's all about relationship, knowing where and how we fit into the whole no matter who we are or where we live. When I was just an infant and our family so hastily had to leave our home in England, I guess that's why our family quickly fit into the whole of our adopted country here. Perhaps that is one of the reasons why my aunt and Dirck's mother could fall in love with Dutchmen and embrace their different beliefs and customs. Not everyone can do that and most haven't."

"Yes, that's true, and I noticed how much you enjoy studying those maps. They are fascinating. No wonder the Dutch here prominently display them in their homes. You both had so many questions I couldn't answer."

"Father, you take such pride in helping Dirck prepare for his exams at the University of Leyden. From what you told me, he has such dreams about that. It is his passion. He couldn't bear the thought of giving up the university to only pursue finish carpentry with his father and older brothers for the rest of his life. I know you were hoping to have more time beyond the three years originally contracted because you have so much to give and have high hopes for such an able student. I've often thought you saw in him something of yourself when you were a young man."

"I did, and so I thought until today."

"What changed all that? It's not like him. He's so serious and focused. You are such a fine tutor that I know Dirck would pass the exams when you thought he was ready if his father would only let him take them."

"Yes, Sarah, but Dirck's father now insists that he is needed more than ever in their shop. We are situated here in the heart of the Dutch Empire—every quay and the entire bay of the *Zuyder Zee* filled to capacity with naval war ships, merchant *fluyts*, and other trading vessels. The *Veerenigde Oostindische Compagnie* is the wealthiest and most powerful commercial force in the world. It and the *West-Indische Compagnie* that trades up and down the Atlantic Coasts of Africa and the *West Indisches* depend on the Province of Holland to provide those ships on which their global supremacy relies.

"Furthermore, Dirck's father was anxious to recoup the losses he never fully recovered when the wild, reckless, speculative bubble of the tulip market burst. His father's brother-in-law, despite his advice, got in at a bad time just before the craze peaked and then abruptly collapsed. All sorts of otherwise reasonable merchants and tradesmen were bereft of all common sense and lost thousands of *guilders*. His cautious father was one of the few who didn't lose all his hard earned savings and bankrupted. He deemed even the reckless loss of a single *styver* foolishness, but he was compelled to rescue from dire poverty the family of his only sister whom he dearly loved. After that he became all the more steadfast in his resolve that not only is the family business finish carpentry—what they've always been good at—it is their only business.

"Dirck always knew that his father considered my young scholar's dream to attend the university just another useless costly endeavor that would do nothing to advance the family's standing in the shipbuilding guilds of Amsterdam at a time when the young man was needed in the workshop. Given all that, it was hard for him to release Dirck from full time commitment to the family business and must love his wife dearly, respecting her prenuptial contract as he did. Clearly Dirck understood all that and diligently applied himself with the dream that he might obtain a grant from the University of Leyden and not impose further."

"Hum, this isn't sounding very good… Good for the family but not good for Dirck."

"Last week, in spite of impassioned pleas from his mother, he was told that he must now work full time under the direct supervision of his eldest brother."

"Oh no, this is so unfair. He has so much promise and always studied hard. There has never been a student who mastered Latin so quickly and responded with so much depth to your questions. You always said he was very brilliant."

Dr. Kent explained, "Dirck knows too well how tightly the guilds control all the trades with standards and rules that are unassailable. He will have to work as a full time apprentice for years and can't possibly support a wife and children. When he becomes a journeyman, it may still be many more years before he will be financially able to marry. It would take a long time to gain the expertise and pay the steep fees the guild requires to be a master craftsman like his father. In any case, the days are long and hard, and any further study will be impossible.

"Even if his father permitted him to attend the University, it will also be three to seven years before he can fulfill all the requirements for advanced degrees and actual experience to earn a post decent enough to earn the income necessary to support a family. In England after my first wife died suddenly, I buried myself in study and pursued advanced studies at Cambridge with single-minded intensity knowing that I could ill afford to get married then given I was not independently wealthy."

"But, Father, I realize that young men would not speak about such things to women especially one as young like myself, but it never occurred to me that Dirck was even thinking about marriage yet, and what has that to do with you and me?"

"Sarah Elizabeth, he is hopelessly in love with you and can't bear to be without you."

"What, what are you saying, Father?"

"Dirck loves you very much and is most unhappy about what his father wants for his life. He decided to leave Holland and sail across the ocean to *Nieuw Nederland* with or without his permission, cut his own course, and not held captive under his oldest brother's critical eye. He also learned that Dutch citizens there have sent letters of complaint because there is only one school master and not a very good one at that. You know the Dutch in the Northern Provinces are proud of their public education since gaining their freedom from the Spanish Catholic Inquisition and suppression of their lands and lives. Influenced by Dr. Martin Luther and his foundation of *sola scriptura* as our sacred authority and not the Pope or the Crown, the Dutch Reformed and other Protestants consider literacy a religious necessity for boys and girls no matter where they live. It's the basis for who we are and what we believe.

"Dirck decided that if he can't attend the University, perhaps the need for schoolmasters across the ocean is a calling and opportunity meant especially for him. Woodworking skills he has already acquired will be useful too and in great demand in a growing settlement. There will be more opportunity for a young man to advance and provide for his family unlike here where the rigid rules for craftsmen are stringent and competition great. His heart yearns for the fulfillment of the dreams that he cannot realize in his father's trade. He knows he will be bound and stifled by its rigid structure and brothers that will wring every last dream from the person he knows himself to be."

"Papa, this is crazy. Dirck and I have only exchanged a few polite pleasantries all this time. There has never been any talk of marriage or any hint of our lives together. Besides, you seem to tire more easily lately, and the long ocean voyage would be too arduous. I would never leave you here alone. Respectfully, Father, I can't imagine such plans, and this conversation has me most frightfully distraught."

"Sarah, Elizabeth, you are the light of my life, and we are very dear to each other. Your future happiness means everything to me, and that is why we must talk about these things. It is I who must leave you."

19

"Have friends called you back to England? The Civil War sounds ghastly. It's all the talk here because the wars on the Continent have already gone on too long and too horrible and now this across the Channel. It has Hollanders worried. Amsterdam and other Dutch cities continue to receive refugees from our homeland and other countries. You told me that King James and the Church of England no longer permitted your congregation to hold services, and they did not take kindly to the ideas you expressed in your lectures and pamphlets and that under his son King Charles the situation even more dire for nonconformists like yourself. Mother, Aunt Alice, and you were forced to leave when I was just an infant. Amsterdam has been good to us, and you have been able to write and teach without fear of punishment."

"I will not be going to Nieuw Nederland or England either, Sarah. You yourself mentioned to me that your aunt's brother-in-law, the physician from Leyden, stayed with their family for a few days when he came to attend Dr. Nicolaes Tulp's anatomy lectures recently. That fascinated you but especially the medicinal herbs from all over the world at the University's *Hortus Botanicus* that he talked so much about, much older and larger than the more recent botanical garden here. What you did not know was that while your aunt kept you quite busy, she arranged for Willem's brother to examine me."

"Well then, Father, does that mean that you were offered a position at the University? If that were the case, certainly Dirck would never give up a chance to study there, and you would somehow find a way to help his father realize that there is another way for his youngest son to bring honor to the family."

"Sweet, darling daughter, you must clearly understand that my days are already numbered, and I will not be leaving here, but I will be leaving. Your mother was much younger than I when we married. I am old now and not well, and we both know you have been concerned and knew something was amiss. We talked sparingly of it because I did not want to trouble you unnecessarily with how grave my condition was thought to be until I was certain. Alice's brother-in-law confirmed the diagnosis of the excellent doctor I saw here a few weeks ago, and he cannot help either. I am not going to get better and am weaker every day. My time appears shorter than I hoped."

"But, Father, I can take care of you and will not leave you, ever! This can't be!"

"Sarah, the kindest thing I can do for you now is to tell you this truth and begin the necessary arrangements for your future while I am alive, and we are all in control of the choices we want to make. Your mother did not get to watch her little girl grow up, nor meet her husband, and cuddle our grandchildren. I must at least make sure before it is too late that the man you marry is a match for you in every way if you truly love each other."

"Dirck and I have only been with each other briefly in your study with you. We have never even chatted together let alone court. Really, we scarcely know each other."

"When your mother died, her sister Alice and her new Dutch husband were kind to take you in so I could tutor and write full-time. You needed more than a father alone could provide, and they did not yet have the many children that have since been a blessing to their marriage. She raised you as she would her own daughter, and when you were older, she very much appreciated your helping hands. We have all admired how you have such a way with their little ones. Your center is strong and self-assured, but you are also kind and loving. I am concerned that as wonderful as your Aunt Alice is, because you are so caring and responsible, that you will remain with her family, striving to meet their needs and never really have a life of your own."

"Papa, at the proper time Aunt Alice would want me to get married and have my own family, I'm sure."

"When I am gone, Alice's husband will be your only adult male relative and must assume full responsibility for you according to Dutch law. Although he is a good man he now has many children. His very demanding work sometimes requires travel, and he is accustomed to making decisions quickly and authoritatively. I can't be confident that he will have the time or keen sensitivity that I, as your father, feel for you nor that you will be completely free to meet and choose a husband for a family of your own."

"How can you be so sure, Papa?"

"I can't, but you are your mother's daughter and like her respect-ful and reverent, but there is also a barely suppressed wildness and inquisitive spirit within as irrepressible as the lovely curls that escape your *kaper*. I can't bear the thought of you not entering entirely of your own free will into a lifetime commitment. Your life with your aunt and uncle's family would be secure and safe, but Willem may feel differently about the best suitor for you. He will face many pres-sures as your guardian."

"Father, I have always completely trusted you, but I can scarcely let you go on."

"Dearest, Sarah, it is because I love you dearly that I must con-tinue and trust you will grasp the full import of what I say.

"Dirck never overtly expressed any affection for you. As my stu-dent, he knew that would be highly improper. He suppressed his most private thoughts from you and me and everyone else. It was his father's insistence that he cannot continue his studies and must now commit fully to the family business and what I just shared with you about my medical prognosis that evoked such spontaneous outburst of both grief and love that even I was stunned. The floodgates so burst through his usual reserve and deference that his feelings must be very deep and real. In a single moment, he realized he could lose his dream, his tutor, and you."

"All these revelations in just one afternoon, Papa…"

"You must admit, Sarah Elizabeth, that you sometimes blushed when there were glances between the two of you that have not escaped me. No wonder he rushed out of here, could not greet you, and as you said, 'red between the ears.'

"It seems to me that you found more reason to leave your aunt's house to hover here to bring me *hutsepot* with *klapstuk* and spiced *kojkjes* before Dirck left than you ever did with any of my other students. You waited until they departed, and then we enjoyed our noonday meal together and chatted about the books I gave you. We always had such good talks, but suddenly it was as if I wasn't the only male presence you desired. I think you thought I did not notice. Am I right, Sarah? Do you have feelings for Dirck too?"

"Yes, Father, I do. I wake up every morning looking forward to my precious time with you, but my heart does flutter a bit when I see him from Auntie's window walking toward your stoep. But now my heart is truly broken because I cannot live without you and cannot bear to hear talk of such things. I would give up a hundred suitors if it meant I did not have to leave you. You can't really mean it's all so final."

"Dearest one, I often imagined you with lots of children of your own and yearned to hold them in my arms because only you survived your mother's pregnancies, and you were everything to us. Dirck is a good man and although young sees more and farther than fifty good men, and he loves you, Sarah Elizabeth. Real freedom is in knowing who you are and then moving forward honestly in the direction of your God-given dream because it is the assignment he has given you for your life. It is the *vocatio* or calling that Dr. Martin Luther taught and that we have talked about.

"As I first told you so long ago when you were a little girl, 'God, in his wonderful wisdom gives us amazing surprises, and he always knows exactly what his creation needs.' It's there for us to seek and find, and I also confidently believe you and Dirck were meant for each other. We certainly have had our surprises this week, haven't we?"

"We certainly have, Father, we certainly have!"

"The sudden dramatic turn of events that we each encountered this week overrode our customary way of responding, Sarah. The veil of secrets, like the cold, gray winter, that hid who each of us thought we were, the false vision for our lives, was torn asunder by this bright spring morning. Honesty won over propriety, and none of us will be the same again. We become most free when we are most honest. This is the essence of our sacred scripture, 'The truth shall set you free.' It is when we fully face the death of our old selves that we open to the eternal and become most alive. You can give in to what others decide for you or you can lose the life you knew to activate what God planted in your heart before you were born. Even though the world tells us otherwise, you are free to decide. The Crown and Church of England denied us and others that freedom, and so we left, leaving most of our worldly goods and home behind not knowing the future that beckoned, yet one we also chose. You are a very young lady, and even by Dutch standards, there are customs your uncle must honor that will affect your future and capacity to freely choose."

"My dear papa, I will marry Dirck while you can still bless our marriage. You must perform the ceremony, and we will never leave you until you first leave us. God willing, we will have lots of children with the names in our family Bible that you and mother always wanted. Now I need you to put your arms around me and hold me ever so tight."

Father and daughter collapsed into each other's arms and wept.

CHAPTER 2

Aunt Alice Gets the News

When tulip bulbs were finally available and affordable again after the Tulip Bubble burst, they returned to their time-honored place in every garden and window box. Aunt Alice suggested planting them at the grave of Sarah's mother every fall. She thought it would be a nice tradition to help heal the loss for all of them, a tangible symbol of the circle of life, of remembrance, and reflective of her mother's beauty that her niece could touch and smell. The family ritual added to the excited anticipation of the first flowers that heralded the beginning of spring and the promise that their beloved tulips would soon burst the bonds of their winter captivity. When they appeared, it was time to visit Mary's grave again.

Every fall, Alice and Sarah visited the flower market to purchase more bulbs, and Alice taught her niece how to diagram where they planted each variety and color noting the date and her age. With the special art supplies her uncle found for the girl, each spring her drawings of the brilliant blossoms became more detailed and expressive of Sarah's gift for observation and artistic talent. It was a special time, just the three of them, Reverend Dr. James Kent, Sarah Elizabeth, and Aunt Alice—a time to remember how Mary was special to each of them.

When they planted the bulbs last fall, none of them could have imagined how different this spring day at the gravesite would be from all the others. James Kent, with all the pastoral, fatherly compassion he could muster gently began to tell Alice about the conversations that took place in his study the day before. Alice knew from Willem's brother that the prognosis of her dead sister's husband was very serious, but she was not prepared for all the sudden decisions about her niece's future.

"James, I'm stunned. Sarah Elizabeth has never even hinted that she might care for someone, and now she is practically betrothed, married, and on her way to some far-off forsaken outpost in the West-Indisches! And they are both too young. I don't believe what I'm hearing. She is my sister's only child whom I've cared for like my own, all that I have of the beautiful sister I adored. Sarah lights up our home like her mother did when we were growing up. She is my sunshine in this often gray world.

"My worry for you, James, was profound. I refused to believe we would lose you too, our rock, our ever solid soul, and now Sarah Elizabeth is going to board a ship with a young man I don't even know and never to be seen again? Frankly, I'm not sure if I'm angry, alarmed, filled with unspeakable grief, or just too shocked to know what I feel. The three of us is all that remains of our family from England. I love Amsterdam. I love my husband, and I love our children but took it for granted that you both would always be part of our home here too. I can't deal with this. This is impossible, unacceptable. You can't be serious."

"Alice, when I returned from Leyden to find my wife dead from another late-term miscarriage and already buried, my heart was torn asunder. You know how inconsolable I was and our poor little Sarah Elizabeth without her dear, precious mother. I should have been with them. It was you who saved us, who found the path through the darkness for all our sakes when this happened to our already small family. It was you who convinced your sister that danger was imminent in England and that we must leave at once. You have never failed us."

"James, I love you and Sarah as much as my own family. Here at Mary's gravesite twice a year it has always been just the four of us, the memory of her and us. What shall I now do? Surely, this is a hasty, ill-conceived plan so unlike you, James. You have always been

26

measured and realistic. You must reconsider. This is not what was supposed to be."

"Dear Sister Alice, it is a hasty plan but not ill-conceived. Because of the professionalism that I insisted on, you know that Sarah Elizabeth has only rarely been permitted to listen in on lessons with the students I tutor and never to interact with them. They were my students, not her friends, and she always understood how this relationship must be. Dirck, however, is different from any student I've ever had, a most exceptional young man. There was a connection that began between the two of them from the very first that neither ever gave voice to, but I could feel it in the air. They both respected the standards established from the beginning.

"When I shared with Dirck how grave my condition had become and his father gave the ultimatum that his studies would have to end for him to pursue the family trade full-time, all the long repressed emotions burst their bounds. He is deeply in love with Sarah Elizabeth and apparently has been for a long time. He also understands the reality of life in his father's guild now that his studies with me must be over."

"Sarah, is this true? Are you just responding out of concern for your father or do you truly love this young man?"

"Aunt Alice, I never imagined that I would be permitted to have feelings for one of my father's students and if I did that I could share those feelings with anyone. We have to accept losing father, but I also love everything about Dirck and now can't bear to lose them both. Haven't you noticed that I always leave a bit earlier with father's noonday meal than I did with the student who used to come at that time?"

"I just don't understand why we can't all live happily here in Amsterdam, the most wonderful city in all of Europe and a place where people share ideas openly without fear. Why this crazy plan to just pick up and leave for that vast, uncivilized, wild, far-off place and risk everything on a dangerous ocean voyage? Crossing the English Channel was enough for this family. The Vereenigde Oostindische Compagnie has traded profitably in the Far East for decades, but Willem and other merchants have a low opinion of the West-Indische

Compagnie's finance and management of their Nieuw Amsterdam trading post populated by employees, not even a real village or town.

"James, Willem and I would do whatever was necessary to help Sarah and Dirck work out things here with the approval of his parents. What's the big rush? They are both still very young. Why right now?"

"Alice, you and I both know that soon I will be gone. Now is the only time I can ensure this marriage between Dirck and Sarah. They would not be allowed to make a go of it by themselves the way things are here for apprentices in the trades, and his father likely will not think it proper or feasible for him to visit my daughter, the niece of a wealthy merchant. For two decades, young couples have gotten married shortly before they leave here for Nieuw Nederland. Better that than getting married by the ship's master at sea. New worlds are for the energetic young, radical, new ideas and ways of doing things most often from them."

"Not to be disrespectful, James, that you were ordained a minister, but you have no licensed congregation here. Your marriage documents alone will not suffice. We both know that. The law is strict and requires that the couple appear before the Court of *Schepenen* to obtain a certificate for posting of their marriage *banns* for three Sundays. Sarah Elizabeth is barely nineteen and will marry with your consent, and Dirck is younger than the legal age of twenty-five for males. He needs his parents' permission. Certainly his mother would be greatly distressed and his father angry with any hint of such a proposal. They put their trust in you. What about their feelings? How can this be?"

"I am very concerned, but this is between my student and his parents, and I had no idea until yesterday that Dirck had such plans. As a fourth son, he fears it will be long, hard years before he can become his own man here, and apparently his eldest brother treats him with great disdain. I was unable to dissuade him.

"Dirck completely surprised me with his desire to leave for Nieuw Nederland, but in retrospect, something was slowly awakening in him that I didn't foresee. Both he and Sarah were so intrigued by the trading maps that your husband provided, geographical marvels and artistic masterpieces hung with pride in many Dutch homes like yours. Dirck wants to start a new life there with Sarah, and he means to do so with or without her no matter what it takes, but together they will have a better chance of success. Alone, neither will be complete here or there."

"James, I need time to think."

"Not to upset either of you further, but devotion to Sarah Elizabeth and my most promising student is what has kept me going these last few months. We both know his parents would oppose such a marriage or a voyage across the ocean. One way or another, however, he will leave them, and that is their very imperfect predicament. Better this, not a preferable choice but better this.

"My certificate of marriage will have to do. We do not have enough time left for the marriage registration and banns. Only a few ships a year leave here for Nieuw Amsterdam, and the next is very soon. Somehow it will work out, or it is not God's plan for them."

"Sarah, we need to get your father home. He looks very tired. It was such a cold winter and now our sunny sky again forbidding, dreary, damp, and gray. Do make sure he is fine and settled in with warm, dry clothes and a foot *stoof* right away when we get there. You stay with him tonight. The older children can carry the evening meal to you and your father that I planned for all of us at our home when we returned. They can help with the youngest ones. I need time to think, to be alone for a while. Now, let's be on our way. The tulips were especially beautiful this year. Do you have your journal, Sarah Elizabeth?"

CHAPTER 3

Looking Back

Dr. James Kent's sister-in-law was right. He had been the reflective, deliberative scholar, husband, father, and anything but impulsive, but he changed after their flight from England to Holland and even more so after the sudden and tragic death of his second wife and the child she carried, a boy.

When they arrived in Amsterdam, a leading port city, they intended to make their way to Leyden where so many other religious refugees from many countries had settled near the highly esteemed university. Twenty years earlier, separatists from England went first to Amsterdam like the Kent family and then to Leyden. Their daring voyage to New England in 1620 was inspirational. The times beckoned the devout and risk takers, the destitute and oppressed to take radical action. William Bradford, early governor and author of the *Journal of Plymouth Plantation* had written, "*All great and honourable actions are accompanied with great difficulties and must be both enterprised and overcome with answerable courages.*"

Scarcely more than a decade later, like so many Puritans before him, John Davenport, a leading London clergyman, left England for Amsterdam, a choice far better than the inevitable retribution of the increasingly powerful William Laud. He deemed the Puritan rejection of elaborate ritual and vestments, centrality of the stone altar for mass, images, stained glass windows, and veneration of saints subversive to the Church and the King's authority. Until Davenport's departure for Rotterdam in 1634, he and James found much to talk about although Davenport's theology would become far more conservative.

A former Cambridge classmate and colleague of James Kent, Dr. Robert Blake, who had leased a small, narrow affordable town house for a year in a comfortable Amsterdam neighborhood, just accepted a position at the university on short notice when a professor died unexpectedly. He was requested to meet students after they debarked from their ships, rowed ashore, and accompany them to Leyden right away, remarkably the day the Kents arrived. Dr. Blake couldn't believe his eyes when he saw the familiar face of a weary, weatherworn man struggle with baggage not far from where Blake was to meet his new charges. Neither man could believe what just happened. They were both alive and well after having lost contact with each other due to their imperiled status as Protestant Nonconformists in their homeland. Suddenly by the raucous shore of the Zuyder Zee and cacophony of dialects, locked together in warm embrace, the men's eyes watered, overcome with unspeakable blessing and gratitude.

Blake was relieved and overjoyed to see his longtime friend James, meet his family, and learn of their hurried escape and safe arrival. Seeing the restless toddler in the tired mother's arms, he immediately suggested they take over his lease—spare but adequate—if the owner agreed. He noticed how little they brought with them, typical of many under scrutiny of the Star Chamber, High Commission, or Church of England. Their next stop could just as readily have been the Tower of London rather than Amsterdam. Certainly they would need a place to stay and such an arrangement might temporarily solve problems for all of them.

The newly arrived Kent family was exhausted, in need of housing, and Blake, summoned to leave Amsterdam at once with the students, did not have sufficient time to adequately manage everything and properly notify his landlord. Robert explained that he did not need to take furniture and household goods as the letter described a fully furnished residence ready for him adjacent to the university. It was evident his brilliant friend had to leave most of his library behind in England. Would James temporarily take responsibility for the books? As Blake did not need all of them right away, Dr. Kent could send them on later after they were both settled. Dr. Blake had already packed the most essential works for his first classes. In the meantime, James Kent was free to make use of the remainder, and once situated in Leyden, Robert could explore more permanent accommodations there for the Kent family. This was truly a day of divine miracle.

Everything about Dr. Kent's academic studies at Cambridge and subsequent work would have also prepared him well for a position at the University of Leyden although not a sure thing. Dr. Blake was deserving and fortunate. Great scholars from all over Europe were drawn to this remarkable center of learning in seventeenth century Europe and certainly one of the most progressive in a country where tolerance was the norm rather than the exception. Keen, visionary thinkers like James Kent could thrive and flourish in such an atmosphere of unfettered intellectual freedom notable for open discourse devoid of cropped ears or the fiery stake.

He secreted a number of carefully guarded manuscripts he dared not publish in England and other papers in progress. Now he could finish those and send them all with confidence to Dr. Blake where his friend could arrange a Dutch translation from the Latin and English and get them to press in all three languages. In Amsterdam and Leyden, there were more publishers than in all of England. It was not uncommon for those with ideas considered subversive to the established state churches, and therefore the monarchies in Europe, to covertly send their work to the University town for publication. Indeed, some publishers in Holland specialized in such endeavors, including many in Amsterdam, but Robert's connections in Leyden would prove more useful.

His friend's fortuitous offer provided much needed relief for his wife and sister-in-law while they tended to little Sarah Elizabeth, already a bundle of energy. They would be warm and safe with all the basic essentials to establish their new home. The small inheritance he had frugally set aside would cover their living expenses until he could determine how best to provide for them. It wasn't long before Dr. Kent learned that one in every four residents of Amsterdam was an immigrant contributing much to the trades, arts, and intellectual ferment. Parents from his homeland sought good English tutors to supplement their children's education in Dutch public schools, a progressive innovation in the 1600s. Not only was he a profound scholar but an effective educator. Word spread rapidly of his remarkable capacity for teaching Latin and perfecting compositional skills until he had to turn away more aspiring scholars from English families than he could manage and still attend to his writing. His family would be well cared for in their new land.

As it happened, their stay was not temporary. Almost four years passed before the now highly regarded thinker was finally asked to speak and participate in a series of lectures and debates at the Leyden University following critical acclaim of his publications that sparked much interest. Robert Blake learned his friend was being considered for a position, and this was a timely opportunity for James to appear professionally in person. Alas, he accepted before Mary shared she was pregnant. Sarah Elizabeth was the only child his wife successfully carried full-term, but when he was to leave for Leyden, her belly was already swollen. Now that he was expected within two weeks at the University, he began to feel uneasy about leaving his family, but he was a man of his word, and she urged him to go.

Several weeks later, he returned home just after the letter was sent that his wife and unborn child died during a premature birth. Mary and the infant were buried immediately. Both his beloved wives had died, and now he was the sole surviving parent of an only child. Of course, her Aunt Alice would do everything she could to meet the needs of the little girl. Newly married to a well-to-do merchant of the Vereenigde Oostindische Compagnie, and living in his spacious, deep town home on the street near the short bridge across the narrow canal with a kitchen garden in back and not yet having children of her own, she would gladly do her best to mother her sister's darling daughter.

James Kent buried himself in doctoral studies after the death of his first wife, but this time the otherwise deliberative and introspective man realized that he did not want to miss a moment of his daughter's childhood. He could have left Sarah Elizabeth with her aunt and accepted the post that was offered him after the debates, what he passionately sought as the culmination of his career, what he and Mary hoped and planned for. This latest tragedy, however, changed everything and reconfigured what was most important to him, his daughter's life. Sarah Elizabeth, so much like her mother, was bright, inquisitive, independent, trusting, and confident. Her ready smile and sparkling eyes lit up their lives, and now all he really wanted was to be her guiding light and protector. For the first time, he fully comprehended how really precious a human life is and what it meant to give a life to save another. He finally internalized the essence of the spiritual quest.

He learned from their hasty flight to the Low Country that it was worth leaving your homeland to live in a more open society less dominated by aristocracy and Crown, a punitive state church, and where upward mobility in Holland derived almost as much from natural ability, vision, and effort as family status. James came to love Amsterdam with its mix of immigrants and the lively artistic, commercial, scientific, religious, and intellectual atmosphere bristling with ideas and such noted philosophers as Frenchman René Descartes and revered Dutch artist Rembrandt van Rijn.

During his many walks and the convenience of the *trekschuyts* drawn by canal horses, James Kent enjoyed the spontaneous conviviality of the passengers whereby he gradually acquired an affinity for the Dutch language, engaged with learned men in Latin, and often conversed with the many other Englishmen who found a home in Amsterdam. It was during one of those outings that an acquaintance introduced him to Minister John Davenport. The three of them had a similar experience with the English and Scottish merchant church, the only one permitted by the Dutch *classis* in Amsterdam. When the minister John Paget became ill, he refused the clerics' offers to assist against the wishes of his own lay members, apparently over differences in authority that put the congregation in inferior relationship with their minister and church hierarchy. The incident would further crystallize the men's views to favor the congregational versus the presbytery form of local church governance.

Remarkably exciting and pertinent to Kent's tutorials were the intriguing ideas about education that John Davenport discussed with him. Forced to leave Poland, Samuel Hartlib joined the minister's St. Stephen's London parish in 1628 where there was an active group on behalf of Protestant refugees from the war torn continent. Jan Amos Comenius, a man forever in exile, fled his native Moravia when the Protestants there were defeated during the decades long war on the Continent. He hoped to find solace in Poland where the two men met before conditions there also worsened. Comenius was passionately devoted to the study of education, particularly language instruction and especially how to more effectively teach Latin, the European universal language for the study and practice of theology, law, science, and trade, and the outgrowth of humanism influenced by the classics. Comenius taught widely during his sojourn in exile from war and persecution, applying his insights, and writing volumes, well-known and highly regarded. Hartlib, Davenport, and others in London were inspired by his observations about nature to influence young minds, educational innovation, and religious reform. It was those fortuitous conversations with Davenport that clarified and enriched James Kent's vision of the possible and how he might better teach and guide his young scholars and inspire his own daughter Sarah Elizabeth.

Even though Dr. Kent never pursued his academic goals at the University, what he received in return for that decision to keep a watchful eye over his only child was the freedom to influence young aspiring minds, to write, and to occasionally lecture without fear of persecution. In fact, although the income was modest it was sufficient, and without the academic demands of a full time professorship, he had more time to reflect and elaborate his ideas. Significantly, through his many pamphlets, correspondence, and major treatises he was well respected and perhaps had indeed influenced others more than he would ever know. The rigors of university responsibilities would have taken their toll on his weak heart, while in Amsterdam Alice ensured that he ate well, could dote on his daughter, and accomplish much.

His wife, daughter, and sister-in-law gave him much pause to rethink how significant were women's capabilities and insight, how much they had to contribute if only the opportunity. In spite of all his heartbreaking loss, Sarah Elizabeth made him feel like the most fortunate man in the world. Given this opportunity to nurture her more than most fathers, he learned the essence of relationship and regard for feminine insight, a spiritual revelation more profound than all his studies with learned men could possibly provide.

CHAPTER 4

James and Alice

James Kent did not sleep well Sunday night after they visited his wife's grave, but he thought it best to wait until Tuesday to visit Alice and talk further. His sister-in-law was grief-stricken and her raw emotions intense. She would need time to absorb the stunning news.

"My dear, sweet Alice, you have every reason to be sad, angry, hurt, and worried. You have been a generous, loving mother to Sarah. Mary could not have had a more devoted sister than you and I a more thoughtful, gracious sister-in-law. Your steadfast kindness deserves more than the anguish you now feel. When Sarah and Dirck set sail, it is you who will be left without the family that journeyed here together from England. Mary has been gone from us for fourteen years. I am getting weaker every day and will soon be gone too, but losing Sarah in this way is asking so much of you that it would be insensitive of me to hope that any real consolation is possible. I am truly sorry."

"James, if only Willem had not left with his brother on business in Leyden the day before we went to Mary's gravesite, perhaps we could have explored other possibilities. I understand your desire to see your daughter married to a brilliant scholar and fine young man you both care about and how urgent that must seem to you now. Certainly Willem and I can ensure that Sarah will find a proper suitor when she is older, or with the permission of Dirck's parents perhaps we can find a way to help with that budding relationship. I often imagined her wedding, and we always thought to provide Sarah and her groom with a traditional Dutch feast. It would have made my sister proud and happy and my care for her daughter complete. If you and Mary were both here and in good health, I can't imagine for a minute that you would let Sarah Elizabeth hastily marry a young man she scarcely knows and inadequately prepared to sail off to some faraway Dutch trading post. I'm terrified over what could happen to her."

"I agree, Alice. If Mary was here and I was not about to die, we would not be having this conversation."

"But we are, James, and this is Amsterdam, the envy of Europe, and like Leyden marvelous and stimulating for bright minds, not so Nieuw Nederland. You teach and write to your heart's content in one of the few places where you need not fear that you will be separated from your loved ones, imprisoned, tortured, and condemned to death or put family in harm's way because of your ideas. James, we have all flourished here in every way possible except for the loss of our precious Mary. We have more than we ever dreamed of when we were forced to leave England—comfort of every sort. In Nieuw Nederland, Sarah and Dirck will face only adversity, not opportunity, in a place where they will have no family, no friends, no one to support them the way Willem and I can do here. The ocean voyage alone ought to be reason enough for concern. Ships are pirated or go down in foul weather with devastating loss of lives and goods. Such is the reality that would have undone us long ago were it not for stock companies, insurance, and the vast profits from his father's early investments."

"Alice, it's so very odd how just one brief moment of spontaneous and honest recognition ignites fiery passion within that powerfully changes the direction of our lives forever. I was content here until I realized how few days remain, and I had to reveal this secret to Dirck and Sarah. She was content with the daily routine of helping care for your children and sharing our noonday meal together. Dirck was content devoted to his studies and dreams of the University. In less than an hour, nothing would ever be the same. In a single instant of clarity, the veils lifted and laid bare everyone's discontent and guarded dreams.

"Dirck realized the lover and adventurer in him was as central to who he was as the young scholar. A flash of self-understanding pierced his soul. He would rather leave everything that was known, secure, and comfortable for the uncertain hardship of a faraway world if he could be his own man, follow his own instincts, and serve his own God-given vision. Sarah discovered it was all right for her to love her father's most promising student. Like him, she no longer had to hide feelings that had been subterranean for a long time and that her dreams, indeed her insatiable curiosity, about far-off lands and strange people were not just make believe. Sarah's fantasies catapulted her toward a daring adventure with Dirck she would never have thought possible, and yes, I learned that to save a life perhaps one has to risk a life. In such moments as these, we are open to inner wisdom that normal expectations of the society in which we live are secondary and do distract us from a life of unique purpose. Now and then we respond to the truth of this still small voice. Most of the time we need a bolt of lightning and clap of thunder."

"James, this is a lot to absorb all at once, and it's going to take a long time for me to accept that all this leads to never seeing Mary's daughter again or holding her grandchildren close. I too have my dreams and wanted one day to plant tulips by Mary's grave and whisper, 'Your daughter is married and now has children of her own. We will teach them about their beautiful Grandmother Mary. We will not forget you.' I've held onto that vision for so long I don't know how to let go. I don't want to let go and somehow feel so alone without the three of us together. No mother, no father, no sister, no niece, no brother will be forever. You were both father and brother to me, James."

"Such loss is a lot to bear and must be very painful for you, Alice, and I've always been touched and grateful for your undying love for my wife, daughter, and me. You are a generous and rare person, yet the consequence of not taking bold action now would be to let two young lives drift along, leaving behind dreams that bubbled up to the surface that one amazing morning. Could those dreams be retrieved later? I will not be here to know, encourage, and support them.

"Yes, it must seem that I am more impulsive now than the man you thought you knew. We've all changed in response to disruptive circumstance, but I believe a timely, singular decision comes to each of us when unbidden and unforeseen, an untold number of cogs in the wheel of life click into place and one leaps forward or falls behind. You must respond to the call of your heart and head or live a life of regret and what could have been. Our life in England would have been one of ultimate tragedy if you had not had such clarity and courage during a moment when there was little time to reconsider. It was a crucial, life-saving decision that made all the difference in the world, and we all moved forward."

"But that was different, James, we were all together and with the exception of little Sarah Elizabeth grown adults."

"Alice, yes, the details were different, but there was a choice between trying to make a troubled past work and an unknown future. As it turns out, either way, there was uncertainty, and I believe this is exactly what Dirck and Sarah Elizabeth face.

"There is more. Can you manage it?"

"No, I can't, James, but time is short, and we should talk alone now as there will be much to do should they sail on the next ship. A few days ago the penetrating chill of our most frigid winter seemed finally over. We looked forward to spring and brighter skies, and I was at peace. Suddenly ill winds of change blow violently. I'm cold again, overwhelmed, and drained.

"And, dear brother, you look pale and exhausted. Are you sure you can continue?"

"Thank you, Alice, I am tired, very tired but must finish one more revelation, something that has haunted me since the night before Sarah Elizabeth was born. I had a dream about the Greek myth of Ulysses and Penelope. We have talked about that story before because I think of it every time we see the women wistfully waiting at the *Schreierstoren* for their loved one's ship return to the Zuyder Zee shore. Your husband is a merchant. We both know, and given what you just said, the awful statistics here in the Netherlands and Amsterdam in particular—since 1600 almost half a million of our young men off to faraway trading posts of the Dutch Empire in

Asia, Africa, Brazil, the West Indisches, and now Nieuw Nederland. How many Penelopes spend most of their lives anxiously hoping and waiting for a loved one who never comes home?"

"I think you underestimate your daughter's future here. She will never lack for available and prosperous suitors, even if young men are in short supply these days. If anything, it is more an issue of keeping would-be lovers away. When we go to the market lately, every male head turns. Sarah Elizabeth has become a strikingly beautiful young lady."

"I was not aware that she draws so much attention. Our walks are less frequent and much shorter than they once were, and I've been preoccupied."

"Believe me, Brother, you have quite a stunning beauty. She is nineteen, not quite legal for marriage according to Dutch custom but no longer your little girl. I just can't imagine life without her, and I can't imagine Sarah off in some ill-kept, unruly settlement, scarcely more than a port of call, on the tip of a vast beaver infested wilderness. That may be fine for fur traders and felt hats but not for a beautiful, educated young lady and my sister's only child."

"Alice, I have had this dream three times—the night before she was born, the night Mary and our stillborn child died while I was still at the University in Leyden, and the night after your brother came to examine me. It means something."

"James, if I do say so that sounds more like ignorant superstition than the words of our own very esteemed reverend and reasoned scholar, Doctor James Kent."

"The Bible is filled with dreams, Alice. Joseph's dreams and his interpretation of Pharaoh's dreams altered the course of history!"

"Just how do you know your interpretation is the correct one, James?"

"In my third dream, the other night I saw Sarah Elizabeth, her face drawn and so alone, staring out into the vast Zuyder Zee. It was she who was waiting for her Ulysses to come home! I understand this sounds crazy to you, but the dream is for a reason. It's a warning to ensure that she is with her husband and not waiting for him. Dirck, Sarah, and I all put at arm's length a relationship that was meant to be close. We were all trying to be very proper and respectful of strict boundaries between teacher, daughter, and student and the customs and laws of Holland. The sudden demands of Dirck's father and my own imminent death created an urgency that none of us could ignore. What we all repressed came suddenly and explosively to the surface."

"I don't know what to say, James. I remember when you and Mary met. The attraction was obvious and compelling. When we first came here, I used to watch Willem and his father leave their grand town house in their fine felt hats that likely cost more than you paid for six months of rent. He was a fantasy, Dutch, and rich. We were poor English immigrants, yet we did meet, we did fall in love, we did get married and now live together in that very same house with your Sarah Elizabeth and lots of children. Love and how it changes our lives really is mysterious. Except for our dear Mary, we were all blessed with lives that just got better and better. Clearly, your daughter and Dirck are deeply in love, but I don't see their life together getting off to a good start and getting better by jumping on a ship and sailing across the vast, treacherous Atlantic. It was terrible enough sailing across the Channel from England, and we both know the Zuyder Zee is turbulent and hazardous. I am so afraid for her, for both of them."

"Alice, from the time you and Mary first dragged me away from England, from the time we were all together in what to us was once a strange land, and ever since Mary's death, all any of us ever thought about was protecting Sarah Elizabeth, doing what we thought best for her, and during that process we also discovered we were doing what was best for all of us. I don't want her to get hurt either. This new journey Dirck envisions is more than a little daunting, but there is also that part of your niece that is resilient, adventurous, self-reliant, and courageous."

"James, that is just it. She is adventurous, courageous, and likely a bit bored here. She loves you so much, and apparently Dirck, that I'm just afraid she will bravely and unselfishly do anything to make you both happy."

"Alice, that is it. She has accommodated everyone for so long, you, me, your husband and children, that she suppresses a secret she unselfishly avoids, her own unique destiny. Sarah is one of those rare spirits who thrive most when they can fly beyond all the spaces and habits the rest of us have grown accustomed to. What I fear most for her is not an unknown future but a stunted one, like a bird with a broken wing. If she stays behind without Dirck after I die, her anguish will be profound, and the part of Sarah Elizabeth that yearns to be free will one day wither and dry up. She will never know the adventure that awaits those who stretch their wings, soar, and truly live their dream even if seemingly impossible or improbable. The entire Reformation was once seemingly impossible and once begun, still in the process of becoming, tumultuous, and of uncertain, anxious outcome. Yet, here we are in a country that is a receptive, open society compared to Spain or France and even our beloved England precisely because of that Reformation. Others and the Dutch here suffered and sacrificed to cast off the oppressive yoke of religion in the name of a Christ married to state churches and monarchies gone mad and vile. Risk is inevitable if we are to move forward as a person or a people."

"James, you would think that Sarah is your son not your daughter. Regardless of your idealism, are you sure about this? Our Dutch trading ports around the world are not Amsterdams. Here in Holland, the richest of the Northern Provinces, women have more rights and wealth than any place in Europe, likely in the world, not a bad place to be at all if you happen to be female."

"It is precisely because she is a daughter that I must support her in the newly awakened aspiration she shares with Dirck. If I don't do this now while I can, who else will? Am I right, Alice?"

Alice had secrets of her own too. To accommodate the rapidly burgeoning population of Amsterdam, a challenging expansion project of three major canals was started in 1612. Still unfinished, prestigious homesites along the waterways had become increasingly available to those who could afford them. Her husband, having become quite wealthy but prudent with personal finances, declined the even more expensive and lavish residences on *Herensgracht* in favor of the still highly desirable *Prinsengracht.* Construction would soon begin. He planned to sell the long time family home he inherited and the shallow, narrow unit leased to Dr. Kent when Dr. Blake left and freely provided after his marriage to Alice.

She had wondered how she would break the news to Sarah and her father. Of course, both would be welcome. Dr. James Kent would have his own street level study but no longer his own separate dwelling to host students. Now it no longer mattered. Her sister's husband was dying, and there would be no grand and proper wedding celebration for Sarah, no shared future. In spite of abundant, brilliant tulip blooms, storm clouds were on the horizon. The Kent guiding light of Sarah Elizabeth and her father, Alice's light, was about to go out with more dull, gray days ahead.

CHAPTER 5

Dirck and What Tangled Webs We Weave

After Dr. Kent saw the Amsterdam physician a few weeks before that fateful day of life-changing revelation, he dismissed most of his students with letters to the parents that he could no longer tutor their sons due to health concerns. Ever the professional despite his own predicament, he included detailed records of proficiency and thoughtful letters of reference. However, he had not dismissed Dirck with the others. Desperate to impart to his most promising pupil whatever insightful guidance emerged as he approached his own death was imperative to James Kent. He wanted quality time with his gifted protégé during the few days that remained.

Kent often wondered if Dirck's father would support his son's aspiration to attend the University of Leyden but did not anticipate the gravity of his own condition or that his father would terminate the studies abruptly with no transition to the University. He hoped Dirck's father would at least allow the exams. Writing the young man's parents had just become a lot more complicated, but the prudent scholar decided to keep it simple. After all, he had not been the one to insist that Dirck give up all hope of furthering his education nor had he compelled him to abruptly enter the family trade full-time and thus evoke such a daring plan of escape across the Atlantic to Nieuw Nederland. With regard to the sudden declaration of affection between Dirck and his daughter, he had never encouraged such a relationship and, in fact, forbid such familiarity between Sarah Elizabeth and his students.

Long before his remaining student arrived that fateful day, all the tutor and loving father thought about was how to make it easier for Dirck and his daughter to grasp that his time with them would end very soon because he was dying. That alone was his intent and responsibility. However, unbeknownst to Dr. Kent, the ambitious young scholar had already made a radical decision that quite properly ought to be between him and his family, especially his father.

Contracted to prepare Dirck Hendricksz for the University, James Kent's focus was what he thought of utmost importance to achieve that goal. Dirck was such a quick, eager study that he assumed this was what mattered most to his student as well. In retrospect, the Latin tutor realized belatedly there were subtle clues that Dirck's insatiable curiosity was also stimulated by what ought to have been more obvious, not the classical past but the adolescent's present and immediate surroundings, not the ships of Greek heroes, but the myriad of masts and colorful flags that crowded the Zuyder Zee. Amsterdam was first and foremost a bustling city of trade and adventure, of seafarer's stories and songs about mysterious people and exotic places beyond the Texel Channel. Dirck could not have made his way from Dr. Kent's study to his father's woodworking shop every day without full immersion in the city's water world, and that world was inundated by comings and goings, goings and comings.

Dirck's mother knew her youngest son was restless and imaginative. She grasped from his childhood drawings of ships and sea that it was not his father's business he was thinking about but where those ships sailed. The boy was lured by the vast unknown beyond the shore apparently from the time he was a little tyke, and his perceptive mother feared he would one day make that fantasy real. She instilled in her bright son, a substitute dream, the University of Leyden, that could ensure escape from his father's business near the *Oude Shans*, the Western Shore, an alternate pathway to becoming his own man. He would seek his destiny not as a shipbuilder, seaman, or merchant but as that kind of educated person who advances forward in a world of rapid change that beckons the humanist scholar of reason and self-examination. Instead, there was that day in Dr. Kent's study when Dirck and Sarah Elizabeth marveled at her uncle's remarkable maps and discovered in each other's eyes and wordless instant a shared dream.

Although forewarned, Sarah's father was alarmed by his rapid decline in the days that followed. More than ever, all he could do now was take one day, one hour at a time to carefully sort through the tangled webs of conflicted dreams, emotions, and consequences now swarming like a hive of bees around everyone's head. It would not be easy. He was tired, yet he needed to rise to what was most essential including a short letter to Dirck's parents reminding his father, a prudent Dutchman, that he already paid the fees for the entire term and two weeks remained. Dr. Kent explained that his health was failing and that per his doctor's advice, he planned in any case to terminate the tutorial at the end of the month when the man's son completed the previously agreed upon three years of instruction and would merit excellent commendation of completion. He, therefore, diplomatically requested that they be permitted these two weeks for the proper closure of his son's studies and preparation of final paperwork for his culmination documents. Perhaps, James Kent thought, Dirck might change his mind if everyone responded calmly and thoughtfully—at least mend hard feelings. He understood how anguished Dirck's mother would be if her son's quest to leave the province succeeded.

The nineteen-year-old, however, applied himself as usual to set his plan in motion and already knew the next date that a ship of the West-Indische Compagnie was scheduled to embark for Nieuw Amsterdam, and it was soon, very soon. He took this as a sign because spring was the best season to set sail, and it was known the *WIC* did not make frequent trips there, definitely not as often as they should with supplies. Slave trading ports in Africa, northern Brazil, the West Indisches sugar islands, and even trade with Virginia Colony were more profitable to their stockholders in spite of the thousands of beaver pelts canoed or sailed down the *Noordt Rivier* and shipped to the Fatherland every year from the deep harbor of his destination. The scholar did his research, and his mind was made up. Apparently expected to spend the rest of his life in a trade not his choice, he would leave home one way or another, now or never.

He adored his mother. Leaving her would be the hardest part, gut and heart-wrenching for mother and son, but they both believed in her dream that his future was with words not lathes, planes and squares; bevels, chisels, and braces; dividers and calipers—a different destiny from that of his father and brothers. It wasn't a bad life. Their trade was better than many by far, adorning the magnificent Dutch sailing vessels, and profitable because of his father's highly honed skills, exacting and efficient, but it wasn't going to be his life. He had long ago laid claim to another vision for his future.

Dirck had already hidden away the large swath of Dutch *duffel* that his mother set aside two years earlier to craft a bag for his belongings should he advance to the Leyden University. Anticipating his father's final decision about his life, Dirck had been stowing away clothing and other items he would need for a very different kind of journey from that of his mother's yearning for him.

Sadly, he could not gently let her down. He could not tell her of his decision to leave or his father would be furious and derail the plan, and it was going to be difficult enough to secure passage. No matter when she was told, she would hope against hope, and in the end have to deal with her grief for days, weeks, months, perhaps years after the ship set sail. Advance notice was not going to change that awful reality.

What he could do, after they read Dr. Kent's letter, was to tell his parents how grateful he was for the three years permitted for his studies. He would write them a letter for a messenger to deliver when his ship was safely through the Texel Channel of the Zuyder Zee. During the voyage he would keep a journal to return with the ship back to Amsterdam, and once settled at *Mannahatta Eylandt*, he would write his mother again and again. What he would not do is mention the marriage to his tutor's daughter. Dirck did not want Sarah's family implicated in any way that would sully the regard of his mother for Reverend Dr. James Kent, even in death.

As it happened, Alice's husband, Willem, was the most conflicted when he returned home to the sudden turn of events. Had their world gone mad? His always lovely and vivacious wife sobbed as she told the sorry tale and their children bewildered by how their loving "sister" could leave them. Willem's brother-in-law, the scholar schooled in rational humanism, was unreasonable and seemed to have gone quite mad. What was he thinking? James Kent was an academic not an adventurer and knew nothing of the hardships hacking out a life in a wild faraway, uncivilized land. Yes, Willem was not the reflective, idealistic type by comparison, but he was pragmatic and accustomed to sizing up the variables in a complex situation with keen clarity and taking decisive action.

Moreover, as a merchant with the *VOC*, Willem knew the very real dangers of ocean voyages. He knew the statistics all too well of how many men died in the service of the stockholders' profits and passengers who sometimes accompanied them. What's worse, Willem, like his partners and other merchants with the VOC, did not think much of the West-Indische Compagnie. The nineteen powerful officers of their corporation and stockholders were at war to eliminate Spanish dominance of their trading interests in the southern Atlantic and were initially enriched by privateers like Piet Heyn who plundered Spanish galleons and extracted gold, silver, highly desirable Brazilian dyewood, other valuables, and took their slaves.

Granted this policy and practice of sanctioned plunder undermined the Spanish, who were their enemies, to the military advantage and competitive enrichment of WIC, VOC, and the Dutch Empire. The most deplorable revenue stream of the WIC in Willem's view, unlike the Vereenigde Oostendische, was from the African Slave Trade, supplying thousands of captive slaves to provide workers for sugar, cotton, and cocoa plantations in Brazil and the Caribbean, or selling them to the North Atlantic colonies. Lucrative as the beaver fur trade was with the river wilden of Nieuw Nederland, it paled by comparison and thus deemed a less significant venture.

Sarah Elizabeth's uncle understood the implication and reality of underfunded attempts to effectively establish the couple's destination during the first few decades of its existence. The Dutch were traders seeking profits, not colonizers. They set up trading posts at water's edge throughout the world where they exchanged goods with local inhabitants. Expansion beyond the shoreline evoked conflict over land, was costly, and tended toward loss of company controlled Dutch policy. Such commercial endeavors required reciprocity to maximize financial gain and advantage. Merchants could not risk strife. Loss of goodwill meant loss of trade goods and poor return on their investment. Thus, initially the fort at Mannahatta Eylandt was to be a defense against competitive English, Swedish, or French intruders, not the wilden, and so provide safety for no more company employees than necessary for the fur trade or farms to provide food. The purpose of the stock companies was trade with the least expense and effort possible, not putting down family roots that required acquisition of more land that led to troubling encounters with native inhabitants. For twenty years, this policy and practice of a powerful faction within the West-Indische Compagnie prevailed.

Another faction within the WIC and the Staten Generaal, however, contested that policy as too limited and shortsighted. They understood that the entire territorial claim of Nieuw Nederland was at risk and that the most effective strategy against English encroachment, or that of any other nation, must be more colonists. The difficulty was that simply put, unlike England, life was good in the United Provinces of the Netherlands and especially in Holland. The divisiveness within the ranks of the WIC led to indecision and delay until it became imperative that something had to be done to attract more settlers. If the Dutch were to hold Nieuw Nederland, a way must be put forth to entice more young, healthy, able-bodied couples intent on raising large families but why his beautiful niece with all the advantage he and his wife Alice offered? James Kent's plan struck Willem as reckless and unrealistic.

Further, he and other Amsterdam businessmen were unimpressed by the way WIC managed their settlement at the mouth of the Noordt Rivier that emptied into the deep water harbor of Mannahatta Eylandt. Perhaps the most jarring critique was that, unlike the highly successful VOC, the WIC for the most part failed to appoint able directors promoted through the ranks based on experience and management skills, and there were some people returning from Nieuw Amsterdam with strong criticism of the current Director-General, Willem Kieft.

Out of respect for his brother-in-law, Willem Pauw never assumed by manner, word, or deed the role of Sarah's father. Yet, it was always understood that given James Kent's age, if he died before her age of maturity and marriage, Willem would assume that role and responsibility. Indeed, James provided him with notarized documents to that effect. All that said, the truth of the matter was he loved Sarah as a daughter. She was treasured as much as their own children.

Willem also had doubts about Dirck's capacity to support his niece even in Amsterdam let alone in an isolated, forested wilderness across the sea. A successful tradesman in Holland could make a good living but nothing in comparison to the sons of prosperous merchants he knew. The decision struck him as impetuous and short-sighted. Certainly a young scholar, however bright and courageous he might be, was no match for the harsh realities of life in a settlement like Mannahatta that struggled to exist since the WIC sent the first small group of colonists, *Walloon* immigrants, barely two decades earlier. Only the wild stretch of an ill-informed imagination could even call it a town. It may be Nieuw Amsterdam, but it was certainly no Amsterdam proper and likely never would be.

When all was said and done, however, if James Kent prevailed, Willem and Alice would provide whatever necessary to make the bridal couple's journey and arrival more comfortable and to ensure the expense of their passage was covered. At least, then, when they arrived, the WIC would provide more of their necessaries without indebtedness to the company. What he would not do was use his influence for their passage. Willem would not overtly support the plan or have his family name connected with a young man disrespecting laws regarding marriage and who likely went against his father's will, especially a master craftsman in a guild associated with shipbuilding on whom his company's success and the crews' very lives depended.

Aunt Alice still thought the ocean voyage to Nieuw Amsterdam would not happen. Certainly her brother-in-law would come to his senses. Certainly Dirck's father would not approve, and they would never be permitted to marry and board the ship. Certainly it was all so inconceivable, impractical, and illegal. Since Hugo Grotius, Dutch law was very well articulated, regulated, and enforced. At least, she had to comfort herself with that, but if all went as James envisioned, would Sarah falter and panic at the last minute? Alas, Alice knew better than anyone else that in spite of their affection for one another Sara Elizabeth would not.

Like her husband, she would not encourage her niece, but if it came to pass, Alice would make sure her sister's daughter had everything it was possible to take—warm clothing and bedding, paper for letters, dried herbs to supplement ship diet including chamomile and dried, pulverized ginger for nausea. She would prepare watertight packages of cinnamon, cloves, nutmeg, mace, peppercorns, and sugar for after their arrival to use for themselves or barter. Sarah would have her needlework necessaries, small keepsakes that were her mother's and, of course, a few tulip bulbs from Mary's gravesite (hopefully not lifted too soon from fading blooms). Willem would generously provide a pouch of guilders. All this would be their last minute gifts of profound, yet heart-wrenching love. There wasn't time to better plan for their needs during the voyage and on their arrival to set up housekeeping.

Strangely, the young lady at the epicenter of the family crisis was calm and in control of her senses and emotions. When her father explained that she tended to accommodate the needs of others, Sarah Elizabeth reviewed her life with newly awakened insight and realized that her task in Amsterdam was finished. Indeed, her mother, father, Aunt Alice and Uncle Willem had loved and cared for her in every way a person could, but that relationship had also given meaning to their lives. Most importantly, her father's dream was fulfilled in an uncommon way not possible in the land of his birth, but now his work was finished.

In common with other university educated men of his day, James Kent's outlook was grounded in the Renaissance that evoked a return to classical Greek and Roman thought, art, and literature while the Reformation liberated millions from the coercive political, economic, social, and religious constraints of the Roman Catholic Church. With that Reformation, there was the commitment of theologians to read the New Testament in its original Koine Greek and the Old Testament Biblical Hebrew. Nowhere in England was there more foment in such matters of faith and reason than at Cambridge, especially Magdalene College where the young James Kent met Robert Blake. When the Church of England became repressive drawing Anabaptists, Puritan Calvinists, Separatists, and other English Nonconformists like Sarah's father to the Northern Lowland Provinces of the Netherlands along with Lutherans from the Continent and exiled Portuguese Jews who survived the Inquisition, many acted to embrace bold new ideas or deepen and extend their own. Others like the Pilgrims sought to preserve their religious practice, averting Dutch ways, and so moved on to the New World to start new colonies. Some became perennial adventurers of the high seas.

Dr. James Kent's family would benefit from the great migration of such profound change. The serendipitous encounter of Sarah's family with Dr. Robert Blake that eventful day on the shore of the Zuyder Zee led to a lifelong friendship with her father. Aunt Alice explained that Sarah's mother, Mary, noticed a rapid transition in her husband's thought after the loss of his library in England and return of Robert's books. The intellectual cross fertilization of ideas in the more progressive Holland evoked penetrating and transformative ideas that churned within and flowed easily without, fresh and visionary.

Dr. Blake was instrumental in getting James Kent's former lectures in England and new writing in Amsterdam translated from Latin and English to Dutch, published, into the hands of influential professors in Leyden like the highly regarded Gerardus Johannes Vossius, and included in the University library. Sarah's father stretched the humanism of the Netherlands' own Desiderius Erasmus and contemporary intellectuals to new heights, heresy in England but welcome in the lively, freethinking atmosphere of Leyden and Amsterdam. The dislocation from England had produced a remarkable, original, independent thinker. Scholars in Holland increasingly took note of his highly evocative ideas, often too progressive for even Dutch theologians and philosophers or recent immigrant intellectuals of note. His arguments disseminated in pamphlets and treatises, however, were brilliant, well-supported, cogent, coherent, and clearly articulated earning scholarly respect if not always agreement.

The two men exchanged letters and manuscripts reviewing and responding to each other's work. When Sarah Elizabeth was older, her father enjoyed sharing their letters that reflected profound regard for each other and their ideas. Thus it happened that such a vital, devoted friendship empowered their capacity for noteworthy contribution. In essence, the scholarly reputation of each was enhanced by their mutual ability to stretch the other. Dr. Kent's life had turned out well in Amsterdam and that of his longtime friend in Leyden.

In a very short time, Sarah would have to go on living without him, but now she was no longer her father's motherless, little girl. She was strong, confident, secure, bright, and beautiful. Her lively, affable personality made the death of Alice's sister bearable, and when Alice and Willem's own children did not come at first, Sarah Elizabeth filled their hearts until their children began to arrive and in rapid succession. Alice and Willem now had a large family of their own. It was time for Alice to put their life together in England, her sister's death, and the entire Kent Family behind her and move forward with her devoted husband, their own children, and fully embrace their lives together as Dutch citizens. Sarah was confident that after her aunt recovered from the initial shock and worry, she would be whole and healed at last. James and Mary Kent's only child was born into a world of danger and heartache. Indeed, they all emerged the better for it.

That child was now grown up and inspired to decide the direction of her own life journey, that door opened by her father's dying wish. A more daring and exciting venture than anything she had ever known was suddenly visible and within reach. It was hers to grasp. Sarah Elizabeth was also in love with Dirck, her perfect match in every way—dreamer, believer, lover. Together they would make it their time.

CHAPTER 6

The Last Lesson

Everything happened so quickly and was most unusual in the Netherlands where young men seldom married before the age of twenty-five and their brides at least twenty-two, but Dr. James Kent was in ill-health, facing imminent death, and a man with a mission and single-minded focus. He ardently believed he was the only person who fully understood the free spirit that yearned to be free in his cherished daughter and most extraordinary student, who James naively assumed had been forthright with his parents.

He planned to spend the entire morning with the groom and his bride in preparation for the brief ceremony that he would conduct in Alice and Willem's home the next and last day of Dirck's tutorial. There was so much the tutor wanted to cover in the privacy of his study, but his rapid decline since Sarah accepted Dirck's proposal left them little time. The young man was deeply moved by her unwavering response and emotional strength to leave the only home she had ever known and where her parents would soon both be buried. The only marriage gift he had to give her was this last special moment between them with his revered teacher and her beloved father.

James Kent talked of many things, first and foremost, the sanctity of marriage and of his own enduring love for Sarah Elizabeth's mother who had been dead for many years and the profound loss he, his daughter, and Alice endured. He wanted Dirck to see his daughter as an equal in every way and to value the perspective that women bring to a relationship and the world. There would be many dangers ahead for the young couple, and he wanted Dirck to value his wife's insight because it could mean life or death.

"We arrived safely in Amsterdam because my wife Mary and her sister Alice understood clearly what urgently needed to be done to save our family and what I failed to perceive. Women often recognize significant subtleties that men do not notice. It is as if they catch the scent of danger we often miss and men ignore at their peril. They fully grasped the profound implications of our predicament in England. We who sought the reform of practices we thought too Catholic within the Church of England were denied significant posts—the first step to losing livelihood and means to support our families. Many were called before the Star Chamber or High Commission and questioned about their beliefs, and some imprisoned, even executed. They were just forcibly taken and never heard of again, but everyone knew. King James died shortly before we left England, but the coronation of his son only intensified conflict over matters of faith and state. In 1633 King Charles declared William Laud Archbishop, a deadly duo, that worsened the clash with Puritans.

"Even after the wary Separatists left for Amsterdam several years before us, many men still counseled courage or naively believed that who they knew, their professional status or titles in English society or wealth would protect them and their families spared. By year's end of 1625, my wife and Alice thought otherwise. It was not enough to keep my work secret. My lectures before losing that right had been noticed, far more suspect than I realized. More attuned to rumors than I, they knew the house could be searched without warning. The evil was real, powerful, pernicious, and persistent, our circumstance far more uncertain than I was aware. No one could be trusted. The women must get everything ready in secret to leave quickly, and they commandeered our escape, secretly packing the most essential items away from the watchful eyes of servants. To conceal their plan, almost everything we owned must be left behind, and we could tell no one except the contact arranging our journey to Amsterdam.

"Not long after we left our beloved home and dear friends for the safety of the Dutch Netherlands and settled here, I ran into an acquaintance who also fled with his family to Amsterdam. He related that indeed our position relative to the Church of England was suspect, and we were in grave danger. Authorities ransacked our home two days after we left. Our two servants were safe only because they were clearly bewildered and knew nothing.

"Therefore, I urge you to respect each other's many natural gifts and use them wisely. If you do so, your lives will be blessed with a happy home and capacity to provide well for your children and their security."

Ever the scholar and humanist, there were so many things Dr. Kent wanted to say, but he realized that all these years would have to suffice. He had counseled his only surviving child all her life and was tutor to her husband to be for three years at the insistence of Dirck's English mother.

Books and pamphlets he acquired while in Amsterdam along with his manuscripts would be theirs to take on their long and much anticipated voyage, forging their destinies into one life. Thus, he ensured that his protégée and cherished daughter would pass his legacy to their offspring and to the students Dirck yearned to educate in that far-off place. Along with Dirck's diploma and letter of recommendation, Dr. Kent also provided his own professional résumé including the invitation to teach at the University of Leyden. Thus, he hoped to ensure the young man's consideration for the position of schoolmaster, naive given Dutch Reformed clergy generally served such positions in their colonies.

Then he read his favorite excerpt from a collection of the meditative poems of John Donne published in England before they left for Holland and was especially apropos before the couple set sail. Opening to Meditation XVII, "No Man is an Island," he read:

> *No man is an Iland, intire of itself, every man*
> *is a peece of the Continent, a part of the maine;*
> *if a Clod bee washed away by the Sea, Europe*
> *is the lesse, as well as if a Promontorie were, as*
> *well as if a Manor of thy friends or of thine*
> *owne were; any mans death diminishes me,*

because I am involved in Mankinde;
And therefore never send to know for whom
the bell tolls; It tolls for thee.

"This collection of poems is my special gift to you, Dirck. We all live on islands of our own making or so we think and act, but we belong to the whole. Never think that one person counts and another does not. Everyone is of value and precious to God. We all belong to our divinely created humanity. While we prosper here in this remarkable center of global trade, the truth that John Donne's metaphors so eloquently penned in England are lived realities in these water worlds of Holland and Mannahatta Eylandt where you aspire to live. Now, my dearest loves, we must soon part. See your new home here on the map, the island we talked so much about yet also to be acknowledged as part of the maine. You must commit the poem from his meditation to memory. Live and teach that the death of anyone diminishes all, even the death of all the strangers from other lands that you will encounter and embrace in Nieuw Amsterdam as we did here.

"Dirck, I know you carry the burden of leaving your family under angry circumstance. Sarah saw your beautiful mother briefly when she came the last time to renew the contract with me. My daughter would have wanted to know her better. I perceive that your father is a very proud man, but he did permit your study with me. It was not what he wanted, but he must have seen in you what your mother also saw even though his acceptance was never complete because he believed as a responsible father that you needed to master a trade. You must try, if possible, one more time to reconcile with him and so spare yourself and him regret.

"Go to your mother again, gently as I know you will. Her dream imagining your days at the university must seem as a nightmare to her, bereft as she must be of son and shared vision. In her core, however, she is a dreamer, and although your departure to the New World is too hard for her to bear now, she will accept the dreamer in you. It was your birthright and her gift. Don't expect too much. She needs to cry and to hold you tight."

"Yes, Dr. Kent. The last two weeks have been very hard. I owe my mother everything and love her so much that at times the venture seems too great for me, but how many times did we speak of Tacitus, the Roman philosopher, *'the desire for safety stands against every great and noble enterprise?'* Every mother wants her children to be safe. She devotes her energy to that, but I believe my mother also had hopes for something great and noble of me. She just did not expect that to happen quite like this nor I. Your beautiful Sarah Elizabeth and I are losing the ones we love most, but you are us and we are you, and nothing can ever change that, not time or distance or even death, but we do ache, we really ache."

"I know, son, I know."

Then James Kent opened the family Bible to those timeworn pages so familiar to his daughter. "From the time Sarah Elizabeth was very little, I took her on my lap, and before I read a passage, I traced her tiny fingers over the names and dates of family marriages, christenings, and deaths until she knew them all by heart."

Sarah continued, "My father James Kent, his father Jonathan, my mother Mary, her mother Sarah, my Aunt Alice and Willem Pauw, her husband. During our voyage, Dirck, I will share their stories." And she took his hand and placed it on the open Bible. "These people are now your family, and your name will go here with our marriage date."

Her father added, "Tomorrow, this Bible is Mary's and my gift to you, Sarah Elizabeth."

"Thank you, Father."

"One more thing. When your mother died, Alice removed her wedding band, placed it carefully in a silk pouch. Yesterday, she wrapped it in one of your mother's handkerchiefs. Dirck, it is yours to give to your bride during the ceremony." The three of them were so overcome with emotion they could scarcely go on.

"You both have the receipts for payment of your passage. Therefore, do not let them insist at any time that you are indebted to the West-Indische Compagnie. Still there may still be an obstacle or two given your age and that your marriage documents I've prepared will not have been issued by the Dutch Reformed Church or city magistrates. However, if you convince them you are English immigrants living here, and it is seen from my Certificate of Marriage that you are not Dutch Reformed but of nonconformist faith, you may succeed. Also, I have included my permission for Sarah's voyage. Dirck, you appear older than your age. Show your reference letters of study and explain your presence is desired in Nieuw Amsterdam to serve as a schoolmaster and to write and translate documents in Dutch, Latin, and English. Hopefully this will suffice."

The bridal couple was speechless with how thoroughly Sarah's father had seen to every detail within his control.

"Dirck and Sarah, I arranged for us to visit our favorite quay at the Zuyder Zee one last time together, a place we love so much. Alas, we have too little time, and I am too tired so we'll just imagine standing near the shore."

"Oh, Father, we had so many lovely times there, didn't we?"

"Yes, Sarah. That Penelope of antiquity waited at the shore of the Greek Isles for Ulysses, King of Ithaca, her husband and true love to return. Mannahatta and close by islands comprise another water world of rivers, inlets, salt marshes, and bays like that Greek one of old and today's Amsterdam. Whenever you feel lost or troubled, go down to the water's edge and listen to it lapping the shore. Partake of the soothing saltiness of the cool sea breeze. It will heal and remind you of our time together here and delight the little faces of your many children to come.

"In Hebrew, *Ruach* is the word for God's Spirit and for wind. The Book of Genesis tells us that in the very beginning, 'the Spirit of God hovered upon the face of the waters.' Close your eyes, breathe deeply, and feel the wind, the breath of God, caress your face. Recall and embrace these words, and you will know you are not alone. My love for you, Sarah Elizabeth and Dirck, is forever."

CHAPTER 7

Guests Arrive amid More Tangled Webs

The marriage day of Sarah Elizabeth Kent, the only surviving child of Reverend Dr. James Kent from his marriage to Mary, was not, understandably, what either he or Mary's sister Alice envisioned for so many years, far more heartbreaking than joyous and in defiance of the "*laws of the realme*" and the "*Solemnizacion of Matrimonye*" according to the *Book of Common Prayer*. Sarah's father, exhausted from all his final duties as the self-disciplined tutor that he was and the stress of difficult decisions that no one involved could remotely consider ordinary, was very weak, scarcely able to stand. Evident to all, James Kent would very soon be laid to rest—sooner than anyone wanted—perhaps before the last tulip blooms of this sad spring gave up their spirit and collapsed into the ground at his wife's gravesite. The day was as much a final contemplation of their lives even as it was the beginning of a new life for his daughter and her husband. Everyone was drawn within, conflicted, emotional, tense, and uncertain.

Uncle Willem's disapproval of the couple's hasty wedding, lack of formal betrothal and marriage banns, and absence of Dirck's parents remained troubling. Hosting the ceremony in his home implied tacit approval. Aunt Alice knew that even nonmembers of the Dutch Reformed Church had to register with the Council of the Schepenen and secure a certificate for posting of the banns for three Sundays.

Thus, Reverend Dr. Kent's certificate of marriage was essentially null and void under Dutch law before the day was even over. Willem's resolve about what he would allow his own children, sons and daughters, only deepened, and he couldn't ignore the gnawing and growing apprehension about the couple's ill-informed plans to board a ship for Nieuw Nederland.

A third generation global merchant, Willem could not romanticize or minimize the grave risks the couple faced crossing the unpredictable Atlantic Ocean and the adversities that awaited them if they survived the long, difficult voyage. After sailing through the Zuyder Zee Channel at Texel, the ship would catch the Tropical Easterlies and sail south past Spain, the Canary Islands, and then across the southern Atlantic toward the Dutch trading ports of northern Brazil, perhaps Recife. The Prevailing Westerlies would then propel them north toward the West Indisches and the long Atlantic northward coastline toward their destination on the tip of Mannahatta, Nieuw Amsterdam, a long, most unpleasant, dangerous trip at the very least, and often deadly.

Yet the fact remained, Willem's brother-in-law was dying, a good and sincere man, respected and loved by all who knew him. Although James would never hold his grandchildren, he knew Dirck their future father well, and that mattered to him. Sarah's father was about to bless their marriage and lives together in a strange, faraway land. Somehow, Willem reflected, he must support and trust the man's vision during this extraordinary circumstance, but he could not dismiss his concern.

Willem, always one to face a situation squarely, also perceived that the young man was ill-prepared for marriage, in every respect, clearly naïve and innocent. Looking around at the small gathering of guests, it was apparent he was the only one who was up to the task of taking the young man aside before the couple was left alone to consummate the marriage, as they must for it to be fully legitimatized.

Willem and Alice arranged for their brother-in-law to stay at their home after the marriage celebration and requested a doctor for the next day. James had already directed that his daughter's wedding day would also have to end with eventide goodbyes. Their years together when it was possible to truly enjoy and benefit from each other's companionship could now only be a bittersweet, loving memory.

Dirck and Sarah's only time alone together would be two days in her father's small town house before their ship was scheduled to sail. It was now time for Sara Lysbet's turn to leave meals not at Dr. Kent's study desk but just outside the couple's door until it was time to make their way to the quay at the Zuyder Zee where a longboat would take them to their ship farther from shore.

The groom was very somber. It was he who first disrupted all the preconceived notions of his bride's small, close-knit family with the idea of such a daring plan. Within less than a minute, he blurted out upset in response to his father's plans, unrestrained love for the daughter of his esteemed mentor, and the escapade to a new world. It all seemed so natural and right at the time, a pure and honest spontaneous outburst of self-discovery. He finally found voice for what he truly felt and couldn't help himself. Now he anxiously grasped how ill-prepared they both were for the mess his outburst created. He was supposed to be rational, reasonable. He was a scholar.

Dirck was also lost in painful recall of the last few moments with his mother the night before and the unexpected news that foiled his plan to tell both his parents during the evening meal how grateful he was for their generosity that enabled him to pursue advanced study with Dr. Kent. He wanted them to know that much although Dirck would not reveal his plans to leave.

As usual, the first thing his oldest brother Teunis quipped, "Well, now you will know what it is like to do real work for twelve to fifteen hours a day like the rest of us." Typical of his and the other two brothers' attitude and comment for the last three years, he was used to their resentment and conceded the jealousy it evoked. This time, however, he responded, "Teunis, you and our brothers will never say this again to me, never again!"

What startled him, however, was his father's absence. It was to be the last night he would ever see him! Even worse was his mother's baffling explanation.

"Dirck, your father left suddenly for Leyden today. He does have a wealthy client or two there and did say that he had some other business to attend to. I asked him to purchase some woolen for the younger children's clothes next winter if he has time and can get a better price for the goods there. They are growing so fast, and yesterday I tried to find the duffel we purchased a few years ago but couldn't find it. It's been one of those days."

Dirck was stunned by her comments, "I didn't know Father had such plans right now. Why didn't he tell me he was going to the University town? When will he be back?"

"He said to expect him back in less than two weeks if all goes well and quickly. Before he left, your father reflected, 'You know, Dirck and I are really very much alike although it may not seem that way to him or the rest of the family, but we are both fascinated by new ideas and want to learn in order to improve ourselves. He seeks that out through his books and prefers to spend his time with the scholar, Dr. Kent. I like to study new woodworking techniques, how to create a more durable, attractive look efficiently, quicker, easier. We both strive to better understand our material, whether it's wood or words and aspire to be more each and every day. Please tell him that when he comes home and that he can be with the dying man, if need be, until I return. I'm very proud of him for all that he has mastered with Dr. Kent, and I very much appreciated his tutor's thoughtful letter.'

"Dirck, it just brought tears to my eyes. I've been crying all afternoon. The two of you always seem such worlds apart, you and your brothers also, but your father and I love all of you very much, just differently because you are different. Everyone should be different. It would be so boring and useless if we were all the same. Let's try to appreciate each other's unique qualities more."

Thank goodness dinner was almost over because it was awkward after Dirck's outburst and his little sisters somewhat confused by the conversation. He was agitated, anxious, and conflicted, and asked to be excused. Here he was supposed to get married the next day and had not told his parents about that or his plans to board the ship *Swol*, scheduled to embark before his father returned from

Leyden! And who knows, had his father changed his mind about the University? If so, how awful would be his departure, such a betrayal of all that was good about his family. He had violated the trust of his parents. He was supposed to be respectful. He had thought himself a loving son.

Full of regret about hurting his parents and doubt about the rationale for his decision to leave Amsterdam, he wondered, "Do I now call the whole thing off? Will Dr. Kent be disappointed or relieved? Have I dragged his daughter into a precarious venture and put her life at risk? What does Sarah Elizabeth really want? What have I done?"

There are times when life plunges forth in unexpected direction with unanticipated force, too fast and powerful to make account of it and can't be stopped like a stormy ocean surge crashing through dykes and dams sucking everything and everyone into its raging waters. Holland didn't seem quite so flat anymore. Dirck just lost his footing and was sinking into a quagmire of his own making and no seeming escape.

His bride Sarah Elizabeth Kent would appear any moment. Unfamiliar guests, recently arrived in Amsterdam, just entered the parlor where the ceremony was to take place. In recent correspondence to his lifelong friend, Dr. Robert Blake, James asked if he could leave Leyden as soon as possible for Amsterdam. He described his health condition, probability of imminent death, and plans for Sarah. Dr. Blake quickly responded and brought his second wife, Jane, who he met in the University town shortly after accepting the professorship. When Mary Kent was pregnant with Sarah Elizabeth in England, Robert and his first wife were asked to witness as godparents for the christening when that day came. By that time, however, Dr. Blake was seriously thinking about departing for Holland, but his wife was resistant to leaving family, home, and friends. When she died suddenly of a terrible fever, Blake wrote the Kents of her death and that regretfully they could not be present for the christening after the baby was born.

He wrote of his decision to move forward in a new direction and recommended his friend do the same, code for leaving England as soon as possible. James Kent knew how much Robert loved and was devoted to his work and immediately grasped that the new direction he talked about was definitely a geographic one east to the freedom and safety of Holland, but James was not convinced nor prepared at that time to take such a drastic step for himself and his family, at least not while his wife was pregnant. She already had two miscarriages.

The Blakes arrived the day before the wedding and stayed with Willem and Alice. Robert was aghast when he saw how much his friend had declined and the couple stunned to learn there was no formal betrothal and the marriage quickly arranged. Although they were not Sarah's godparents in fact, James considered his friend Robert a godparent by intent and asked them to sign marriage documents stating such. They agreed because of Robert's profound regard for his devoted friend. Such haste, indeed urgency, to conduct the wedding ceremony of his daughter, once the toddler in her mother's arms Robert met eighteen years ago at the shore of the Zuyder Zee, was uncharacteristic of the reflective scholar and reverent theologian. However, the penetrating focus, despite his illness, revealed more than words that something bigger than all of them was at work, but there would be no lively discussion this unusual day. Sarah Elizabeth's father was exhausted and quiet. The bells had tolled for their beloved James, and they all knew it.

Dr. Blake had the foresight to request that his good friend Philippe Rapalje accompany them. Blake's second wife Jane left England with her family and settled in Leyden where she and Philippe's wife became good friends. The two women saw each other frequently at the market place. Jane, educated and multilingual, conversed easily in French with the Walloon Rapaljes. Their grandparents left the Spanish Netherlands for England in 1570 while others escaped to France and Germany due to the severity of the Catholic Inquisition under the Iron Duke of Alva and his Blood Council. Many, like the Rapaljes, eventually settled in Leyden and worshipped at the Vrouwekerk.

Joris Rapalje, a cousin of Philippe, hastily married Catalina Trico, both very young, a few days before they joined a small group of Walloons in 1624, the very first group of colonists to leave Holland for Nieuw Nederland. In the Walloon community of Leyden, the couple was legendary and rumor had it both were still alive and prosperous, and parents of the first child born in the nascent colony.

Philippe, however, didn't think much of Nieuw Amsterdam. For most, colonization had not gone well. Since 1640, supposedly under instruction from the *High Mightinesses Staten Generaal,* the West-Indische Compagnie was finally providing better incentives to ordinary people for settlement. Based on information he and other Walloon relatives received, however, he had reason to doubt their status would improve significantly under the present Director, Willem Kieft. Blake thought Philippe might talk some sense into his friend and the bridal couple about their plans to leave Amsterdam and board a ship for Mannahatta. He certainly understood the history of persecution they all shared and the imperative to make quick, uncertain, life-changing decisions. This, however, was different. No one was in danger so both men were puzzled why Blake's remarkable friend would encourage the young couple to marry so soon and leave such a prosperous and vibrant city where they were all doing quite well with a bright future for a place so unlike what they knew and were accustomed to.

The bride's aunt had good reason to be anxious. Once the couple married and consummated the marriage, life would become very complicated for them all if they could not embark for Nieuw Amsterdam. Still, Alice consented to sign the marriage certificate as witness and use her maiden name, quite common on Dutch documents, and simply identify herself as aunt. Like her husband, she still did not approve of the whole arrangement and was concerned about Dirck's parents. Where were they in all of this and why not present? A very troubling situation, but something inside her knew Sarah's father had a more profound view of the moment at hand.

There were a few close friends Willem and Alice might have invited, but that would have engendered unpleasant speculation about the necessity of such a quick wedding and getaway with too many prying questions. There was enough upset to go around not to deal with that. She would see to it that her niece's good reputation and that of their family remained intact.

Still unable to accept the reality of it all, nevertheless, Alice managed her emotions with the distraction of ensuring a wedding feast for the small wedding party. There was an abundant assortment of North Holland cheese, Gouda, Leyden spiced with cumin, and Edam, plenty of bread and butter. Kibbeling, a battered white fish, soused herring and mussel, and pea soup graced the table. The children loved their mother's *rodekool met appeljes* and gherkins, and delighted in the spiced sweets including marzipan, *zoute drop* of salty licorice, and many with *kojkjes* like *stroopwafel, gevulde koek,* and *nougatientjes.*

The older children, Christiaan, Wilm, Sara Lysbet, and the younger ones Kees and twins Geertje and Maritje remained perplexed and sad. Sarah Elizabeth was part of their family before they were born, always the older sister and good for extra hugs, help with reading and getting ready for school. She could always be easily persuaded to tell a bedtime story or two. During the dark cold months of winter especially, they eagerly looked forward to her imaginary tales of faraway places with strange sounding names, peculiar people, and all sorts of creatures they never saw in Holland, mostly only familiar with horses and cows, fish and fowl. What were these furry creatures called beavers with big floppy tails anyway, and were the wilden dangerous?

But her stories were always supposed to be just for fun fantasy, made up, not real life. Were they really true then and how could she leave their family for somewhere so different from the canals and *polders* and market places of Amsterdam? Their mother feared they would never see Sarah again, the first time they ever saw her so unhappy. Maybe they would all feel better when they got to eat her scrumptious meal and sweets after the ceremony. Maybe.

Alice guided Christiaan and Wilm to either side of the parlor door. It was time. "Everyone, please stand, the bride, our sister, is here." It was Sarah Elizabeth Kent's time, and she felt exquisitely alive, radiant and beautiful in her mother's best dress that Alice saved for her. The world whirling without and within everyone only moments before was stilled at last, the room hushed with only the tiniest whisper between Geertje and Maritje. Dr. Robert Blake walked over to the bride and accompanied her to Dirck Hendricksz. where she would soon place her hand in his.

Sarah Elizabeth's striking moonstone eyes and confident smile framed in her soft golden curls lit up the entire room. Together the impossible was possible, the improbable certain, and Dirck silently pledged his utmost to love and protect her and their children in every way a man could. With her beside him, Dirck was healed and whole. Holland's gray sky lifted, doubt vanished, and the long awaited bright spring sun entered into the celebration through an open window infusing them all with light and love.

"*Dearely beloved frendes and familie, we are gathered together in the sight of God, and in the face of his congregacion, to joyne together this man and this woman in holy matrimony, signifying unto us the mystical union that is betwixt Christ and his Churche.*"

The good reverend interrupted the ceremony and paused to steady himself and recover his composure before explaining that he met the previous morning with the bridal couple in the quiet and comfort of his study. Although most Puritans had rejected the *Book of Common Prayer* that included the traditional wedding service, he shared with them the portions he valued and should be retained and that, if stronger, he would have liked to extend to all present.

"Before my strength and spirit fails completely, this much must be said. In England, the doors of our hallowed church were locked, our devoted congregation dispersed, and my license to preach revoked. That was the way of it for those of us who would not conform to the doctrine and ritual of the Church of England. Alice remembers those days of fear and uncertainty all too well. Our small family then became our only congregation until we fled. Although we need not fear for our very lives and were permitted liberty of conscience without interference of any sort, Dutch authorities did not permit our own public place of worship. Again our loved ones have been our only congregation hosted in this very home where I have been accorded every respect by my very dear brother-in-law, my brother indeed, Willem, and my wife's loving sister, Alice.

"We once thought that God would always provide bread on our table, but there may not always be butter on our bread as the

Dutch say. Happily, the generosity of Willem and his father filled our soul with charity and our bodies not only with bread and butter and cheese, but such as Alice graciously prepared for us to celebrate this blessed event.

"All of this is to say that pure circumstance impelled us to consider and live what is most essential and enduring for the practice of our faith. We gave up much once thought to be binding, unquestioned. With the loss of my strength and health, again more was stripped away. What now remains is the love that Jesus, our Lord and Savior, gave to the world. What now remains when all else is stripped away is grace freely, generously given, the Spirit of God that infuses us with love and blessing.

"When Sarah Elizabeth was a very little girl her mother Mary was pregnant again although I did not know that when arrangements were made to debate and lecture at the University of Leyden. Two months later, when it was time to depart, she insisted that I promise to ensure a loving, capable husband for our daughter and to serve as minister for their marriage. Her entreaty left me most uneasy. Nonetheless, she insisted that I keep my commitment to the University and keep this promise to her. Alas, as you know, that was the last time we were together.

"Thus it is that we find ourselves in this perplexing predicament that we must yet view from the perspective, 'in God's good time.' I myself began to despair that I could not keep that final promise to my wife yet one that I would not void. So as it happened, a way for its fulfillment was made, yet in so doing it was not possible to regard the law of the land that has been our happy home these many years. I am profoundly aware this is a troubling matter for all of us and that within this, our small congregation, you find yourselves witness to this blessed union under unusual and anxious circumstance. However, I trust completely that everything has happened as meant to be and ask that you open in faith to this larger realm of purpose and grace.

"This is what appeared to me when one young man, our Dirck Hendricksz., with childlike faith blurted out what was most honest in his heart, most true in his mind, and most right to the integrity of what he newly and most clearly understood in his very soul. Suddenly and seemingly unbidden, the letter that is his life was opened. The immediacy of this inner reality was like that treasure hidden in the soil of his soul and so strikingly imagined in the parable of Jesus and exacting a price, the willingness to give up everything else. Dirck was at a point of no return, to seize the moment or forever betray and discard what was most essential to his very identity— his God-given talent, commitment, vision, and passion. In a single moment of divinely inspired clarity, we discover our truest heart's desire grounded in the profound awareness of what we are called to be. Thus, we find ourselves in this consequential moment so that…

"We are stripped to the core of our belief, that this man and this woman will simply take their *trouth* to the other hand in hand, according to '*God's holy ordinaunce*' in your presence, our loving, faithful family and friends."

Dr. Blake gave Dirck the ring that Alice placed in a silk pouch so long ago, wrapped in her sister's white handkerchief, and with Reverend James Kent's blessing, "man and wife."

It was the last time James Kent would stand unaided. He was spent and like Alice overcome that it was as if Mary herself was present in the person of their beautiful, loving daughter. The bridal couple enveloped their dearest father and teacher in their arms, sobbing with great joy and great grief until they knew they must support him arm in arm to a nearby chair.

They thanked and chatted with Philippe Rapalje, Robert and Jane Blake until they were besieged by the children, the girls tenderly touching Sarah's beautiful dress, and all just bursting with pride and love at the transformation of their sister into a dazzling bride. Sara Lysbet, her namesake, beamed, "Oh, I hope I will be so pretty on my wedding day, just like you!"

The couple saved Willem and Alice Pauw for last. "How can I ever thank you for all you have done for me. You saved my parents and you saved me, and now my husband Dirck."

Her Aunt and Uncle spontaneously responded, "No, it is you, Sarah Elizabeth, who saved us and our family. You filled the empty spaces of our lives and made the full ones brighter."

"Dear Uncle Willem and Aunt Alice, it is now time for your Sara to be the oldest sister. It is best for her, best for you, and best for the other children. I can't imagine going on without all of you and will never forget your love and generosity, but as Father always says, 'in God's good time.' You deserve the very best. I love you and my cousins so much."

"Sarah and Dirck, the Staten Generaal require that all captains follow regulations for food provisioning to the letter of the law for every passenger and crew member. In fact, many foreign sailors sign on our ships because we provide better and more food than other countries. After a few weeks at sea, however, they have to rely on foods that keep reasonably well for long distances and not really adequate for good health. You will only have fresh food for a short time then followed by salted herring and other salted foods, dried peas and beans, hard ships' biscuits, porridge made of groats in the morning, dried fruit, and lots of cheese often moldy. Chickens and other livestock on board, perhaps pigs will then be provided. The reality is this food can't possibly offer everything you really need to stay well, especially the last half of the voyage."

"Sarah Elizabeth," added Alice, "at that time put some of the dried herbs I gave you and some of the spices if desperate for more flavor in with whatever beverage they provide to soften them up, then mix that with your food. Be sure to keep the herbs and spices dry until then. They will help make up for the loss of fresh fruit, greens, and vegetables later in your voyage."

"Remember when my brother was here from Leyden? He brought medicinal herbs from the Hortus Botanicus and wrote instructions for Alice to use, but he will send us more."

"Thank you, Uncle. You have always been thoughtful and generous. Our family was so blessed to become your family. It is indeed right that we end this day with a song of thanks and praise. Father requested that before eating we all sing the Dutch hymn written after the United Provinces gained their independence from Spain. He was moved to tears by what your people endured and how that struggle was expressed with such simplicity yet profound depth, gratitude, and reverence by the composer."

"We will, Sarah Elizabeth. We will!"

"Alice, please wrap Father in the cloak that Mother made for him our first year here. He faithfully wore it whenever there was even the slightest chill, and now it is quite worn. Promise me you will do this. Papa told me that when I was a little girl that I wanted to put a blanket over Mother's grave to keep her warm during the long winter. Do you remember that?"

"Yes, I do, Sarah, very much so."

"Please keep my father warm for me, Alice, please. I know you will."

"Dirck, we don't know you very well, but there is something in you that is deep and steady. I'm just now beginning to understand my brother-in-law's confidence in you and Sarah Elizabeth's unwavering love. You are courageous and strong, yet tender and genuine. We give you both our blessing and prayers for a safe journey and long life together with many children. We will never forget you."

"That means a lot to us, Mr. Pauw. Thank you."

"Call me Uncle, Dirck. Call me Uncle. We are family now."

"Thank you, Uncle Willem, it is an honor, sir."

*****

We gather together to ask the Lord's blessing;
He chastens and hastens His will to make known;
The wicked oppressing now cease from distressing;
Sing praises to His name He forgets not His own.

Beside us to guide us, our God with us joining,
Ordaining, maintaining His Kingdom divine;
So from the beginning the fight we were winning;
Thou, Lord, was at our side all glory be Thine.

*Unknown Netherlander and published in 1626

Penelope's Song

PART 2

Lynn, Massachusetts Bay Colony, New England, 1643

Turning and turning in the widening gyre
The falcon cannot hear the falconer;
Things fall apart; the centre cannot hold;
Mere anarchy is loosed upon the world,
The blood-dimmed tide is loosed, and everywhere
The ceremony of innocence is drowned;
The best lack all conviction, while the worst
Are full of passionate intensity.

—William Butler Yeats
"The Second Coming," 1919

CHAPTER 8

Point of No Return

The Tower of London and fiery stake, edict and excommunication, banishment and exile, or oppression by any other name, fragile boundaries breached. Ancestral lands confiscated. Families alienated. Economic life lines ruptured. Community places and congregational spaces plundered. Personhood violated. Bodies tortured, minds twisted, souls tormented. Unpredictable landscapes beckoned. Strangers sojourned in strange lands. Dreams imagined and dreams aborted. Disruption.

Heresy was deadly, the stuff of treason. The marriage of monarchs with matters of money, state, and church produced a perennial existence of agitation and anxiety, endless persecution, and war without end. For the unfortunate many, life didn't get better and better. Sometimes the most resilient survived, and the just plain plucky or lucky perhaps prospered. Some possessed of large vision and uncommon resource assessed their predicament, planned accordingly, and departed for a *"city set upon a hill,"* Salem, a place of peace; or looking heavenward, a *New Haven*; and Lady Deborah Dunch Moody was in the middle of it all.

For Dame Deborah and her friends in faith and reason, the frigid winter of 1642 just got colder in Lynn, Massachusetts Bay Colony. The very independent, aristocratic widow and two married women were charged and admonished by the Salem Quarterly Court for *"…Houldinge that the baptizing of infants is noe ordinance of God."*

Unwilling to renounce their *"error,"* Puritan ministers and magistrates were compelled to condemn Lady Moody and John Tilton's wife, Mary. Since the New Testament said nothing about infant baptism, the women, like others of independent thought claiming liberty of conscience informed by scriptural interpretation, concluded it ought to be a decision derived from the mature understanding of mind and heart. The women did not coerce others to adhere to their Baptist beliefs but neither would they recant their position nor present their infants at the baptismal font. Like the Augustinian monk Martin Luther more than one century before them who would not recant his declaration against unsupportable doctrine and practice, excommunication and exile was only a matter of procedure and time. They were forewarned, and this time the culprit was not the Spanish Inquisition, Pope Leo X or Catholic Queen Mary, James I or Charles I and the Star Chamber or High Commission. It was not the furies of Reformation and Counter Reformation, the High Church of England and Archbishop Laud, or marauding armies gone amok. It was the up close, personal, and ultimate betrayal of Puritan against Puritan, friend against friend, and the dignified Lady Moody, adverse to spectacle, was in no mood for public trial.

Many in New England and back in the homeland were appalled by the 1637 outcome of another trial—what happened to Anne Marbury Hutchinson, daughter of the much-respected Francis Marbury, Puritan Vicar of London and previously minister in Alford, Lincolnshire, where she grew up. Charged with heresy and imprisoned for seeking reform of the Church of England to abandon popish appearance and ritual, her father was an inspirational role model. Well-schooled by him in the Holy Scriptures, an articulate debater, and possibly the most brilliant theologian in Puritan New England, Anne skillfully defended her spirited and intricately reasoned beliefs during the proceedings but to no avail. John Cotton, the minister the Hutchinsons once revered and who inspired them to leave the comforts of their beloved motherland and flourishing affairs to follow him and brave the Atlantic crossing with their brood of eleven children, distanced himself from previous praise for Anne's theological insights, long-standing friendship, and regard for the Hutchinson family. Devoid of support for his once devoted and prosperous church members, Cotton clearly lacked the Hutchinsons' loyalty and integrity. How then could the widow Lady Moody and her friends possibly hope for a satisfactory outcome?

William Thorne, Deborah's friend in Salem and Lynn who was fined in 1641 for hiding and helping Francis Hutchinson, Anne's son and son-in-law, William Collins, and aware that worse was yet to come, left for Sandwich. He didn't wait around to be pilloried or purged by courts in Boston, the city set upon a hill.

Another friend Thomas Savage, married to Anne's daughter Faith, was unwilling to take back the courageous and powerful defense of his mother-in-law. Encouraged by Roger Williams, the thriving and ever-expanding, highly regarded Hutchinson clan with more than thirty-five families traveled south beyond the reach of the Bay Colony to Aquidneck Island rather than remain silent witness to the unjust and cruel fate imposed by the "*Saints*" of Boston. Williams, a minister of Salem, likewise condemned for his civil and religious views three years before the Hutchinsons were banished, was forced to leave his wife and children and flee into the wilderness during another frigid winter night.

Rescued by the Narragansetts who saved him from certain death, he remained steadfastly loyal to them and in good relationship. In 1636, on land they conveyed to Williams, a new dream emerged in the form of Providence Plantation that was to become a safe haven for his family and other nonconformists of the established Bay Colony Puritan Way. Thomas Savage, Anne's husband Will, and others devised and signed the Portsmouth Compact prior to their departure from Boston in 1638. They would be the beneficiaries of the friendship between Roger Williams and the Narragansetts and his knowledge of their language that enabled these exiles and others to obtain land on Aquidneck and begin anew.

How was it then that Lady Deborah Dunch Moody, formerly of London and Wiltshire Garsdon Manor, found herself in a similar predicament so far from her ancestral home? By 1629, four years into the reign of Charles I, Parliament, already disputing powers of the Monarchy over the rights of Englishmen, had become increasingly

Puritan. During the 1630s, conflict with High Church Archbishop William Laud and the devotion of Charles I to his Catholic Queen Henrietta Maria escalated. Daughter of Catholic King Henry IV of France and Marie de' Medici of Tuscany, historically passionate patrons of arts and letters, she was the target of Puritan ire. Increasingly embroiled in political, military, economic, and religious dissension, the Stuart King dispensed with Parliament in 1629, the year that Lady Deborah's husband, Sir Henry Moody, a member of that deposed Parliament, became deathly ill in London as did Thomas Fones, apothecary to her husband. Fones was married to the sister of John Winthrop, elected Governor to Massachusetts Bay Colony in October of the same year before leaving England in 1630. Winthrop was personally acquainted with Dame Deborah and thus very aware of the lady's tragic loss when Sir Henry died, yet thirteen years later the most influential man in the Puritan colony would abandon support for her.

Sir Henry's grandfather, Richard Modye, while a footman in the court of Henry VIII, saved the king's life when the monarch, then much overweight, fell off his horse landing face down and would have suffocated in the mud had Modye not responded quickly. When the king, still without a male heir, broke with the Catholic Church to divorce Queen Catherine and marry Anne Boleyn, he dissolved its vast holdings in England and rewarded loyal subjects, such as Richard Modye, with former abbeys and other properties. Thus it was that Sir Henry Moody inherited Garsdon Manor, two miles from Malmesbury, the manor houses of Lee and Cleverdon, twenty houses, ten cottages, one thousand acres of meadow, five hundred acres of pasture, twenty acres of wood and other acreage. Further, he was entitled, as his father and grandfather before him, to rents from these properties and a portion of the income from corn, grain, and hay. His wife and son were also to inherit Whitchurch Manor.

Unfortunately, Sir Henry died deeply in debt, a not unusual circumstance given many peers and gentry were land rich but cash poor. When Parliament refused to finance the wars abroad of King Charles, aristocrats and gentry were increasingly subject to the crown's excessive taxes including the despised ship's tax previously not required of inland gentry and aristocrats, additional fees, and fines. Prices for basic domestic goods set by powerful monopolies enabled by the king became excessively high and further threatened financial stability with high inflation.

Technically considered a tenant of the Crown, all of Sir Henry's holdings were subjected to *Inquisitions Post Mortem,* a jury of eighteen to determine the extent of an estate derived from the largess of the monarchy. Fortunately, at that time, Lady Moody's son was twenty-three. When fourteen years old, he matriculated at the prestigious Magdalen College of Oxford University and received his bachelor's degree on his eighteenth birthday in 1624. He then pursued the study of law at Lincoln's Inn of Court in London. By the time his father died, he was an accomplished young man prepared to assist his mother through the intense legal and financial wranglings that continued from 1629 through 1638 including the sale of Garsdon Manor to Sir Lawrence Washington. He was knighted by King Charles thus becoming Sir Henry the Younger and inherited his father's baronetcy with its privileges, responsibilities, and expense, but by then, a vastly smaller portion of the family's former wealth remained with mother and son.

Lady Deborah's father, Walter Dunch, provided generously for his daughters' dowries enabling her to contribute the marriage portion to the wealth of her husband's estate. According to the custom of the time, she retained that portion after the death of her husband. When all was settled, she was entitled, therefore, to the use of Whitchurch Manor during her lifetime and to twenty pounds sterling every year thereby providing some relief to the beleaguered widow.

Severely isolated, however, she sought the solace of religious discourse, friends, and son in London, a lively place—the intersection of foreign diplomats, courtiers, artists, musicians, dramatists, scientists, merchants—that drew the enterprising and the poor for commerce and became increasingly overcrowded. The wealthy enjoyed their elegant estates and lavish lifestyle along the Strand of the River Thames, close to theaters, shops, apothecaries, booksellers, and other attractions, a place to see and be seen, but the dense population of rich and poor was all the more therefore susceptible to plague and other downsides of a large municipality. King Charles, aware of the dangers of a crowded city and always in need of more revenue, believed the country estates of the wealthy would fare better and thus contribute more taxes if their lords and ladies spent more of their productive time at home than in the capital. A season of visit was acceptable and encouraged but even his most important appointees were required to share responsibilities on rotation between their manors and London.

Thus, it was that the Star Chamber ordered Lady Moody to return to Wiltshire having long overstayed in London. Now much reduced in land and wealth, the status and life she once enjoyed with husband and son at home and in London vanished, doors closed, and few would open in the future. Her mother did not fare well after the death of her husband when she married Sir James Mervyn. Self-indulgent and proving unfaithful, he took unfair advantage of the wealth the woman brought to the marriage. Certainly, this Lady Deborah would not seek to remarry.

John Winthrop and other friends and associates from London had already crossed the Atlantic for the city set upon a hill, a place of new beginnings and thought free from the constraints of religious persecution. Along with some of her servants and friends from London and Wiltshire, the courageous and resilient woman would join others who had already found their way to a new world. Thus it was that Dame Deborah provided power of attorney to her son to conclude their financial and legal affairs in her coming absence.

Shortly after Lady Moody's arrival from England, Governor John Winthrop opened his home to her until she could settle in a small house at Salem, an amazing busy place for about one thousand inhabitants and mostly a tight cluster of four hundred homes. On April 5, 1640, she was accepted into Salem's First Church, the town's most impressive structure, innocently pure white with its nearby whipping post and pillory, a foreboding reminder of persecution she thought left behind in her troubled country. Had she been subjected to the usual examination of doctrinal details of one's conversion and faith, she may not so quickly and easily have been counted a member in good standing. According to her reading of the scripture and in discussion with others back in London, it seems her nonconformist views were not exposed. Perhaps in the eyes of Dame Deborah's examiners, her highborn status as a lady of worth and the reputation of her mother's family of highly regarded clerics was deemed sufficient. What really mattered to the Saints, however, was evidence by experience of genuine conversion and relationship to God's saving grace. In that regard, Lady Moody was indeed genuine.

However, to a manor born and bred and to a manor wed in the southern English countrysides of Berkshire and Wiltshire, the in-your-face immediacy of Salem neighbors was certainly a bit too close and intrusive for a woman who would soon realize that the understood imperative to conform was not why she left everything that was familiar and crossed the turbulent Atlantic. It was liberty of conscience, to interpret Scripture as she understood the words to mean—the freedom she sought in New England—that fully impelled such a radical departure.

Scarcely a year later, Providence seemed to offer a solution to her desire for more autonomy when she learned that Deputy Governor John Humphrey planned to return to England by way of Barbados with his wife, the Lady Susan, daughter of the Third Earl of Lincolnshire. Their farm with its thirteen hundred acres a few miles away in Lynn, originally called Saugus by its original inhabitants, was a smaller community supported mainly by farming and fishing. Certainly, it was more removed from the scrutiny of prying eyes and ears and suddenly available to her. The sale gained the Humphreys a more than tidy sum, and one perhaps too generous, more than was warranted to the disadvantage of Widow Moody. However, with a view to the several tenant farmers already working the land, a relationship she was familiar with as a child and wife, the solitary but astute woman must have thought it worth the risk to her diminishing resources.

Whatever the rationale, like Anne Hutchinson before her, many of the scattered local Lynn residents were drawn to Lady Moody's resolute conviction and charisma. They came to appreciate her views in opposition to infant baptism, alas, a profound influence that would all too soon come to the attention of ministers and magistrates in

Salem and Boston…and so it went with all its vexing reverberations. It was something that they and Governor John Winthrop, now the most highly regarded man in all of the Massachusetts Bay Colony, could not countenance. Rigidly entrenched in a narrowly defined Puritan Way to ensure stability and success and deemed a loving act to guide them into the fold of the holy Covenant, they were impelled to persuade her and the Tiltons to reject their *"error"* even as they unsuccessfully tried with Roger Williams and the Hutchinsons. Lady Moody, John and Mary Tilton remained steadfast during the early months of 1643. Excommunication would surely follow. So ostracized, thousands of fellow Puritans must refuse them solace and shelter or face disciplinary consequences. One seamless web of civil and religious solidarity would prevail. That which Roger Williams had so ardently argued against, leadership deemed imperative priority. Among powerful authorities, contested arbitrary boundaries of faith posed a fatal threat, a breach of that community order.

Even King Charles and others in England were dismayed by the controversies and severe punishment in New England towns. Long before Lady Moody arrived at Salem, leaders of the Massachusetts Bay Colony had pursued a road of self-rule and viewed themselves beyond the need to swear allegiance to the King such that their charter might even be withdrawn.

By 1640, two decades of massive migration of Puritans fleeing England had come to an end. The days when hundreds of ships arrived every year carrying people, news, and trade goods were over. In response to the confrontation of the King in the House of Parliament, London erupted, His Majesty and Queen forced to flee. What happened there happened to Atlantic on shore colonists beyond the seas. With friends, associates, family, and economic interests still in England, life in the Bay Colony was once more uncertain as trade with the mother county all but dried up, and young men drifted back across the ocean to support the Puritan Parliament Cause. The tides had turned, and the Great Puritan Migration to Massachusetts had come to an end and with it a new exodus of open minds and daring souls begun to other Atlantic shores.

During the first weeks that followed the late December 1642 decision of the Quarterly Court, it was time to review the situation. Warmed and comforted by the fire of her commodious Swampscott home, Lady Deborah privately analyzed her course of action, the choices she could make, and reflected on the stories her mother, another Deborah, recounted to her when she was just a girl. Deborah Moody was not the first in her family to face exile, and that fact inspired hope and strengthened her resolve.

Her mother's father, the highly esteemed Right Reverend James Pilkington, was a prominent Protestant cleric who fled the fiery stake of Catholic Queen, Bloody Mary, for a life of service. During most of the 1550s, he sought refuge in Zurich, Geneva, Basel, and Frankfurt where he educated children of other refugee Protestants until Mary's half sister was crowned Queen Elizabeth I, and he could safely return to England. Pilkington secured a post of divinity professor at Cambridge and increasingly known for his preaching and oratory, he was summoned in 1560 to preach before the Queen at the Royal Court. Consecrated Bishop of Durham the following year, he revised the *Book of Common Prayer* and continued his mission to promote the Protestant education of children founding the Rivington Free Grammar School.

Religious conflict again threatened the trajectory of the good bishop's life in 1569. When the Earls of Westmorland and Northumberland plotted to overthrow Elizabeth I in favor of restoring Roman Catholicism, the Right Reverend Bishop was forced to flee again, this time with wife and small children in tow, including Lady Deborah's mother. The earls raised an impressive cavalry and army of six thousand soldiers. Storming Protestant churches and Pilkington's Durham Cathedral, they destroyed English Bibles and *Book of Common Prayer*. He and his family escaped to London dressed as beggars. When the rebellion failed and peace was restored, Elizabeth the Queen retained the Crown, and Bishop Pilkington resumed his work.

After his death, his many books were passed to his schools and daughters, his sons having died as little boys. In death as in life, he was magnanimous providing generously for family and others.

Forever revered, he left a legacy of devotion to education and the family traits of sacred wisdom, fortitude, resiliency, and renewal.

Like her exiled grandfather, the sooner Lady Moody and her friends made plans to leave of their own volition while they could the better, but in Virginia the Anglican Church prevailed. Seasonal disease took an alarming toll on newcomers of that royal colony. The not so inclusive and Separatist Plymouth Colony to the north struggled and did not bode a warm welcome. Villages founded by Puritans along shores of Long Island Sound were just more of the same judgments and control. Thanks to the Narragansetts, the single exception were the settlements of Roger Williams and worthy of consideration but somewhat in a state of chaos and at risk of wreck and ruin by the aggressive Massachusetts Bay Colony seeking more land.

It was rumored Williams planned to leave for England to secure a formal charter and so keep his colony safe from such incursion, but in order to secure a seaworthy vessel denied him by Massachusetts magistrates, he was headed to the Dutch Island of Mannahatta to wait a ship from Virginia bound for England. He gambled on such a journey to protect his colony's future autonomy. A few months after he successfully departed for London, colonial ports were just receiving news that Reading, site of a major Royalist garrison near Oxford and the King's Civil War capital, surrendered to the Earl of Essex's Parliamentarian forces. One of many unfortunate outcomes to years of contention between the prerogatives of royal authority and the rights of Englishmen vested in Parliament, England was increasingly a precarious destination. For Lady Moody and her friends returning to homeland was clearly not an option.

Undaunted, like her parents and grandparents before her, Lady Moody, too possessed of large vision and uncommon resourcefulness and resiliency, assessed their predicament, planned accordingly, and given the unfortunate fault lines of homeland and English colonies, looked outward to still another strange land. She and her friends of kindred spirit were at a point of no return, but that only called forth a surprising path to plant her dream.

Edict and excommunication. Expulsion. English and European enmity. Once again unpredictable landscapes beckoned. Strangers sojourned in strange lands. Such was the state of affairs in all of Britannia and Continental Europe long before Deborah Dunch Moody was born and during her long, remarkable, and at times tumultuous life. Would it be such after her death?

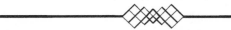

Penelope's Song

PART 3

Atlantic Shores, 1643

A dream which is not understood is like a letter which is not opened.

—The Talmud

CHAPTER 9

The Letter

Amsterdam
April 5, 1643

Dear Father and Mother,

I made a burdensome decision without your approval. You are generous, loving parents and not to blame in any way for what I alone am now accountable. Please know this with absolute certainty.

Alas, I am not a first, second, or even third son but your fourth, the last one forever trailing after the others making it more difficult to become the independent adult I want to be. You know I've always been more restless, more driven to cast about, learn new ideas, and pursue my own aspirations. That doesn't mean I don't respect what you have accomplished and want for us, the imperative to master a trade. Father, I am proud and impressed by your commitment to your craft and your remarkable expertise. You supported our large family in comfort with great love, but I must follow the powerful prompting that impels me to seek a future different from my brothers. There were signs of that from the very beginning that must have made you both anxious.

Father, you were very generous in supporting my studies with Dr. Kent, who died one day before I wrote this letter. That opportunity meant everything to me not only because of what I learned but because you so lovingly supported Mother's dream that I should study at the University and sacrificed much for our sake. I can never repay either of you according to what you deserve and should be respected.

I was very touched, Father, by the parting words you shared with Mother before you left for Leyden. My departure without our last embrace or your permission will understandingly be deemed betrayal and for both of you almost too much to bear, certain to hurt, and make you angry. However, do not be bitter. It simply had to be. From the time I saw my first ships, began drawing them, and heard the songs and read stories of far-off lands, this future was mine to touch and now must set out on my own. I thought myself content with study but recently grasped those musings were more than just a small boy's past time.

When you receive this letter, I will be beyond the Zuyder Zee and the channel at Texel aboard the West-Indische Compagnie ship, *Swol*. May the name in Dutch for you, Father, and for you, Mother, in English, *Sturdy, Well-Built*, at least be of some comfort. I do recall when you received the commission for the *Swol's* finish carpentry, Father. Although your work is not about the structural strength of our Dutch ships, it is you who contributes to their grace and beauty, and through such extraordinary workmanship, you will be with me on this journey.

There is always much talk in Amsterdam, as you well know, about our trading empire overseas although less is bantered about my destination, Nieuw Amsterdam. I learned they are much in need of schoolmasters, and my capacity to read and write Dutch, English, and Latin will be valued where few have this ability. Located between the English colonies in Virginia to the south and Massachusetts to the northeast and that Latin is the written language of the highly educated and government officials, I expect to fully support myself and eventually a family.

Father, the skills acquired during my apprenticeship with you will also be useful as there is now a need for more housing, and in the forests of Nieuw Nederland I will find the finest quality wood you require since Holland increasingly competes for lumber from the Baltics. I want to make you proud and one day ship you the very best.

Mother, I took the duffel you purchased to craft a bag for my belongings in anticipation of my matriculating at the University. I feel badly for your distress in not finding it. I was selfish and unkind.

Not to follow my dream would yield a life of regret, but please know that although I do not deserve your forgiveness, I do love you both with all my heart and will forever hold you dear.

During the voyage I will frequently write in a journal and send it to you via the *Swol's* return or another ship to Amsterdam and letters from Nieuw Amsterdam once settled there.

Please tell the girls their Dirksje loves them very much and will miss their giggles, affection, bright eyes, and endearing smiles. They are very special and will grow up to be beautiful young ladies.

Respectfully your loving son,
Dirck

CHAPTER 10

The Swol

It was Willem's sad task to confirm for his wife that the newlyweds Sarah Elizabeth Kent and Dirck Hendricksz. had indeed boarded and embarked for the West-Indisches and Mannahatta on the merchant ship *Swol* under contract of the WIC as Dr. James Kent believed with certainty would happen. The circumstance, however, was most peculiar.

When Willem walked in the door, Alice was waiting for him, anxious and distracted. She knew, somehow she knew, and unhappily resigned to the awful, awful before he returned. His immediate embrace and tears confirmed the worst. His wife's beloved niece and her sister's only child was gone, likely gone forever. There was now no measure of hope left that the improbable would be the impossible. In the view of Willem and Alice, the couple sailed away to a far-off island port hacked out of the wilderness and scarcely replaced by a struggling, poorly funded, unkempt, raucous settlement.

"Alice, I think we must accept that perhaps your sensitive brother-in-law was correct after all that the two young lovers would make it aboard. As he said, 'if it was God's will in his own good time' it would be so."

"What do you mean, Willem?"

"Apparently, when the couple first arrived at the harbor with Dr. Blake and Philippe Rapalje, their names were not on the manifest as Sarah and Dirck expected, but they had payment receipts of thirty-five *florins* for each of them. Since the West-Indische Compagnie, at the behest of the Staten Generaal, started offering more attractive incentives for colonists, ships sailing to Nieuw Nederland transported larger number of passengers. Given the *Swol* had a full manifest, the Chief Officer did not feel compelled to accept a young, not quite properly documented couple. He did not complete the final entry.

"Well then, Willem, what happened to change all that, just what we hoped?"

"Sarah and Dirck were incredulous and panicky, refusing to return home with Philippe and Dr. Blake. Now with her father dead, Sarah Elizabeth was determined not to remain here—could not bear it.

"Dr. Blake showed the officer Dirck's papers from your brother-in-law that certified his mastery of three languages and qualifications to assist with official documents and serve as a much needed school-master. The officer was not fully convinced because of Dirck's youth, but Blake said he was too rushed and impatient to carefully examine all the documents. Then your brother-in-law's friend explained that the young man learned woodworking skills as well from his father, a master craftsman. The officer looked at Dirck's hands, noted his muscular build, and remarked, 'Well, I would believe that. I'll record his occupation as carpenter.' Philippe then handed him a letter of introduction to his cousin Joris Rapalje and wife Catalina Trico who had lived and done well in Nieuw Nederland for twenty years. In effect, he somewhat exaggerated the young couple's relationship to them whereas in Amsterdam Sarah's mother was long since deceased and her father just passed away."

"Then what?"

"Still, the man wavered, but just as the newlywed's hopes again appeared thwarted, a stately, well-attired couple with many trunks and piles of baggage were helped to leave the *Swol* and into the long boat to shore where they paused to chat briefly with the Chief Officer. Apparently, for reasons they did not explain, their travel plans to Nieuw Nederland changed at the last minute, and according to Blake and Philippe, the man seemed quite relieved."

"Why would that be, Willem?"

"I don't know for sure, but what I can tell you from one of the merchants I know with the West-Indische Compagnie they were sending one of their very analytical, pragmatic officers to Nieuw Amsterdam to thoroughly investigate ways to make the colony more enticing to settlers and more profitable to the WIC. The site of the deep water harbor is too valuable to lose. The High Mightinesses of the Staten Generaal are very concerned about threats to their Dutch claim because of the English Virginia colonies to the south, and the heavily populated, ever encroaching English Bay Colony towns, their English settlements on the eastern end of Lange Eylandt, and on the maine opposite those settlements. Something different has to be tried, or our only trading port and hold on that region of the Americas could easily be lost to the English, and even conceivably to the French or to the Swedes just south of Nieuw Nederland.

"Likely, neither the Captain, nor anyone else would have been too thrilled if the couple that debarked is the one I think it is. They are arrogant and demanding, and he would scrutinize every detail of the officers' command and crew's conduct. The ship's manifest would likely have been meticulously examined. That is probably why Sarah and Dirck's names were initially dropped from the manifest that routinely includes brief notes about each passenger.

"Clearly, if the prominent and powerful stockholder brought his wife, they planned a long stay, and the Captain would not have been pleased about all the baggage. Even his quarters are very tight. With the ship filled to capacity—trade goods, supplies, crew, passengers and livestock—responsibilities would have been especially many, and with the WIC official and his wife on board, a far more stressful voyage than usual, especially if longer than anticipated.

"The good news, Alice, is that the WIC would have utilized one of their best captains and ships for such an important person. Certainly, the name of the ship, *Swol,* at least bodes well symbolically. Why the couple left so suddenly, however, is perplexing. That's what I would like to know."

"So is that why the chief officer then decided to take them on board?"

"Yes, according to Robert and Philippe. Accepting them would have solved the awkward dilemma that the company had not yet refunded the money James paid for his daughter and gave to Dirck. There wasn't time to manage that whereas the couple was likely covered by the compagnie. The WIC also urgently needs more housing for the recent increased influx of settlers so apparently the officer felt confident enough in Dirck's much needed carpentry skills that the manifest would pass muster and the number aboard remain the same. The last minute delay caused by the couple's hasty departure clouded and likely influenced his quick judgment call as he returned abruptly to the ship with Sarah and Dirck, the entire situation an exception to customary protocol. The *Swol* embarked within a few minutes of their boarding suggestive that the ship's Master was not happy with the delay and anxious to leave. The tide had turned in more ways than one."

"Or as my brother-in-law was fond of saying, 'in God's good time.' Who would have ever thought? Willem, when could we realistically anticipate word from them?"

"Of course, that all depends on whether the *Swol* is mainly a supply ship headed directly for Nieuw Amsterdam or will follow the longer, more lucrative trade route to our trading posts on the Brazilian coast and north to the West-Indisches for more trade and supplies, up the Atlantic Coast, possibly stopping at English Virginia to acquire tobacco, and finally further north to Nieuw Amsterdam. The return to Amsterdam follows a shorter, more direct route across the North Atlantic and then up the English Channel, a voyage of about one month. Sometimes the ship may have to take the longer route north around Scotland then over to the Noordt Zee and south to the Zuyder Zee. There is so much I don't know right now but will make every effort to learn more about the itinerary.

"Simply put, Alice, since voyage conditions are unpredictable and I don't have sufficient information, it could be five months or more for Sarah's letter back to us on the *Swol's* return trip or another ship. If it is a more direct supply vessel to Nieuw Amsterdam, it would be sooner. Either way, I know it will be an anxious time for you and seem too long, but the best you can do is to keep very busy with lots of outings for the children during the warmer weather now. As much as they loved ice skating the canals, we're all relieved the terrible winter is well behind us. Now they can enjoy getting about by trekschuyt on those same canals. It will perk you all up and make the waiting pass faster and in better spirits. Let's do our best to just love each other and our children. That's the finest way we can honor Sarah Elizabeth and her parents and to appreciate how blessed we all have been."

"You're right, Willem. We are very fortunate to have each other and our beautiful, happy children, and that's exactly what they would have wanted. What's done is done, and the fact of that somewhat relieves the anxiety of these past unsettling and exhausting weeks."

Willem did not want to unnecessarily alarm his wife and kept more troubling thoughts to himself. He didn't know if the captain or its crew had ever sailed up the often problematic Atlantic Coast toward the entrance to the harbor of Mannahatta where it was known to be treacherous in places, possibly the most unpredictable stretch of the ocean journey from the Texel Channel. Of course, the captain would be so advised, but that does not favorably compare with actual knowledge of dangerous coastal conditions. Willem hoped the WIC would at least hire a pilot familiar with the treacherous shoals and sandbars. Most disconcerting, however, was why would such an important couple on the ship leave in such haste given the weeks or even months of discussion and planning that would have preceded arrangements for such a journey? He would be on the alert to any talk of the *Swol* along the quays as ships arrived and at the *Bourse* where news of ships was often exchanged amid the trading of stocks and other financial transactions.

CHAPTER 11

Shipwreck

Still in the throes of the Little Ice Age, the winter of 1642 was extremely cold even for then. Finding and taking down wild animals proved especially difficult with the endless, heavy snowpack, and the *Navesinks* like everyone else had precious little meat that dark winter. When the late spring finally arrived, the soil warmed slowly, and their women worked long hours to make up for lost time to plant the three sisters—corn, beans, and squash. Most of the men were already at Sant Hoek Bay protected by the spit of land, *Racko Rumwaham,* to fish and gather clams and oysters, everyone more anxious than usual to replenish the food supply.

Four boys noticed unexpected fresh deer tracks near the wild beach plum shrubs that retain the sand dunes. The white blossoms in full bloom promised juicy jewel-toned fruit at summer's end after two more full moons. Two warriors took off in fast pursuit pausing now and then to catch their breath. The size and depth of the tracks indicated their intended prey was a very large buck, permissible to kill now that mating season was over, and the swollen bellies of the does already yielding the first fawns promised another generation of good hunting, but where was he leading them? The tracks were always fresh, yet in all that time not even a glimpse of the creature was to be had as if he were a phantom of their imagination. He never seemed to tire, always out of reach and sight.

Suddenly, an almost naked pale woman covered with blood emerged cautiously from the hollow of a large buttonwood tree where she apparently sought shelter. The young warrior raised his bow and took aim, but the older man intervened quickly preventing the arrow's release. The two argued briefly until the younger one responded to the gestures of his companion and saw the enormous white stag for the first time. It was forbidden to harm or kill the legendary white stag. Tales were told of rare momentary encounters of the sacred buck, and it was known that such were considered a gift from the Great Spirit *Kishelemukong*. The man of striking bearing perceived immediately that it was not they who were tracking the remarkable animal but that he had been leading them to this very place and to the terrible spectacle of this mutilated woman. She was to be protected, her life spared.

Even more extraordinary than the steady and massive presence of the white stag was the look in her eyes and the total absence of fear, for she seemed to welcome the old man. She seemed to know him, to love him. Never had he seen such tenderness in the gaze of a *Swanneken*, the Dutch salty people he despised.

Sarah Elizabeth survived her terrible wounds from the brutal attack along shore but scarcely remembered making her way to the stand of trees beyond the dune grass and plumb bushes that offered protection from exposure to the cold winds of Sant Hoek Bay and wild creatures. What was real, what was nightmare? Weakened from shock and loss of blood, with little sustenance but the sap from the tree, she found the strength to call out to the strangers,

"Papa, you came for me, and you're wearing the cloak Mama made for you. How I've missed you. You came for me! Let's go home, Papa, let's go home!"

The older Indian removed the deerskin draped over his shoulders and protectively wrapping the young woman with it gently supported her in his strong, sure arms as she slipped into unconsciousness. Raising her up, he draped her limp body over his broad shoulder and carried her on their ancient trail to *Ramesing* where four waterways met and two of five ancient trails passed through its town readily connecting the inhabitants to other villages throughout the region and where their *sakima, Popomora,* wielded considerable influence.

A few days earlier they heard about the ship that hit a sandbar and broke apart during the storm when the South Grandmother Wind defeated the North Grandfather Wind. Survivors who made it to shore were attacked and killed by young warriors, possibly Raritan, still bent for revenge despite the truce following the war begun by the Swannekens. She must be one of them. For hundreds of miles around, villages up and down the great river, on islands near coves, inlets, and bays, and even further inland were aroused from their accustomed alliances and set aside historical animosities to take vengeance for the senseless and brutal murder of innocent villagers at Pavonia. Inhabitants of that small, peaceful village were massacred by the very Dutch who by treaty were to protect them from their upriver enemies. Every warrior took up the tomahawk, and he too would have killed what remained of the lone woman if the white stag had not intervened, if he had not seen the trust and love in her eyes. The loss of his own son, who according to custom moved out from Ramesing to marry into another clan, was among those slaughtered when the violence began that compelled retribution. Alas, the Great White Stag was a warning, a sign that must be respected.

CHAPTER 12

Two Letters

Scarcely a year after Lady Deborah Moody's move to Swamscott, and clearly no longer a Salem Puritan member in good standing, she decided it was time to leave, would be in command of those choices, and prepare accordingly on her own terms. Thus, we find the woman who was warned that cold December day during the harsh winter of 1642 finally ready to depart. With the spring thaw and once massive snowdrifts gone, ice that blocked Salem Harbor broke up.

Behind her, once flourishing *Agawam* villages peopled the land before they were decimated by disease that arrived at their shores. Where they once cleared, tended, and harvested corn, beans, and squash, New England Puritans flourished barely a decade after their own abrupt harsh encounter with starvation, deprivation, disease, and death. The sentinels of once dense forests, silent witnesses to the demise of ancient peoples and hardships of new arrivals, still extended down to the stony beaches but now supplied English shipwrights. The sloop, with John Tilton's family and other close friends of Lady Moody from Lynn and Salem, left behind that thriving town, the rivers, necks, and wetlands. It breezed its way through the Atlantic seaside watery hub of tall masts and sails alongside a few Algonquian canoes and dugouts and caught a strong wind south to Boston for a larger vessel with more friends. Sailing east into the Atlantic Ocean, around Cape Cod, then toward Long Island Sound's New Haven, the Dutch Director General Willem Kieft awaited their arrival at Mannahatta Island with his promise of land and autonomy.

The West-Indische Compagnie failed to attract sufficient settlers to leave their secure and comfortable lives in Holland to serve as a buffer between the Swedes along the Zuid Rivier and the English Virginia and Maryland to the south. English settlements to the northeast continually encroached on territory long claimed by the Dutch on either side of Long Island Sound while colonists from the aggressive, rapidly expanding Massachusetts Bay Colony of twenty thousand people increasingly posed a threat. Walled off in the fort at the tip of Mannahatta, Willem Kieft had no choice but to reach out to disgruntled Englishmen disillusioned by preaching, policy, and practice of the all too rigid Puritan way. In order to hold and protect Dutch territory, he needed and wanted them to keep his population deprived colony intact and ensure its growth, not the best option for the Dutch but a necessary one while Lady Moody and her Anabaptist friends sought sanctuary far from the scrutiny of their beliefs and how they wanted to live their lives.

If the widow Anne Hutchinson with her now smaller family of young and unmarried children and John Throckmorton's association of thirty-five families had courage to settle in remote wilderness alongside the Dutch, both formerly of Massachusetts and Rhode Island, certainly the dauntless Lady Deborah and her friends could do the same. Inspired by the vision of their daring venture and bold action, she had inquired of the Director about such a possibility for herself and those who wished to travel with her. Willem Kieft's letter, in which he not only replied but affirmed that she was welcome, was well secured for safe keeping during the voyage.

Lady Moody was directed to assemble a group, as had Throckmorton. They would be allotted sufficient land for their own town and surrounds, not as part of an already settled Dutch village but with enough *morgens* to establish their own English town in exchange for loyalty to the Dutch West-Indische Compagnie and the High Mightinesses Staten Generaal of the Netherlands. Kieft knew of Englishmen already at Nieuw Amsterdam accustomed to Dutch manner, language, and trade with local wilden. They could be useful and were at liberty to complete thirty-nine patentees. He was prepared to grant them a coastal site with a good harbor on the southwest tip of Lange Eylandt. Called *Sewanhackey*, land of shells, by the Algonquians, it was the coastal area of the most highly prized clams for *zeewant* used as currency. Willem Kieft confirmed they would *"enjoy the free libertie of conscience according to custom and manner of Holland"* for the practice of their faith. Suddenly the dream, beyond Lady Moody's wildest imagination and as vast as the Atlantic Ocean, was realized.

Impelled to leave London, where she was born when her father was a member of Parliament and ancient barrister at Gray's Inn of Court, and she later married at St. Mary Aldermary Church in 1605; bereft of the enormous Moody country estate in Wiltshire and most of their wealth when her husband died deeply in debt; chastened by men she once thought her brothers in Christ; forced from a home she had only recently purchased for a price all too dear to secure future income from tenant farmers; and condemned to seek a foreign land where she would have to start all over on what likely would be primitive, undeveloped land was surely a life interrupted. Unbelievably stunning, is this what is required to reach one's dream? Is it just possible that big dreams require big sacrifice? That struggle is as much the journey as the visions of what we can be and hold so dear? So it seemed.

That spring of 1643, Lady Moody carried another very precious letter with her the day of departure—one that almost did not reach her in time. The news was grim. Her son, Sir Henry, who she sought to include as a patentee, was detained in England, not what she wished and another devastating blow.

A few weeks before she and the Tiltons were warned by the General Court in December, news had just reached Boston and Salem that Parliamentary forces and the Royalist Army of King Charles met in pitched battle at Edgehill in Warwickshire. Apparently, each side assumed they would emerge victorious, gain the day and control of the divided country, but both armies were ill-prepared for battle with mostly inexperienced men, lack of supplies, and poor organization. The carnage between them lasted three days until exhaustion, shock, and the loss of dead and wounded men forced a stalemate. With no clear winner, New Englanders wondered if more battles were inevitable. Had civil war just become the new fact of life in an already uncertain England? When Lady Moody heard the news, she prayed fervently that Henry had already taken a ship to the Bay Colony, but that was not to be. The seventeenth year in the reign of His Majesty Charles Stuart, 1642, ended badly for the Moodys, the English people, and their monarch.

Far beyond the seas, such a state of affairs was known when Hugh Casswell found Lady Deborah Moody at the Swamscott home she was about to vacate that unusually cool and cloudy spring day of 1643. The widow scarcely recognized the handsome but tired man at her door, having last seen him before he went off to Oxford, like her son a fourteen-year-old lad, and now like Henry a man in his mid-thirties. Clutching the letter close to her heart that he delivered that day, and gazing beyond the horizon, she recalled that extraordinary yet anxious encounter.

"Meladie Moody, I bring you news of your son, Sir Henry."

Stunned, she could scarcely find the courage to inquire, "Is he alive? Is he well? Please come in and rest. My servant will provide you something to eat and whatever else you require. In the meanwhile, let's sit by the fire."

"To alleviate your anxiety, he is alive, but Sir Henry insisted that I first identify myself beyond a doubt. Besides my name and thought that you might not recognize me after all these years, he insisted that I tell you two things so as to remove any doubt."

"How strange. What would that be and why?"

"First, I see that you are wearing the beautiful brooch that your mother gave you and that she received from her mother. Almost every time we visited when I was a little boy, you wore that brooch and was told it was very special to you. Second, I was to remark about the camera obscura Sir Henry enjoyed while living on the Strand in London in 1634 and that a remarkable traveler and merchant of the British East India Company, Peter Mundy, stopped there to see it for himself when he arrived after several years in faraway, exotic places. Certainly he told you about the visit when you were there.

Lady Moody, I am the Hugh Casswell, your Henry's lifelong friend and son of the woman who was always so grateful for your assistance during a time of great need for our family. She insisted that I never forget your kindness and generosity."

"Thank you for your compliment and hers, but I only responded as any true friend would. I miss your mother very much, but why would my Henry require that you identify yourself in such a way? I do see something of his favorite childhood friend in you and always trusted the integrity of your family. It was a sorrow to me when they left for New England, but here we all are. It was my understanding that you were to remain behind in London to take care of family business and personal affairs as Henry did for us. How is it you came to be here now and for the sake of Henry and myself? Hugh, please, do come in at once. We have much to talk about."

"Meladie, much has changed in England since you left. The country is now terribly divided between Puritan Parliamentarians and Royalist supporters of King Charles. Certainly, it is all the talk here with fewer trading ships from England and young men returning to fight. Long before that, he did share with me that given your husband's death and out of concern for you and the expense it would incur, he did not depart for a grand tour of the Continent like many young fellows do when their studies were completed at Oxford and Law at Lincoln's Inn of Court. Such would have been of great advantage for him to advance in position at the Court of His Majesty. However, after you left England, I do know he fully embraced the life of a courtier.

"Yes, Hugh, after Henry received his degree at Oxford's Magdalen College, his father and I thought it advantageous for our son to study law at Lincoln's Inn where we occasionally visited him during our stays in London. It was deemed important for its young men to attend and even organize and act in the dramas to gain confidence, acquire presence, and become more fluid in their use of rhetorical skills necessary to succeed in law and government. As you know, it was after my husband's death that he was also called upon to compose poetic commentary about some of the plays, something of my mother's gift he displayed even as a child."

"That brings back happy memories. He often turned our funny and not so funny escapades into catchy verse."

"He once accompanied me to Massinger's *A New Way to Pay Old Debts*, where we saw it performed by the Queen Majesty's servants at the *Phoenix* on Drury-lane in 1633. The commendatory poem he was asked to write was printed on the program. What a surprise he managed to keep secret from me. I was so proud of him although Massinger's title was rather ironic as we were still in the throes of settling my husband's estate. I rather thought then that Henry's views personally and poetically were very much affected by that burdensome fact of our lives. Indeed, it was an impetus to establish himself further in London theater and court life. What we both thought would be our lives and responsibilities at Garsdon changed almost in an inkling of the eye when his father died suddenly. Henry was also requested to write a commendatory poem for one of Fletcher's dramas. We both loved the theater. It was a special time in our lives that filled the absence of our loved ones. The Court Masques of the Queen he was honored to attend stirred his creative temperament and the muse within."

"While Sir Henry lived on the Strand, meladie, he occasionally came to the book and manuscript establishment I inherited from my uncle. He especially asked me to keep an eye out for Italian dramas of quality as both King Charles and Queen Henrietta were especially drawn to them. He mentioned once that they were motivated by the ideal of art patronage of her de' Medici family, and he wanted to become fluent in that language. He loved to peruse my books while you were in London although you and I did not see each other then. In recent years, Sir Henry and I saw less and less of each other although he still lived at St. Botolph Without Aldersgate on the Strand in 1638. While he was finalizing matters of concern to both of you including arrangements for your voyage to New England, he clearly was pulled further into the life of a courtier as you know all too well."

"Yes, we were completing the sale of Garsdon Manor to Sir Lawrence Washington. Originally, I was to have use of Whitchurch manor during my lifetime and receive rent from its tenants for the marriage portion provided by my father. Interest and tithes were due me for the dowager portion of the *advowson* with its right to appoint the parish priest. However, we realized that our income there would be exceeded by necessary expenditures, debt, more taxes, and fines, and become a lonely, desperate way to live with diminishing income and fewer servants. I assigned my rights to Henry should any further action be required and resolved to leave for Boston where there were friends like your family. Even if the Star Chamber would have permitted me to return again to London during the visiting season, it was always an expensive and increasingly difficult place to live and the shadow of the Star Chamber problematic."

"Dame Deborah, I am truly sorry for all you and my friend suffered at that time. About a year after you sailed, Sir Henry came to me quite agitated over the changes taking place in London. The depth and passion of emotions aroused made him nervous. Parliament itself was alarmingly contentious by 1641. I gave serious thought to leaving England to join my parents and had completed the term required in my uncle's will to either continue as proprietor or sell his former bookshop. By that time, Sir Henry was also much involved with the Royal Court. He seems to have been particularly taken with the poetry of Richard Lovelace and the music of William Lawes, a favorite of the King who composed *Beauty in Eclipsia* with words by your son. William's compositions for viol always lifted my friend's increasing despondency, a noticeable change in his demeanor. Clearly, Sir Henry was worried."

"Hugh, you still haven't explained all the mystery behind identifying yourself."

"During the stays in London with your husband when he was an MP and later during the early thirties, the Court of Charles was a busy place, a mingling of nobility, foreign dignitaries, and influential persons regardless of religion or politics. It was the place to be seen and make important connections as well as a place to be entertained as you, your husband and son well understood. That has changed, meladie. Suspicion and dangerous discord is pervasive. Only His Majesty could determine when Parliament would be called to session, and it was hard for him to understand why the woman he loved so much, his wife the Queen, could be so hated because she openly displayed her Catholic piety. Such wanton abandon was an affront to Puritan values and sensitivities who wanted all vestiges of Catholicism removed from the Church of England, the Court, and the land. The King was not able to comprehend the depth of the intense criticism her behavior evoked and suspicion thus leveled toward his presumed popery. Failure to do so could only have serious consequence. After you left, His Majesty recalled Parliament in late 1640 to fund his wars. In that he was unsuccessful. He could not realize how powerful the more extreme Puritans had become and how determined MPs were to not support his demands.

"Sir Henry grasped that life could become very difficult for a courtier like himself who remained loyal to the King and carried the burden of profound foreboding. He came to me with all his books, entrusting them and private papers for safekeeping. When I told him of concerns I already had for my parents here in the Bay Colony, we talked a bit how I might sell the shop, set sail, and leave behind what may yet come. We both suspected that I might be searched at port, but given I'm a bookseller, no one would question me about a large cache of books. We decided that his sensitive papers, the carefully prepared document giving you power of attorney for his legal and financial transactions should they be needed, and hurried letter he wrote to you could be packed in my luggage and tucked under another lining stitched in place. By that time, he was aware of your Swampscott purchase here, how I do not know. A good thing it was that he was so prescient.

"In early January 1642, King Charles set out for Westminster and naively tried to arrest five men in the House of Commons, guilty of treason in his mind, but they were forewarned. The King's hasty, ill-considered and unprecedented intrusion made him seem a fool and poorly advised. He and his troop of courtiers, possibly Sir Henry, and soldiers were deeply resented. The act set off a volatile reaction in an already incendiary situation. A few days later, the King and Queen had reason to feel threatened and hastily fled their beloved Whitehall and Banqueting Hall. With their involuntary departure, his Majesty's dreams of a London that would reflect the artistic beauty, grandeur, and ceremony he loved was aborted. Sadly, according to Henry, the King's good qualities and cultured, loving family were overshadowed by his inability to effectively deal with the obvious and highly charged religious, political, and economic dissension in a city and country desperate for more balanced and competent leadership. Charles failed to understand the fractures between a monarchy grounded in the presumed divine right of kings and the people's rights, especially the more factious Puritans and Presbyterians. Moderates like your son still hoped for some kind of peaceful realignment. When the King was hastily forced to leave in disgrace, Henry was much distraught.

"Right after that happened, my dear friend stopped by for only a few minutes and quickly scribbled a poem for my eyes only and to memorize for your ears only. We embraced one last time, and he left."

"Please tell me, why was that, Hugh?"

"The poem was meant to reveal his intentions without being direct should I ever be questioned about him."

"Please tell me."

> "Remember well our boyhood days
> and our repose of courtly ways.
> So much has changed and so have we
> that now no path to normalcy.
> Though, dear friend, we must depart
> alas unsure, remain stalwart.
> A man once grand and now in need
> has sealed my fate,
> but, you my mate,
> are destined surely to succeed.
> Remember well, remember well.

"Meladie, Sir Henry was a Royalist caught in circumstance that would of necessity transform him into a Cavalier, a warrior for the cause of the Crown. His short poem recalls the courtly progress of King James in Wiltshire that so impressed us when we were boys and pretended we were courtiers. Given his integrity and loyalty to the oath taken when knighted to serve the King, he would not do otherwise. That oath was inviolable to him, if not to others. He expressed deep affection for the Royal family and was especially fond of the children and concerned for their safety and welfare. I never saw him again and could only surmise from the poem, as he intended, that Henry followed King Charles and his family to Oxford and would be at the then unforeseen Battle of Edgehill discussed in newspapers and pamphlets that arrived in Boston just recently, very much from the Puritan point of view like London's *Weekly Intelligencer* I should think."

"Oh, Hugh, I'm so frightened for Henry and despair now of seeing my dear son soon, if ever. It became clear that we could not have the life his father and I enjoyed when he was a child, studied at Oxford, and before his sister Catherine died, Lincoln's Inn of Court, and the theaters. The absence of his father was filled with stimulating court life and the influence of older learned men, fascinating diplomats from afar, intellectual pursuit of science, and the joy of inspirational music, art, and poetry. Indeed, such was nourishment for his mind and balm for his soul. Henry moved so graciously with such congeniality and sensitivity. With the loss of his inheritance, it became home to him, and he thought the Queen's singing and dancing during the grand masques with their guests a very lovely thing."

"I do believe, meladie, if I may be so bold to say that my best friend is very extraordinary like yourself. He possesses that quality beyond words to describe that puts others at ease and valued. It's no wonder that he ingratiated himself even in the company of more aristocratic and powerful attendees at Court not by insincere flattery like so many but through genuine loyalty, appreciation and regard, rare indeed."

"Thank you, Hugh, for sharing this. I had hopes he would join me at Swampscott but did not fully grasp the influence of his growing relationship with the Royal family and other courtiers and how committed he was to them. I assumed too much and perceive now this was his dream, apparently now even to the point of risking his life. Is this the reason for his secrecy?"

"In part, Dame Deborah. Sir Henry wanted to protect you from his letter falling into the wrong hands or from writing anything that would expose his identity and thus yours in your very

Puritanical world here. Rather than divulge these things in his letter to you he felt it best for me to tell you in person although there was the possibility that you and I might not meet. He understood what the Puritan sentiment would be here and the gossip that would find voice if it was known that your son was a Cavalier rather than fighting with Parliamentary forces. He took great pains to protect you from ill-thought and regretted there was no stretch to a middle way by either side. It was becoming apparent that brothers would fight brothers, fathers and sons, cousins against cousins, uncles and nephews thus tearing English families asunder only to break her people, her economy, and stability to the detriment of all.

"Considering the prevailing hostility, I will tell you also that Sir Henry wanted to protect me as well knowing that I would be questioned or searched prior to boarding a ship for New England and possibly on my arrival in Boston. Our last conversation was deliberately left vague so I would not have to lie if questioned. Therefore, he had to leave much out of your letter, if discovered, and could only say there were more personal matters to attend on your behalf and that he would remain in England for that reason trusting you would understand."

"How is it you came to be here now? I've had no correspondence from your mother for a long time. Is your family well?"

"My dear Lady, I crossed the Atlantic as much to assist my family as due to the circumstance of civil discord in England. I received a letter from Mother a few days before Sir Henry came to me. Only a few months after my family moved from Boston to Roxbury, my only surviving brother William, on whom my parents relied, died leaving behind his wife and young children. Mother and my youngest sister, although almost grown, were in need of more strong hands as my father was not well. I had long concluded all that remained of their personal affairs in England, and our family benefitted much from the quick sale of the bookstore. Certainly, without my favorite London customer, Sir Henry, and theaters closed by the Puritans, life would never be the same anyway, indeed, already dull and unpleasant. Now I can be of service to my family.

"Although I departed just as summer ended with hopes of still favorable weather, we sailed into Boston Harbor during a powerful storm. I arrived at my parents' home where they were in desperate straits due to the early and extremely cold winter that as you know never seemed to end without any relief. Please forgive me that it was such a long time before it was possible to visit you."

"Dear, dear Hugh, you have shared sad but much appreciated news and must not apologize. It was an untimely sacrifice for you and your family to think of Henry and me. I can't tell you how much your visit does mean just now. You must greet and embrace them for me. You must also thank your parents for the kind of young man you have become, clearly my son's devoted companion in courage. They were among my closest friends in Wiltshire and such a significant part of those long-ago happy days at Garsdon.

"Now I too have stunning plans to share. Friends and I will leave shortly for Dutch Mannahatta where we will meet with Director Willem Kieft. He promised a colony of our own on the shore of Western Long Island. The General Court in Boston issued a warning in December and will soon excommunicate us for our differing views on the baptism of infants and refusal to conform to their way of it. Should my Henry be able to make his way to Boston, he will have no difficulty learning of my new whereabouts. I understand that word has already begun to spread of our anticipated departure and destination. There will be rumors aplenty, and Swampscott will soon be in the hands of Daniel King and his family who, short of funds, will lease it until they can offer us more favorable arrangements."

"Meladie, my parents knew about the Quarterly Court's decision and talk that followed. They were much dismayed and alarmed for you. Insistent that I see you in spite of their predicament, I dared not leave until Father was stronger and knew him to be well. Sir Henry would be much taken aback. He was relieved and grateful that you were no longer in England, believing it God's good will to have spared you from the unrest and danger that appeared imminent when last we talked. He thought you safe with John Winthrop and fellow Puritans you knew long before your departure for Boston although there was much talk in London that they had become too extreme in their discipline of Bay Colony nonconformists like yourself."

"That they definitely are, Hugh. At least when I arrived here, both Boston, Salem, and other settlements were well-established towns, with houses waiting for me. I do admit, this new venture is rather daunting. After our arrival and meetings with the Dutch Director, we will leave for a place that is not settled. It is virgin land, but it will be ours, an English town in a Dutch world. Most importantly, it will be our own community with liberty of conscience and our own magistrates, free from the intrusion of narrow minds and cold hearts."

"And to think, your son believes you to be English through and through and settled down in vast Swampscott holdings of your own at last. Apparently your family is not yet finished with sojourning in strange lands. I recall the story of your mother's Pilkingtons."

"That is just as well, Hugh, just as well. Certainly we have both lifted up our hearts and concerns to our Father in Heaven who knows all things and hears the words of his devoted servants. Now I insist that you spend the night before I send you on your blessed way well-fed and rested. Meanwhile, I want to gather some things for your mother and write her a letter. I am ever indebted to you for your devoted friendship to Henry and myself. If everything is as you say, then knowing he could trust you is a precious gift to us. Now we really must spend some time recounting our days together, the days of your youth, and I want to hear more about that dear mother of yours."

"My wonderful, Lady Deborah, I would love that, and one day we shall tell Sir Henry all about our brief time together, just as he wished. Although anxious knowing he is in grave danger, I do believe he will endure. He was determined to hold his beloved mother in his arms once more, his intention real and strong. He will come to you. Surely he will."

Thus was the remarkable visit of Hugh Casswell, her son's lifetime friend, deeply impressed on Deborah Moody's mind, piercing her heart with thoughtful, caring words, just the thing her sagging spirit craved—word of her son, hard news but word of her son and words from her son, in his own hand, however guarded they may be.

"Dearest Mother…"

CHAPTER 13

New Haven

"Good morning, John. How are Mary and the boys today?"

"We're all doing very fine, thank you, meladie, especially since we should arrive in New Haven tomorrow. The boys need to run about, and it will be a pleasant change to go ashore and visit with old friends again. The weather has favored us."

"Yes, it will be welcome. Although I was disappointed at first to learn that Roger Williams had already left for Nieuw Amsterdam, perhaps it was best for all of us that we did not expend our precious time at Providence. That would have made our trip from Salem longer and perhaps unnecessarily inconvenient. There was much I hoped to learn from him about the founding of his settlement and how it is he has such a good relationship with the Narragansetts. It is said that he speaks some of the local dialects better than any other Englishman."

"I agree, meladie. It's remarkable how his life changed for such a marvelous purpose. Salem lost a valuable man when he was exiled, and as we learned before sailing because of that exile, he can't even leave for England from a Bay Colony harbor. Possibly, he will still be in Nieuw Amsterdam when we arrive. It is said that he became familiar with the Dutch language through his father's business when he was growing up, and the fact that he travels long distances by canoe, often alone, has made that man quite a legend."

"Yes, imagine that, John, but a canoe will hardly take Williams across the Atlantic. It would be very helpful if we could talk with him before he embarks. That opportunity may have come and gone already. We've learned that Virginia merchant ships frequent the Mannahatta harbor and especially now with that awful cold winter behind us. I'm eager to see the plans John Davenport drew up for the layout of New Haven. Our settlement will have fewer patentees but more manageable from my point of view."

"Meladie, I agree with you completely, and I'm grateful we will have the opportunity to discuss the list of questions we drew up at Lynn to discuss with Minister Davenport and Governor Eaton. It is said they are even more harsh and restrictive than Massachusetts magistrates and ministers, but their recent experience of founding a new colony will be invaluable to us especially since we will likely miss Williams."

"While my son and I were in London, John, I learned that Samuel Hartlib, a friend of Jan Comenius in Poland and fellow refugee, joined Davenport's St. Stephen's parish. It seems that Comenius was quite a remarkable educator and inspired Hartlib who then shared some of the man's innovative educational ideas with John Davenport. Since my mother's father achieved much with his free school, I wonder if the minister might have knowledge that would be useful for the school we will eventually have. Some people are beginning to think differently about the best ways to teach children, and I'm told the Dutch teach boys and girls in their schools."

"I did not know that, meladie."

"When the thunderstorms of winter's human conflict come to an end, we can open to the springtime of a new creation. Unencumbered by the burden of turmoil, we are reborn to a world of the dreams we forgot and the ones yet imagined. My son Henry had an insatiable appetite for the many wonders, inventions, curiosities, plants, and animals that merchants brought to London from their trade all over the world. The remarkable collection of artefacts the Tradescants put on display to the public at their *Ark* and plants they brought back from all over the globe to their botanic garden in Lambeth and to enhance the royal grounds were cherished by King Charles and the

Queen. They carried ideas that taught us how much there is yet to discover or learn anew.

"Minister Davenport also worked tirelessly on behalf of Protestant refugees of many countries like my grandfather Pilkington. That effort and apparently his views drew the ire of Archbishop Laud. His life threatened, he was forced to flee to Holland where he may have stayed a few years before returning to England and then sailed for Boston. I hope he will provide useful information about Dutch law and what we can realistically expect in our relationship to Dutch Reformed Church authority. Perhaps, John, we can thus avoid a few nasty mishaps."

"I agree, Lady Deborah, it was hard enough avoiding censure in Massachusetts. The Bay Colony was not what we thought it would be. Ministers and magistrates fashioned their world in the image of themselves, what they think is the only way to salvation. Blind obedience to the dictates of Catholicism, High Church of England, or the Puritans is not what God intended. With Bible in hand, reason does direct us to interpret those words each in our own way according to conscience, but in that they see only potential congregational disorder that would threaten the unity of their very communities. We left before they issued a formal excommunication, but I have no doubt the magistrates of Boston will proclaim it soon just to make our banishment a lesson to others. Director Kieft promised no such interference in our religious beliefs—and will be written into our legal documents—but more information can only serve us well, meladie.

"More worrisome is that we do not know everyone who will join us. There will be risks to meet the minimum Kieft requested. A serious concern is the character of a few men who now reside in Mannahatta. Previously, at least one who is quite capable drew criticism of others in Lynn and was admonished not for nonconformist religious belief but for ill-tempered behavior. These men may not be motivated by higher purpose but solely to advance themselves without restraint and potentially problematic, but we will require a lot of strong arms and backs to clear the land and build our homes that must be done before winter sets in."

"John, I overheard such comments after I moved to Lynn from Salem and agree with you. If what we heard is true, we must then be more vigilant, more prepared to manage come what may, and not divulge anything that individuals of their ilk might use for self-advantage only. We cannot afford to be naive but be as wolves in sheep's clothing. We shall reflect and talk about how to ensure everyone's natural inclinations and skills best serve the needs and goodwill of our entire community. May prayer guide us to be servants that move forward in a spirit of greater accord without coercion. Liberty of conscience can only be supported by mutual regard for one another.

"Your attention to detail will serve our colony well. Our sure safety is your capacity to generate deliberative yet diplomatic correspondence and maintain good records. What's in writing, whether with Dutch authorities or decisions and actions we take within our own town, cannot be denied or thereby misunderstood and what's agreed and recorded not later retracted except by mutual consent. I am exceedingly grateful for your assistance as we prepared to leave Lynn and am confident your part in this new venture will surely be significant for years to come. You and Mary are very dear."

"Thank you, meladie, your trust is truly gratifying, and I am profoundly moved that you should so honor me. I will not fail you or the others who become part of our community. Fortunately, your capacity to enlist many elsewhere in the Bay Colony and Rhode Island through your diligent and persuasive correspondence are individuals much respected. As soon as they put all their affairs in order and prepare their families for the move, we can anticipate their arrival and full support. I have their letters of intent should they be delayed.

"One more thing, your livestock is in good hands until we are settled and ready to request transportation. The contract you asked me to draw up is firm, and I am confident we can count on these men to properly care for your animals and secure a vessel for them to our new farms when the time is favorable."

"Thank you, John. We face many challenges perhaps even greater than our departure from England. This is not what we envisioned then and did not anticipate such complications, but we are fortunate to have a place to start anew. We are blessed to grow our own community on virgin soil unpolluted by those who lack the imagination and heart to allow others the God-given right to interpret Holy Scripture according to reason and conscience reflective of genuine search for the truth. Honest persons willing to work hard and respect others are welcome."

What Lady Moody did not share with John Tilton nor anyone else was her concern for Governor Eaton's wife, Anne, who she first met in London. Anne's letters were not those of her husband's impassioned dream but the drudge of daily nightmare. He and Minister Davenport may have been the highly regarded founders of New Haven, but the lot of Governor Eaton's wife, and of so many like her, was a hard one and often lonely. Sailing to New England was not her dream.

Anne, well-educated and from a highly esteemed family like Deborah Dunch Moody, married Thomas Yale, a very successful merchant. After his death, she married Theophilus Eaton, a widower, while they were still in London thus joining together children from each of the couple's previous marriages. By the time her second husband decided to leave with John Davenport for New England, the Eatons had more children.

Once settled, within a short time due to their wealth, prestige, and position, they had the largest home not only bursting with their many children but Anne's domineering mother-in-law, servants, two African slaves, and numerous others. All in all, a large household by any measure of about thirty people. To make matters worse, Theophilus was so taken with his passion for the new colony and the importance of his duties that he had little interest in helping to sort out his wife's domestic difficulties. It was too much for Lady Deborah's friend who had corresponded frequently and clearly became more desperate and erratic.

The good lady feared that Anne was crumbling under the weight of it all and knew from her letters that she had no one to turn to. Even though most Puritans were of the middling sort and aristocrats rare, for the few ladies of distinction, the disruption and dislocation from family and grand country manor or sumptuous London estate on the Strand by the River Thames was especially jarring. Harsh realities of the new world and abrupt loss of elite society with all its attendant support, cultured refinements, latest continental fashions, many servants, and courtly grandeur had undone more than just this once happy, confident woman. Such happened to the aristocratic wife that first occupied the Humphrey Swampscott home Lady Deborah acquired and just vacated. If only for a few days, Lady Moody would visit with her friend, listen, and do her best to soothe the lady's troubled soul and weary body.

In her last letter, Anne also requested Lady Moody's copy of the recently published Andrew Ritor's *A Treatise on the Vanity of Childish-Baptism*. Needless to say, it would have to be shared and read secretly and certainly one more unacceptable fact of Anne Eaton's life in the narrowly scripted Puritan settlement by the *Quinnepiac* River where the People of the Long Water Land, themselves much diminished by European diseases, provided life-saving assistance to New Haven's first settlers scarcely five years before.

Penelope's Song

PART 4

Gravesend, Lange Eylandt and Sant Hoek,
Nieuw Nederland, and England, 1643

Ubi solitudinem faciunt, pacem apellant.
(They create desolation and call it peace.)

—Tacitus
Roman historian, writer, and
orator, first century A.D.

CHAPTER 14

Deborah

While wars raged during times of great crisis, two Deborahs separated by the Mediterranean Sea, massive continents, the Atlantic Ocean, and almost twenty-five hundred years of human history emerged leaders of men to secure for their people a place to live and each according to their belief in one God. The Deborah of the Israelites during the period of the Judges, when she herself was a judge, prophetess, poet, and warrior, urged her general Barak, son of Abinoam, to join her in battle to subdue the Canaanites.

Our second Deborah, agile of mind and inner vision, courageous and determined like the prophetess of old, sought a home for her people, a place where they could live and interpret their Holy Scripture—with its ancient account of Deborah—according to their own conscience unmolested by any worldly power, faith informed by reason rather than by doctrine or dictate alone. Removal from the land of their birth in response to religious persecution led most of her future followers to towns situated in the Puritan Massachusetts Bay Colony of New England. There they encountered even more rigid insistence on compliance, for the sake of order, until at last Lady Deborah Dunch Moody sought the protection of the Dutch in Nieuw Nederland for them and herself. It was here, unlike the Deborah of old, her task would be not to subdue the nearby *Canarsees* but to find a way to live in peace with them on the southwestern edge of Lange Eylandt, an assortment of English inhabitants straddling a

Dutch world where trust between them and numerous villages of Algonquian peoples had completely broken down.

Her grandfather, William Dunch, served as high sheriff and Justice of the Peace for Berkshire and was Auditor of the Royal Mint for Kings Henry VIII and Edward IV. The daughter of Walter Dunch, barrister-at-law with Gray's Inn of London and Member of Parliament whose prominent family were committed proponents of the rights of Englishmen, would lead her generation to greater freedom of religion. Driven by a potent dream to this time and place for good, she was now Lady Deborah Moody of Gravesend, preeminent leader extraordinary. Founder and guiding spirit, she was the first female patentee and woman to vote, create a town plan, and so establish a settlement in the New World.

From the very first, Gravesend was conceived as an English town by Director Willem Kieft. Most of the original thirty-nine patentees she gathered about her did not arrive directly from England but like Lady Moody were exiled, disillusioned, or simply disaffected with the Massachussetts Bay Colony towns where they first settled. Captain Nicholas Stillwell, Richard Stout, three men from Lynn like Deborah Moody and the Tiltons, and a few others had already settled near the fort at the tip of Mannahatta. Uniquely, Gravesend was the only town in Dutch Nieuw Nederland granted self-rule with town meetings, as was the English tradition, and empowered to elect its own magistrates authorized to maintain records in English. These concessions, and most importantly for Lady Moody and her associates in faith and reason, secured absolute freedom of conscience and practice of religious freedom within their town "*without magisterial or ministerial interference*" specifically noting that "*no other ecclesiastical minister might pretend jurisdiction over them.*" This was no tender crocus tentatively poking its blue bonnet through late winter new fallen snow. It was a lightning bolt from heaven.

In many respects the location of Gravesend selected by Kieft was fortuitous. Its own natural harbor was protected by *Conyne Eylandt* nearly opposite the Verrazano Narrows, entryway to the upper harbor of Mannahatta. The generous triangular grant was well placed at the crossroads of two wilden paths winding toward the ancient

Mechawanienk Trail that became the main route for the new English arrivals with Dutch towns north and east on the island. The site was flat and laying within well-watered woods and along its southwest coast abundant marsh grass for livestock, including forage for Lady Moody's pigs on Conyne Eylandt. The location, once the site of *Massabrakem*, a Canarsee village, was no longer forested and long since uninhabited. Thus, conflict was avoided. Canarsee villages further away and much diminished by European disease would retain rights to some of its shoreline resources although they had more immediate access to other coastal areas.

What was achieved under Deborah Dunch Moody's aspiration and guidance was something entirely new and novel in colonial America. Indeed, Gray's Inn of Court, with its tree-lined walks planted by Francis Bacon, where the family sometimes lived with her barrister father during the reign of Queen Elizabeth; Berkshire's Avebury Manor not all that far from the largest stone circle in the world; the London of her husband's Parliament days during James I; and her son's life at the Court of Charles I; the Moody Wiltshire Garsdon Manor with generous holdings and agricultural land; and even Salem and Swampscott at Lynn, Massachusetts, were now lifetimes gone by.

CHAPTER 15

The Summons

"*Patroon* De Vries, welcome. Your visit honors us. What brings you and our patentees Sergeant Hubbard and Ensign Baxter here this morning?"

"Meladie Moody, we beg your pardon for our sudden arrival with no invitation from you or prior request on our part, but urgent matters necessitate that we meet with you immediately."

"Please do come in right away. I'll ask my servant to prepare something at once."

"Thank you for your kind hospitality, but that will not be necessary."

"How can I be of help?"

"The Patroon is conversant in English, but he asked that I accompany him should you and your magistrates have any questions of Director Kieft later," responded Ensign Baxter. "When the two of you were introduced briefly after you first arrived at the fort, he noticed your integrity and generous spirit. He wants you and your friends to be well but is anxious for your safety."

"Thank you, Ensign, we are fortunate to have your commitment here in Gravesend even as you serve at the pleasure of the Director. I sincerely appreciate the Patroon's compliment and thoughtful concern for our welfare."

"I am pleased to be part of this new venture here. Director Kieft reaffirmed your authority to conduct town meetings and maintain all records in English, but do know that should you or your clerk John Tilton have need for translation, please call on me."

In his thick Dutch accented English, the Patroon addressed the founder, "Meladie Moody, I have reason to believe you and your new village may be in grave danger. I fear that Min Heer Director General did not fully inform you there still remains risk of attack. I see that men here scarcely had time to construct a secure structure for your home, and much remains to be done to make the settlement more safe for everyone."

"Forgive me, but I don't understand, Patroon. Fortunately, this southwest portion of Lange Eylandt was cleared by the Canarsees long ago. Still much was required of our men to prepare their lots for houses and cultivation, provide stakes for the palisade, and build homes before winter arrives. We scarcely had sufficient time to plant crops in time to harvest this fall although women and children did their best to help. We knew of the terrible war between the Dutch and the many wilden peoples in the region but were told that a successful treaty was achieved. It was said that before Roger Williams sailed from here for England that he had some helpful contact with a few of their leaders and that you were able to persuade the Canarsees and others on Lange Eylandt to meet with Director Kieft and river wilden leaders at the fort."

"Yes, that is true. You and your friends arrived shortly after the treaty was finally signed in March, but only after it exacted much patience and required diligent diplomacy to earn their cooperation. The war that the Director inflicted on all of us—wilden and Dutch— was unprovoked and unnecessarily tragic. Not only did Dutch families, who did not anticipate war nor prepare for it, lose farms and loved ones, but the local villagers suffered much larger numbers of warriors, elders, women, and children who were wantonly massacred without warning and without cause. The toll on their present and future well-being is catastrophic."

"It's hard to fathom the horror of it all."

"Yes, it is, meladie. We urged Heer Director General to be very generous, indeed magnanimous, with gifts to ensure the peace treaty is honored, an authentic act that would show them he understood the impact of their profound loss and grief and was truly sorry. They were to be compensated accordingly to help us all heal and be reconciled for the sake of peace between us."

"Did he not then do so?"

"Quite the contrary, sakimas and other leaders were insulted because what they received was very insufficient to disperse adequate gifts that families bereft of loved ones deserved and expected. This is how they manage to forgive and rebuild relationships fractured by the atrocity of war. They perceived his neglect demeaning, disrespectful, and a failure to express genuine sorrow by the Dutch for the immense tragedy that befell them when they were attacked in such cruel ways without cause. This offense cannot be understated and will not be ignored. I believe the treaty will not hold.

"Understandably, they know they were wronged and that Willem Kieft's apparent indifference and inadequacy as a human being revealed he was incapable of grasping the depth of the suffering he inflicted and implication for their future—wisdom lost elders imparted to the village gone, life sustaining skills of healthy adults gone, keepers of stories and sacred traditions gone, women and their offspring gone and thus their generations gone. Hopes and dreams for the continuance of their previously reduced people from disease was once more shattered. Heer Kieft fell far short of making even a lesser tragedy right. Every village knows his attack that started the war was unjust, and his failure to take full responsibility to help them recover was again unjust."

"I am deeply troubled, Patroon De Vries. We did not know that. He is a leader with no conscience or regard for those who suffered by his command, a man without honor or human decency let alone repentant in the face of such horrific deeds."

"There is a sense among those few of us who have cultivated trust with these people and who truly understand their way of gift giving and receiving for treaties, protection, transfer of land, and recompense for wrongs against them how great must be their dissatisfaction and anger. At best, the treaty is a temporary truce."

"What then are we to do?"

"Ensign Baxter and Sergeant Hubbard will stay with you rather than returning to the fort. When we finish here, I urge them to blow the horn for an urgent meeting. Everyone must be fully informed and grasp that it is critical to immediately determine strategies, responsibilities, and actions including what bare essentials to take if need be. Lieutenant Nicholas Stillwell was at the fort and will arrive shortly. He has already been briefed, and his experience is invaluable as a military leader, but he is one of the few who is also in good relations with the wilden who lived near him on *Staaten Eylandt*. They respect him.

"If an attack occurs, it will most likely come from the north and not from those the lieutenant knows and with little warning as happened to my holdings and people. He can assess the most effective defense but also determine, if need be, that your women and children must leave for the relative safety of Amersfoort at once. One man traveling alone can go faster and should quickly advance ahead of them on the Mechawanienk Trail to alert the people there of your predicament and so be warned themselves. It would also be advisable to have more dugouts, canoes, and other vessels at the ready if an escape route is necessary along the southern coast of Lange Eylandt to the Atlantic side and thence overland."

"We will do as you have instructed us and are very grateful for your warning and guidance, Patroon. What else would you suggest not only to be prepared for such eventuality should it occur but to avoid misunderstanding and conflict in the future?"

"Meladie Moody, most of the inhabitants here in Gravesend are inexperienced and do not know how they must consider the values of their wilden neighbors. There is much misunderstanding about arrangements for their land. They believe the land is a gift from the Creator for their sustenance and so live their lives. The concept of private land ownership is not practiced by them. Many lower river villages west of here have been subject to burdensome tributes forced by more powerful enemies further north of Mannahatta and Lange Eylandt. They may gift land not as a permanent purchase but rather an agreement as one of mutual protection from these more aggressive peoples. Such was the understanding of the inhabitants at Pavonia who were attacked by Kieft's soldiers. Thus, destruction of their village and brutal murder was ultimate betrayal.

"The Canarsees near you reason that they have given the Dutch permission to settle while they still retain right of access for fishing, collecting clam shells for *zeewant*, or access to the shore for other reasons. Their lives depend on this relationship to the land, water, and its natural resources. To secure and retain their trust, they need to be accorded this respect and their needs met.

"The gifts Director Kieft gave them for this land, apparently more generous than what we have seen since and long before you and your friends arrived, are part of long standing ritual and deemed very important. Indeed, the WIC requires that the company purchases all lands from the wilden first. You and your magistrates will also be expected to make the same gesture for Gravesend when the time is appropriate. Although there has been no wilden village here for a long time and the local Canarsee now at some distance, they still view the harbor entry, shoreline, inland, and Conyne Eylandt as their ancestral right and responsibility."

"Patroon De Vries, we will do everything in our power to ensure the basis you explain for good relations is well understood."

"You must understand that Penhowitz is Sakima of the Canarsee, very powerful in the region, and not an easy person. Honesty, generosity, and fairness is central to how wilden judge others and themselves, values your Roger Williams well understood and practiced among the Narragansetts which is why he is respected even here. Such reputation becomes widely known among them. Penhowitz, however, had a very different experience. He is most resentful of all the things his people have done for the Swannekens since we first arrived here in our big boats only to receive cruel blows to his people in return. Near death, he will have influenced the younger kinsman Tackapousha.

"Prior to the treaty negotiations in March, three hundred warriors and sixteen sakimas were gathered at *Rech-qua-aksie* when Jacob Olfertsen and I arrived. Penhowitz was testy and set us down for tedious hours while he drew sticks from a large bundle one at a time for each act of dishonor. He would not even consider leaving Lange

Eylandt to attend negotiations with Heer Director and other wilden sakimas already gathered at the fort until he had thus stated his case. If you and all the English here in your settlement treat him with genuine respect, you may have a more positive future. If not, you will face much difficulty. He is very powerful and related by marriage or blood with other influential village leaders in the upper and lower harbors, islands, and lower river villages. He will either be your ally or your worst enemy—nothing in between."

"The situation is more worrisome than we were led to believe. We are very blessed to have the counsel of your vast experience and wisdom, Patroon. How can we ever thank you adequately?"

"Meladie, I will leave Mannahatta in two weeks when I serve as pilot for a trading ship to Virginia and then to Holland never to return. I worked tirelessly for years, but in spite of my best efforts to build positive relationships with the people who lived here long before us, I and those closest to me, including my trusted wilden friends, lost everything because of Heer Kieft's ill wind. You can thank me by heeding my advice. Perhaps you can influence him better than I. You made quite an impression at the fort and seem to bring out the best in the man. I wish you and your friends better fortune than was my demise here.

"Sergeant Hubbard and Ensign Baxter, I need just a few minutes alone with Lady Moody. In the meanwhile, do please pull together key directives for the emergency town meeting. As I have another imperative commitment, I will not be able to join you. Thank you, gentlemen.

"Now, meladie, there is one more matter of grave concern and another reason to act quickly."

*****

"Richard, thank you for coming so promptly after the meeting."

"Lady Moody, it is a privilege to respond to your request."

"It would not have been my way to add to your concerns right after such an urgent meeting that will require even more of us in the days ahead. Please forgive me.

"Patroon David Pieterszoon de Vries, Sergeant Hubbard, and Ensign Baxter stopped here first before initiating the emergency meeting. As you know, the patroon is highly regarded. Given our recent arrival, I was surprised by an additional request that must involve any of us during these dangerous days that imperil what safety we have left. A life may be at stake, and I'm honored he entrusted us with this task. We who have lost loved ones know most of all what that means. I regret to lay another burden on you, Richard, given the tragic death of your wife during the recent hostilities, but I believe you are the best man for the job."

"Meladie, the patroon was the most vocal man of stature and influence on the Council of Twelve and strongly protested Director Kieft's order to attack the wilden village under promised Dutch protection at Pavonia. One young Weckuaesgeek killed an innocent wheelwright and farmer to avenge the senseless murder of his uncle by a Dutchman several years before when he was just a boy. Apparently, according to their custom, he deemed this act of retribution his obligation when he became a man. De Vries warned that Dutch aggression would only cause dire consequences. The patroon was right.

"Before you and your friends arrived, Kieft's heartless attack evoked the anger of all the villages in the region previously not united in common cause. Their massive retaliation took us all by surprise. Everything happened so quickly. None of us who made our homes here were prepared to fight, including us poorly prepared soldiers conscripted by Kieft. Even Patroon De Vries himself, who knows much about Indian ways, their manner of diplomacy, and much esteemed suffered the destruction of his own well-tended properties at Staaten Eylandt and Tappaen by Algonquian warriors situated farther north who did not know him. No wonder he plans to leave."

"Yes, Richard, when Ensign Baxter was here he lamented that De Vries now plans to set sail for Virginia in two weeks and then depart permanently for Holland where he will have much to say to the High Mightinesses Lords Staten Generaal. This already uncertain Dutch enterprise will lose its finest leader, and those who survived are almost undone and thinking to leave, he said, just when this colony had substantially improved with more settlers arriving than ever before. Surely his witness to events here will be significant."

"Many have sensed that he would leave. Few had say in the matter and believe that had Director Kieft heeded the patroon's sound counsel, lives and property on both sides would have been spared and my wife alive today. Tenuous trust was broken. What's begun will be hard to end. By all accounts, Patroon De Vries is much disgusted and disgruntled."

"You're right, Richard, he wants nothing to do with Kieft and has lost all motivation to rebuild. However, he just learned from his closest ally Oratam, Sakima of the *Hackensacks*, that a white woman may have survived a shipwreck at Sant Hoek about the time my friends and I arrived from Lynn and our stopover in New Haven. A man already here near Gravesend saw a ship he thought to be Dutch below Sant Hoek just before the heavy southeast gale struck."

"I was not aware, meladie, a ship had gone down. What happened to those on board?"

"Apparently the ship's crew had not yet raised its flag for approach to Mannahatta when it was last seen. After the storm, the man, concerned for the safety of its crew and passengers, reported the sighting, but the harbor watchman never saw it enter the Upper Bay or heard a salute fired nor did anyone else. The patroon's Hackensack informant said he was told that the ship ran aground on a sandbar after it rounded Sant Hoek and broke up in the pounding sea. It's as if the ship fully disappeared possibly with everyone on board except this lone woman. Even if the damaged vessel and survivors were sighted from Staaten or Lange Eylandt, according to De Vries, no one would have dared leave to cross the bay to Sant Hoek. They could have been at the mercy of younger warriors who neither trust the treaty or believe it was just."

"One tragedy just seems to follow another. What else did the patroon say?"

"The woman is said to be under the care of a Navesink healer who discovered her in a hollow tree near the shore. The patroon is much concerned that the treaty he arranged with Oratam, Penhowitz, and many other sakimas will not hold after his departure, the reason he came to warn us this morning. De Vries is also willing to make one trip to see if the rumor about the woman is true and attempt to peacefully bring her here before he leaves. If the treaty does hold, there will be an exchange of captives. He believes she would be far better off here with me than in what's left of Nieuw Amsterdam and that she might be even more vulnerable there than with the Navesink, especially if young and certainly indentured to cover costs to live with a Dutch family or in debt to the WIC. He is the only man now who would even consider such a risky venture."

"And what would you ask of me, meladie?"

"Patroon De Vries left quickly to meet with Penhowitz, Sakima of the Canarsees, as an initial step to initiate a relationship between him and Gravesend. Not likely to live much longer, he will leave his impression of our village. This is the patroon's last chance for some hope of peace for all of us. At the same time, Penhowitz is closely related and allied with the leader of the Navesinks. The Canarsee sakima will not necessarily give his blessing to the visit, but since the patroon learned of this matter from another ally and Penhowitz was not the one to divulge such a sensitive matter, he will at least provide a translator, a hearer/speaker, De Vries knows from their March meeting. As a sign of trust, you and the patroon will travel with powerful Canarsee rowers in their own large dugout the seven miles across the lower bay to Sant Hoek rather than sail in a sloop or other Dutch vessel."

"Meladie, I am happy to assist in any way I can, but I don't understand how I can be useful."

"David de Vries requested my choice of one man from Gravesend well suited for the task to accompany them and to serve later as my liaison if the woman is not well enough to travel or the Navesinks won't release her right away. If that is the case, this person, if permitted, will need to return again. Therefore, it would be useful to meet under calm circumstances with their sakima who has her at Sant Hoek Bay while the patroon they highly respect can still be of assistance.

"He explained that such an individual, Richard, must convey strength but not arrogance. He must be calm and courageous enough to accompany De Vries right away and return alone later if need be. He must be that kind of man they will trust. Right now, such persons are in very short supply. I know this is asking a lot after what you suffered, but I will take good care of your two little boys during your absence. Do I have your consent to accompany him and do what you can to bring her here to me if the rumor is true?"

"Meladie, I do not mean to be disrespectful, but I do not see those qualities in myself. You suggest more honorable attributes than is merited. You know that all able-bodied Englishmen residing in and near Mannahatta were conscripted in case of crisis. We were not volunteers. That awful night I was ordered to kill. Many soldiers considered they had done '*a deed of Roman valor.*' It was all so twisted and torments my very soul. Never during my seven years on British ships of war had anything equaled such heartless and unjustified barbarity inflicted on innocent people and while asleep in their own village. It was a nightmare, a world gone mad. I can't bear to think of it."

"Yes, Richard, I know. There is that kind of man that is hardened by such experience and becomes only more brutal, but such a man is not you. You told me that you knew in every fiber of your being that the slaughter of those poor innocent men, women, and children that horrible night was wrong and terrible. Since then, you evidence greater insight into the human condition. We see such fear and hatred on both sides now, but the brutal murder of your own wife seems to have made you more sensitive to everyone's plight including the wilden who surround us now and with whom the Dutch sought their trade. Everyone else remains on edge, afraid. Trusted company and personal trading relationships were severed. You, however, have become stronger, more present and aware. Patroon De Vries speaks English and you also have some familiarity with Dutch and a rudimentary grasp of nearby *Wiltse* dialects as does he. You are needed, Richard, urgently needed, and more valuable than you credit yourself. I trust you as will the remarkable man who made this request of us."

"Meladie, it is you whose presence is sure and trustworthy, your counsel wise and highly regarded. Apparently, Patroon De Vries possessed the insight to recognize you as a lady of honor. If this is what you ask of me, if I can learn anything of use from him, if any real hope remains possible with the wilden villages with whom we now must struggle to nurture reciprocated trust, and if this woman is that opportunity and what you deem necessary, then, yes, I will go and gladly."

"Thank you, Richard. God will mercifully restore your family, and your two sons will know another mother even as you so generously give yourself to this extraordinary task. Love will find you again. I believe it. We will all be healed."

"You overwhelm me with your blessing, Lady Moody. When do we leave?"

"Patroon De Vries described a cove that you can reach by canoe and not observed by others. He will meet you there in a dugout with powerful Canarsee rowers in two or three days. One more thing. He insists that you reflect a spirit of trust, goodwill, and without display of power. No guns. No weapons of any kind. The Canarsee companions will then trust your peaceful intent, and he believes the Navesink will honor the treaty as well, and you will be safe while you are with him.

"No one else is to know of our plans. If anyone asks about your absence, I will intercede for you and explain Patroon David Pieterszoon de Vries required your assistance. Godspeed."

CHAPTER 16

The Men Go to Sant Hoek

Patroon David Pietersz. de Vries warned Richard Stout that he must appear serene, respectful. His heart could not betray him. The wilden were good at assessing who they could trust, and fear reflected lack of sincere respect. The patroon prudently chose to use a wilden dugout with powerful Canarsee rowers he met in March. Their presence would reflect that the peace treaty still held and that De Vries and Stout could be trusted. Although the patroon possessed some facility with the dialects of the local villages, one of the Canarsees was an especially skilled translator, a hearer/speaker, and would discern any nuance that De Vries might overlook as the matter of their visit was very delicate. During such tense times when lack of trust and good will on both sides was tested daily, always at risk, there was no allowance for misunderstanding.

As the men approached the shore, they saw a few warriors near the water's edge and knew most certainly that many more were watching from behind rocks and at further distance in the dense cover of the forest. The memory of recent massacres on both sides was fresh and all too vivid and tragic for everyone present. The patroon, however, had been one of those men who had come to appreciate and respect the inhabitants of the local villages and with whom the Dutch had, with some exceptions, tenuous, fragile relationships to accommodate trade until Kieft's series of senseless, tragic blunders. He knew that while the treaty held—not much more than a truce—both men could expect their mutual but wary regard and must appear at ease and recognize their own diminished status as uninvited guests. They must be deferential to the Navesinks.

Slowly, De Vries, his translator, and Richard got out of the dugout to acknowledge the warrior who stepped forward to greet them. He explained that they wished to speak with their sakima about a matter of grave concern and that they brought gifts selected with great care for his consideration. Would it be his preference to meet here on the shore or should they follow to their village? Told to wait, the warrior turned and walked toward the forest where he disappeared for almost an hour. Suddenly an impressive looking man emerged from among the trees and made his way to the shore accompanied by ten powerfully built and well-armed warriors.

The hearer/speaker assisted.

"I am Popomora, Sakima of the Navesink. Why are you here?"

In a steady, calm, and respectful tone, Patroon De Vries replied, "We have been told there was a shipwreck after the war between your people and ours and that a young woman from that ship might be in your care."

The patroon could see that the sakima was not pleased by the inquiry, yet his expression did not reflect menace or anger. The request, however, did seem to have made him uneasy. All those present knew that while the treaty was in effect, there was always the opening for exchange of captives.

"Why do you ask this? Does this woman belong to your family or clan?"

"It is my responsibility to learn about the fate of the passengers. We think many were lost at sea when the shipwreck occurred during the storm and that others may have been killed on shore. We learned that at least one person may yet be alive here, possibly among your people. We would like to know if that is so and have brought gifts to express our respect and gratitude."

De Vries motioned to Richard to retrieve the gifts they brought reflective of wilden time-honored diplomacy while the other rowers remained with the dugout. "Lady Moody, honored for her truthfulness and generosity, provided these gifts. She arrived after the war and lives now at Gravesend, Sewanhackey." There were several handbreadths of Dutch duffel, an iron kettle, two blankets, some awls, and her brooch while the Patroon brought a generous length of highly desirable Lange Eylandt zeewant.

Satisfied they were sincere, Sakima Popomora replied, "There is a young woman among us who must have survived the shipwreck, but we found her hidden in a hollow buttonwood tree. Horribly mutilated with a deep gash almost severing one arm and across her belly, she was partially scalped and scarcely alive. The White Stag led us to her, and she is under his protection. We call her *Woman Who Lives in Tree*."

"What do you mean about the White Stag?"

"Another warrior and I followed the fresh tracks of a deer for hours but never saw the animal until it stopped near the tree where we found her. It was the Great White Stag who led us to her. Guided by our Great Spirit Kishelemukong, he is very sacred and not to be killed. She must remain under our protection.

"The women who care for her now tell me she is also carrying a child. The woman and her unborn infant are at grave risk until she is more fully healed. She should not be moved."

"May we see her?"

"It would be well for her not to have any visitors yet."

The sakima was becoming increasingly nervous. What he dared not share with them is that he had become as devoted to her as any father would be for his precious daughter. He did not want to lose her. The Great White Stag led him to her for a reason. He was confident she would live and in spite of her wounds bear many children for their village, perhaps more resilient to the white men's diseases and so strengthen his people, and he would never forget the trust and love in her eyes before she collapsed unconscious in his arms.

Likely, the truce, as De Vries had explained to Richard, would not hold. The salty people have a way of creating conflict when a more honorable way is possible, Popomora thought to himself. It could be a matter of days or weeks, and then the men could not return to take her away. He must delay their efforts.

"She will need much more time to heal, and by then her belly will be big. You have our promise she is well cared for and that she and her baby will be safe with us."

"Can you show proof that she is with you so that we can reassure Lady Moody who provided these gifts?"

"My words are straight, and that should be enough, but how do I know that you can be trusted and that we will not be attacked by others after you return to Mannahatta?"

"I cannot say what others will do between our people, but you have my word as a brother in peace that we shall speak of this to no one except Lady Moody. She is regarded by all who know her as a person of honor, and I will report your concern to her. You may feel our hearts and know that we trust you as you would trust us. Lady Moody wishes to know if such a young woman is alive and knows if that is so that you would care for her as one of your own."

"When I first learned of your visit, I knew why you were here and sent one of our warriors to get something that belongs to Woman Who Lives in Tree. He will respond to my signal." A young man emerged from the woods carrying an object wrapped in soft deerskin.

"When the Great White Stag led us to her, she was barely clothed, and used what she had to bind her wounds. Woman Who Lives in Tree fainted just after she came out of the large hollow in the tree that provided shelter. I carried her back to the village where she remained unconscious for days while we performed healing ceremonies of appeal to Kishelemukong. The women and I cleaned her wounds, stitched the gashes on her arm and belly, and applied herbs and oils there and to her head where she was partly scalped. When she awoke, we gave her special foods to eat.

"This object must have been of great importance to her because it seems she spread it across her body and lashed it tight around her waist when the ship crashed. Certainly the Great Spirit must have been watching over her because it prevented the hatchet from going deeper saving her life and the life of the child within. It was soaked in seawater and blood, but when she awoke we could not tell if she had any knowledge of it. We feared that if she saw it, it would only awaken the horror of the wreck and attack that nearly took her life.

Before the ship even hit the sandbar, Kishelemukong intended to send his White Stag to watch over her. We were meant to find her. There must be great purpose for her life."

Richard could not understand everything that was said, but he understood enough to grasp that something unusual happened and that this young woman's welfare was the sakima's genuine concern and her life of extraordinary importance to them. Popomora displayed uncommon accountability for the injured woman in his care and exuded an inner strength that held the center of himself and his people together in spite of all that happened between them and the Swannekens. Richard's heart warmed to this man.

Everyone was quiet for a long time before the patroon decided to respond. Clearly no one could escape the painful pervasiveness of the gut-wrenching mutilation and death of loved ones. Richard struggled for control of his emotions, guilt and sorrow. Here this young woman, obviously a new bride scarcely ashore in a new world far from home, was also brutally attacked. What happened to the pregnant woman and her husband must have been traumatic.

Sakima Popomora carefully and respectfully removed the deer skin wrapping. The men were shocked when they saw what remained of a Bible. It was handed first to David de Vries who opened it only to hand it to Richard. It was printed in English! The young woman was English as was he! Perhaps he could find a name somewhere that would reveal more of her identity. Alas, if not the seawater, then blood wiped out what would have been the customary ink entries of family births and marriages…not a word could be read, and all of the pages were rent asunder by the blow of the attacker's weapon. No wonder the wise sakima never brought it to her when she finally awoke.

Patroon De Vries then asked the Navesink healer if his tall companion and Canarsee companions might return again.

The sakima replied, "When it is the season of the fall of the leaf and the days grow shorter and colder, we will no longer come to this shore to prepare for the cold to come. If the treaty remains fast after the return of the leaf and the corn-planting season begun, he may safely return. We will welcome him as friend. The woman's infant

143

will have been born and will be strong. If war breaks out again, the tall Englishman must not come at risk of his own life."

"What will become of her? Is she your captive to later be adopted or released?" were the patroon's final questions.

"The village at Pavonia was under protection of the Swannekens. Our Real People there were not captives or enemies, yet they were attacked. They were innocent men, women, and children even as Woman Who Lives in Tree was innocent yet attacked. She received the same treatment as the villagers near your fort. The hands of parents were hacked off so they could not save their infants and children who were cut to death before these helpless adults. Soldiers slashed the bellies open of the others who had to hold their insides with their hands. Almost all of them died a brutal death that awful cold night.

"This woman who is with us was fortunate to have survived such deadly injuries from warriors who sought revenge. Instead, the Great White Stag led us to her, and so she is neither captive nor enemy, but she is under our protection, and it is our sacred duty to appeal to Kishelemukong for her healing and for us to keep her safe.

"When my father took me on my first hunt, we saw such a creature for only a fleeting moment, but he said that it was a sign that my manhood was to begin with its blessing and that if it ever crossed my path again, it meant that I was given special gifts and responsibilities and must pay attention to what is happening. The White Stag crossed my path one more time after that when I was needed to heal many who were sick in our village.

"The White Stag appeared a third time when the young woman came to us not as a captive but was entrusted to our care. We cannot decide for her because she does not belong to us in that way. Our family is her family, our village her village." Sakima Popomora anticipated that with time she would want to stay with them and hoped that no Swanneken family waited to claim her during an exchange of captives. To him, she was already a much loved daughter and to his children a courageous sister. She could be useful in teaching them her language and to improve relations with her people.

Patroon David Pietersz. de Vries was deeply moved by Sakima Popomora's account, conviction, and extraordinary dignity and character. "We are honored to have been in the presence of your wisdom, compassion, and capable healing. We appeal to the Great Spirit that our people shall be in peace. May others be spared the pain that has come to your people and ours and this young woman." The three men turned toward the dugout with their waiting rowers to begin their homeward journey to the cove at Sewanhackey.

The perceptive, caring sakima watched them depart with a sigh and heavy heart. He knew that once the treaty held, an exchange of captives would be expected, and he understood that in time, the tall silent man with the honest but sad eyes would come again suspecting that he too lost loved ones in the recent war. Woman Who Lives in Tree would have to make a choice. Until then, he would do whatever he could to ensure a warm welcome fire for her in their home. After all, they were her family now, but the Dutchman and this Englishman were only strangers. The Great White Stag had led him to this severely injured woman and entrusted him with her life.

CHAPTER 17

War and Rumors of War

While Gravesend patentees awaited official approval for their formal charter from the High Mightinesses Staten Generaal at The Hague, the warning of Patroon David Pietersz. de Vries cast a pall over their emerging village. They hastened to make their settlement more secure, their men better prepared for its defense, and celebrated their first harvest. Had it not been for the fast response of Richard Stout and two companions, crew and privateers of the *Seven Stars* would have made off with Lady Moody's hogs on Conyne Eylandt a few days before the pleasantly warm, late October day when Stout and Lieutenant Stillwell arrived at her home and knocked loudly. She opened the door to their urgent message. The fragile truce between the Dutch and most of the Algonquian villages in the region, as predicted by the patroon, fell apart.

Alas, at an isolated area on the maine northeast of Mannahatta, Siwanoys attacked and murdered the family of Widow Anne Hutchinson at their home and many others in John Throckmorton's settlement. The full extent of the damage and how many killed was not yet confirmed. The attacks were sudden and brutal. One could assume war between wilden warriors and more Dutch colonists was imminent. The most vulnerable at Gravesend, women and children, must evacuate without delay while most of the men, utilizing Lady Moody's home as a fortress, stayed behind to defend and save what they worked so hard to build.

Forced to flee to the more distant Lange Eylandt Dutch town of Nieuw Amersfoort where news of fighting in England might be more spotty and delayed, the good woman's newly settled English followers would be cut off from news arriving from Virginia, the only Crown Colony loyal to His Majesty and most likely to obtain and share issues of the *Mercurius Aulicus* supporting him and his Royalist forces. They would also have less sustained contact with Long Island Sound trading ships who would tend toward biased newspapers like the *Mercurius Civicus* and pamphlets from English Puritan sources. One could not be certain what was propaganda what was truth. Nor could one be sure about the more limited but not insignificant news from the Dutch who would have preferred the country across the Channel not destabilized by internal struggles between King and Parliament and who had well placed statesmen on the ground in England reporting the violent civil conflict. Whether news from printed sources or from recent arrivals and all much delayed about the rapidly deteriorating situation, such information received was also as perceived by those reporting and much subject to bias.

The Lowlanders were proud of their republic of seven semi-independent provinces and most ill at ease with monarchs, whether their own rather reduced House of Orange or more powerful kings and queens of England and Continental Europe. For more than a century, the Netherlands had more than their share of oppression from the Crown of Catholic Spain for the Dutch to be complacent about Queen Henrietta's French and Italian Catholic influence on her husband Charles Stuart and none more critical than English Puritans. Contrary to Martin Luther's view of Scriptures that man was saved by God's grace and faith alone, Presbyterians, Puritans, and Dutch Reformed were grounded in John Calvin's interpretation with its reliance on good works as evidence of predestined genuine conversion and thus salvation. It might be thought such religious affinity and Parliament's recent claim to be a republic would incline the Dutch to favor the Puritan Parliamentary Cause, but is that certain?

Since the unexpected visit of Hugh Casswell to Lady Moody's Swampscott home earlier that year and his disturbing revelation about her son, she hoped the violence in their motherland would be short. Indeed, by the time Dame Deborah and her friends from New England arrived at the fort on the tip of Mannahatta that spring in 1643, Englishmen there cautiously engaged in talk about springtime Royalist victories including the Battle of Roundway Down near her former home in Wiltshire. Guarded and despite their favored cause, some may even have opined that the King's Court would soon be restored in London. She could anticipate then that Sir Henry was safe.

That was not to be. By the time Lady Moody and her associates abandoned their newly acquired Gravesend and fled to the nearby Dutch village of Amersfoort, the tide of war had drastically shifted and worsened. Long before then, hard lines were drawn between conflicting visions, prerogatives, and stratagems of Crown and Parliament. Their worlds collided, unable to occupy the same space. How is it that a people, a society, a country seemingly hold contrasting values in tension within the ship of state on calm and turbulent seas perhaps for decades, generations, or centuries? To be sure, change and shifts take place, internal balance of power swings back and forth with some displacement, a vessel forever in motion seldom resting. Somehow the fabric of accommodation woven of shared and disputed values expands and contracts, but the ship remains intact and sails on. There are times, however, when deeply embedded stresses are too great, human psyches rigid, unyielding, refusing to credit the other of equally profound principles and loyalties worthy of regard. Even to spare loved ones mortal anguish and for the sake of survival as a people, they were too contentious to share the same ark.

It was passionate adherence to these contested principles and the convictions of sacred inheritance that evoked the death knell. Royalists like Sir Henry Moody were grounded in the traditional hierarchy of church and state with its divine right of kings, a legacy to be preserved and link to past, present, and future. They had pledged their deeply emotional devotion to King Charles that was inviolable even in the face of ultimate sacrifice. Disloyalty was unthinkable, dishonorable. Parliamentary Puritans recalled the sacrifice of the many for the sake of radical reform within the Church of England that never happened. When King Henry VIII sought a divorce from his

Spanish Catholic queen over the lack of male heir and infatuation with Anne Boleyn, he rejected the Pope's once all-pervasive authority and declared himself Supreme Head of England's Anglicans, but longtime Catholic doctrine and practice remained in place that was abhorrent to Protestants who diligently studied their English Bibles, for them the sole authority in matters of faith. Into the mix were competing regional and economic interests and the volatile issue of whose rights ultimately mattered—the Crown or the people?

To be certain, measured individuals would struggle to find a balance between changes in values that had diverged over time and could grasp that for most it was a matter of emphasis of one over the other. Once King Charles incited Scottish rebellion with a prayer book too Catholic they did not want and sought financing elsewhere to put it down when Parliament refused him funds, hotter heads prevailed. As so often the case, those whose intense passions were stirred to words and action at either extreme polarized the populace until few could manage a middle way. By 1643, and with the 1642 sorry scene of carnage at Edgehill behind them, such differences would not be resolved peacefully. There would be no encounter of further debate on the narrow ridge of hope and compromise, no cessation of arms. Bloodshed rather than reconciliation inexorably claimed the day. When Parliament negotiated an alliance with the Scottish Presbyterians accepting the *Solemn League and Covenant* in opposition to the King, their action was a point of no return for a Stuart Monarch of Scottish birth.

The anxious Cavalier mother could readily imagine gentry families she once knew in Wiltshire and others with whom she was closely connected in London declaring for King or Parliament, relatives and longtime friends maiming and killing each other. The fine lady reflected, as did others of her newly formed community, how unfathomable it was that religious war on the European Continent bloodied its way through a third decade. It wasn't supposed to happen in England, but now their own Civil War would sever the heart and body politic of their motherland while hostilities with Algonquians up and down the Atlantic Coast of English and Dutch colonies resumed and intensified. Internal conflict, external conflict, what the matter—bloodied bodies, tormented minds, broken hearts, and fractured families. Is peace a figment of the human imagination, redemption and resurrection a hazy theological, inconsequential concept after all?

And so it was. Dreams imagined and dreams aborted. Disruption. Disturbance. Death.

No word of Henry.

Penelope's Song

PART 5

Ramesing, Sant Hoek, Nieuw Nederland, 1643–1645

The Great Sea
Has sent me adrift
It moves me
As the weed in a great river
Earth and the great weather
Move me
Have carried me away
And move my inward parts with joy.

—The song of a female Eskimo shaman
for healing from helping spirits
T. C. McLuhan, *Touch the Earth: A Self-
Portrait of Indian Existence*, 1971

CHAPTER 18

Woman Who Lives in Tree

Sarah Elizabeth Kent Hendricksz. and the Woman Who Lives in Tree wrestled within. She did not choose the timing of her father's death. She did choose to marry Dirck, a hurried union that meant she would likely leave Old Amsterdam forever. Right after the ceremony, the three embraced for a very long time, wordless, as they felt the light of Reverend Dr. James Kent's life transition to another space and time. After they helped him to a chair, he told them their embrace was the last thing they were to remember, the embrace of father to daughter and now son. He exhorted them to nurture each other's happiness in whatever life brought their way.

That night they each wrote a letter of love and gratitude to Sarah's father, the last words they would ever share with him. Just as they were about to leave the quay for the ship that would take them to a new world and life together, Dr. Blake gently told them with tears in his eyes that the man they all deeply loved was gone and that the last words he heard were their loving letters that Aunt Alice read. James Kent smiled, closed his eyes, and departed from his earthly family. Sarah Elizabeth did not have to be told. She already knew it was so. The bell had tolled for her beloved father long before his final day, but he willed it to be still until his purpose was fulfilled.

The bridal couple did as he asked in the privacy of Dr. Kent's study and home for all their years in Amsterdam. For two days they nurtured each other's happiness as only a bridal couple can do and the last two such days in their very young lives. After they boarded the ship and not yet through the Zuyder Zee Channel at Texel, Dirck became seasick. The Zee was vast and often wracked by terrible storms and strong tides and could be far rougher a transit than even the Noordt Zee. Despite the dried chamomile flowers and ginger Alice packed away for her niece to treat nausea, Dirck could barely eat, often succumbing to dry heaves. Sarah did everything she could to ease her husband's discomfort to no avail. Although he later improved a bit and sometimes able to keep food down, the family stories she hoped to share during their ocean voyage scarcely reached his discouraged spirit and weary mind. His once strong body wracked by convulsions was perilously weakened by the voyage and vulnerable to ship fever. Even the *Krank-besoecker*, consoler of the sick, died on the open seas before land was sighted.

Sarah did not choose to be shipwrecked on an isolated shore with a dying husband or to be mutilated by vicious, howling wilden vastly different from the peaceful, colorful ones on her uncle's maps in her father's study. Certainly, she too expected to die and never dreamed that her New World home would be a Navesink village of bark wigwams and longhouses rather than that odd assortment of buildings on the tip of Mannahatta.

One might say, however, she did choose to live with them or more accurate open like a blank slate not fully recovered, not fully remembering. Her essence, however, was still Sarah Elizabeth, daughter of that extraordinary man, James Kent. Except for Popomora, who learned some Dutch while trading with Swannekens, she and the others in his village could not understand each other's words, but they did understand each other, and it surprised her. Her beloved father prepared her to meet strangers unlike herself, asserting without reservation that we are all more alike than different, and deep under our skin, we all have hopes and fears and dreams. We all want to be loved and respected. We want to provide for our families and plan for our futures. We all wonder about life and death and what comes after death. This was familiar.

Nothing, however, could be more different from this wilden way of life in the Americas than Amsterdam, the most prosperous, advanced, enlightened city in all of Europe, but she liked it. Her inquisitive spirit thrived here, and she loved her new found intimacy with nature. This was a thrill she never experienced in that vibrant Dutch capital, a perpetual and noisy marketplace and vast seaport, the repository of rowdy seamen. She and her infant son possessed nothing in this world so new to her, but they had everything. She didn't know life could be like this.

It was love that saved her, and it was love that compelled her to do what she set out to do in any world, have lots of children with lots of Christian names and read lots of Bible stories to them. Her father would have his grandchildren, but the grandfather's lap that would nestle and the arms that would embrace and make them feel secure and loved was someone other than either Aunt Alice or Dirck and she imagined when her father pronounced them husband and wife.

By the time Sarah's Navesink rescuer found her in the tree, she had lost all touch with reality; the deep black vortex of tortured unconsciousness and pain were the warp and woof, back and forth, to and fro, of a coarse singular fabric. A deerskin draped over his shoulders, she took him for her father warmed by the cloak her mother made for him long ago. Sarah Elizabeth Kent Hendricksz. didn't know if she was alive or dead, in heaven or hell, or somewhere in between. She knew only that her father had come for her. All her pain, consumed by love for him, was gone. There was only love. That was what Popomora saw in her eyes, and she never thought it necessary to tell him anything different because when she finally woke under the tender, healing ministrations of this wilden *metewak*, it was love that she felt for him. Her father's spirit was alive in such a sakima of the Real People, and it would never leave her again.

Now she had to tell this man that she must leave because it was the only way that she could keep her promise to her father. She had to pass on the legacy that he nurtured so diligently for three years in her husband, his favorite, most promising student. Papa's books were all lost during the shipwreck even John Donne's recently published *Meditations*, his gift to Dirck, and the family Bible, but she remembered her father's words and what he was about. Now it was up to her to teach his grandchildren those Bible and Kent family stories, recite their prayers, and live lives of compassion worthy of him. But Woman Who Lives in Tree was not an island. She was one with her father and his fading world but also one with this remarkable sage, her Navesink father of the ancient ones, now destined to impart his wisdom and the stories of his people to his pale daughter and her children. Sustained and nourished by the ebb and flow of their water worlds, they were all connected to each other and to the maine. This was the only choice worthy of them both.

CHAPTER 19

No Man Is an Island

Sakima Popomora approached Woman Who Lives in Tree. "You have been very quiet for many days deep in thoughts that you keep to yourself. You do not share with others, and there is sadness about you that we have not seen before. Are you not happy here with us?"

"I have been very content here and very grateful for everything you and your family have done for me. You are generous, kind, and wise. Every day I feel the love of your people," she replied.

"Then why are you sad. What have we failed to do?"

"You are as dear to me as my own father who I would have never left."

"How can that trouble you when you pay me such great honor? I do not understand."

"More and more memories of my life before the shipwreck return to me in dreams, things I had forgotten when you first found me and saved my life.

"My father was very grateful to be in Holland where he could write and teach what he really believed without fear. He and my mother fled England where there was such cruelty. People were taken from their homes in the middle of the night, put in prison, tortured and killed because they wanted to be free to think and live out their own thoughts, their own beliefs just as your people want to do. Like you, he was a wise teacher and opened the whole world to me. Shortly before he died, he told my new husband and I that none of us are an island, we belong to each other, and what we do affects others so we must be kind to one another and thoughtful of our differences."

"Then why are you sad and have become like an island? Have we not accepted you into our village with open arms and large hearts like you say your father taught?"

"That is why my heart is so heavy and full of care. If my father were alive today, he would thank you for what you have done to make me a whole person again. He would have respected and wanted to learn from you. He would have understood the sorrow of your people's loss from the diseases we light people brought to your villages. When he was just a boy, his own mother and people too many to count died from those frightful diseases long ago, but he and his father could do nothing to save her or others.

"When I was very little, my father had to visit another town for many days, but my mother was having a difficult pregnancy. He never forgave himself for being gone when the baby came too early, and they both died. She and the unborn child had to be buried right away, so he never saw her again. He did not want to leave her, but he made a promise and committed to a responsibility before he knew she was in difficulty. He taught me that a person's word was one of the most important things about their life and who they are. Sometimes when we keep a promise another person we love dearly may be hurt and bewildered. He felt guilty because they loved each other very much, and he was gone when she needed him the most."

"Do you want to return to where you came from?"

"Oh no, my father and husband had dreams about this land, and I did too. The only family I have there is my aunt, who took care of me after my mother died, and she now has her own family. My father loved me so much that I thought that was enough, but here I belong to an entire village and it belongs to me, a happy and loving home for my little son and me. The agonizing attack that I suffered on the shore and the death of my husband was terrifying, but it brought me to you, and my heart is full here, and I am whole."

"Then how can you be sad and withdraw from us?"

"Before my father died, I made him a promise. I gave him my word, a part of myself that I can't take back. It is all that I have left to give him. Everything else was taken from me."

"Tell me more. What was your promise?"

"He and my mother wanted lots of children. Instead, he looked forward to the day when his only child would bring him the blessing of many grandchildren. He arranged for my marriage knowing that he was dying and sought the assurance that his daughter had a good husband and that another male guardian after he died could not make that decision for me. I promised him, that if God willed it, I would gladly bear many children and pass to them the memory of my father and mother and what they taught."

"You already have a healthy son who will grow up to be strong and brave, and certainly it is time for you to choose a husband from our people who will be his father and with whom you can have many children and keep your promise to your father. Your memory of him will become a part of our stories too."

Silence.

"Woman Who Lives in Tree, you do not speak. Your eyes are filled with great sorrow. I apologize for walking into your private space. Do you want me to leave?"

"No, my Real People father, we must talk of these things. The promise to my English father is a great burden here, and my heart is troubled. After my mother died, every day my father took me on his lap and opened a very holy book we call the Bible. First he turned to the pages where, according to our tradition, the names of our ancestors are written with the days they were born, married, and died. He took my little fingers and let them touch those names while he read them to me so I would always remember. Then he chose a story from the Bible where all those names came from like Mary, Elizabeth, Sarah, James, and Jonathan. He said I must never forget these names and these stories."

"That is very beautiful. I did not know that about your people. We have customs like that, too, but we pass them down from one person to another. Our stories do not come from a book. They come from those who told them before us."

"Yes, I think that is how our stories came to our people long, long ago, and then men we call scribes started writing them down as did we. When my father married us, he gave me that book, the Bible that had belonged to his father before him. It was a few days before we boarded the ship for Mannahatta. It would grieve him to know that it must now lie at the bottom of the sea."

"Hum, you can tell the stories that you remember to your children in our village."

"You have no Bibles here, and I promised my father that our children would be given the names written in his Bible. There is much I need to teach my children that is different and strange for the people here in your village. My heart is cut in two. It now belongs to two worlds whereas before it belonged to only one. It is like the hard way when my father left my mother before she died.

"I can make no further promise here unless I first keep my promises to my father. Without my good word, I am nothing. You saved my life, and I would give you everything that I was capable of sharing. You must know because of whom I am that if I made a promise to you, I would keep it. That's how it is, and I must honor my first promises before I can make others."

"You are in much conflict, my light daughter, and now I see why you have become so quiet. These things are not easily sorted out. Among our people a person's truthful word is held in highest esteem."

"My destination was the Island of the Mannahatta where many come from the great city of Amsterdam where I lived, but they are all strangers. I have no husband now with whom to share that new life, no husband who can give my father many grandchildren. Here in this village, there are many new friends and a large wonderful, loving family, but I am not free to take back my promise. It is already given, but I don't want to leave you."

"While you were still recovering from your wounds, Woman Who Lives in Tree, two men from Sewanhackey came to our shore. They heard that a woman from the ship that crashed in the storm was living with us and came to ask about you to learn if the talk was true. One was the Dutchman De Vries. In spite of the war with the

Swannekens of all our peoples by the bays, on the islands, and up and down the river, he is much trusted by our closest allies and makes our speech. The tall man was English I think. We know nothing about him, but I could see that his heart was honest, open, and respectful."

"I did not know of their visit."

"We knew your body needed much time and care to heal and so save your baby and that your heart would need even more time and tender devotion. I wanted you to stay always with us and feared the day that we must have this talk."

"I told my father in Amsterdam that I could never leave him, but he said that it was he who must leave me to die, and I tell you now that I could never leave my Navesink Real People father. You are the two wisest men I have ever known. Whatever hardships I have suffered are nothing compared to my love for both of you. My heart is breaking, but I must find a way to keep my word, and I struggle with that."

"It seems then that I must lose you soon. You must find the way back to your promise. The tall Englishman will return here now that the final treaty has been made with the Dutch. It is safe for him to visit, and he will want to meet you and see that you are well. The Great White Stag watched over you, and that means you are free to make your own choice. We do not own you. You are not captive. After this man visits, we will give you from full moon to full moon to decide with whom you will live and have your children."

"Thank you, Father. You are generous as you are wise and loving."

"Woman Who Lives in Tree, in spite of all your pain when we found you, there was a love and trust in your eyes that lifted you from your suffering. I have never seen that before and knew that you were different. Your trials and torment have been great, but you walk and talk straight. I will always love you for that, but it is your pure goodness that will ultimately bring me my greatest sorrow. I could send you away when the Englishman first comes, but you have two hearts, and you must have more time to think after you first see him. To keep your promise, you must leave your family and friends here who love you for strangers you do not know. You carry a heavy burden and risk much. Such a choice should not be rushed. It must come of your own free will after much quiet thought."

"Your kindness is too great for me and so dear. I would be honored if you will always be the grandfather to my children that my father wanted to be. As he used to say, 'Wisdom is in short supply these days. When you find it in another, never let it go.'"

"I would have been honored to meet your English father. If what you say is true, and I believe it is, he is like the Dutchman De Vries who asked about you and very unlike most salty people who come across the big water."

CHAPTER 20

Sakima Popomora

Now it was Sakima Popomora's turn to be quiet and withdrawn, a remote island, far from the maine. He knew that if the tall Englishman survived the long conflict between the Swannekens and warriors from every village in the region, he would return. He was the kind of man who, like Woman Who Lives in Tree, keeps his word. If he agreed to return, he would return. Popomora, a metewak accustomed to healing guidance from the spirit world, had keen instincts about people, even the Swannekens, the salty people. Every human being is wrapped in an invisible blanket of spirit. You can feel it, sense it, and it reveals their real character. It doesn't lie. This Englishman's blanket revealed an honest man, a sincere man, but he carried a deep sorrow. His wounds were not visible on his body like the woman protected by the Great White Stag, but they were deeper. He was a man who had not always felt loved the way she did. Every human being suffers and must choose to be bitter or compassionate. Many feel their loss gives them the right to destroy others, but Popomora's ancient people use their loss as a bridge to join their island with the maine. The Dutchman did all the talking, the Englishman listened, as well he ought, but he was the one reaching out. He would return.

The sakima did not want to lose Woman Who Lives in Tree. According to their customs, under normal circumstance he could keep her against her will, but the Great White Stag led him to her hiding place. This situation was no normal circumstance. Kishelemukong intended this encounter for good. Everything was to enfold as was meant to be, no coercion, nor violation of individual free choice. During the agonizing days of the young woman's long healing, he had come to love her as his daughter, the first child, who was lost to disease. He had come to respect her courage and resiliency and would never forget her first real smile. Her eyes sparkled like the sunlight through a crested ocean wave, and her whole face lit up all the dark spaces of his own grief. He was changed forever too. How could he let her go now and endure the deep void of her absence?

She had transitioned to their way of life so easily. After her wounds were healed and her baby safely delivered, Woman Who Lives in Tree, despite the terrible scars, grew more beautiful every day, that kind of person who is at one with whatever the world gives her. She took such delight in every new discovery and like a child often came running to him with a plant she had never seen before. Full of curiosity and wonder, she was fascinated by their use of plants to ease the pangs of childbirth and for healing as Popomora had done for her. Until she withdrew into her island and revealed the inner turmoil of her heart, the metewak truly believed the White Stag meant for her to become one with his people. She came the hard, cruel way, but she came willingly and without fear or anger. Why could she not stay with them forever willingly?

Woman Who Lives in Tree explained that her father was a man of great learning, compassion, and honest character. Clearly she was her father's daughter and the kind of daughter he would want, but that kind of daughter lives the truth that necessitates hard decisions.

CHAPTER 21

The Tall Englishman Returns

Richard Stout was a man definitely comfortable in his own skin. Seven years on the high seas, a hard life and survived by few, had made him strong, confident, and daring. He was used to adjusting rapidly to different nationalities and languages whether among the ships' crews or at different ports of the newly expanding British Empire. He adapted easily to the wilden from various villages that came and went to trade in the fort town of Mannahatta where eighteen languages—Dutch and English, German, Polish, Norwegian, Finnish, Swedish, French, Creole, Wiltse dialects and more—could be heard on the streets. He may not have been as educated as many of the men at Gravesend, but he certainly had a natural capacity for sorting out meaningful and useful phrases among the cacophony of the ever varied multilingual world in which he found himself since leaving his father's ancestral Nottingham home.

Richard was astonished when he first learned that a stately, aristocratic lady was offered a site on Lange Eylandt for an English town on Dutch soil and required a few more patentees. Despite a woman would be their leader, he realized a remarkable opportunity and committed himself to doing his part to make it a success. Soon he found himself in the frequent company of Lady Deborah Moody when they drew adjacent farm lots. Her unconditional regard for the dignity of others derived from her compassionate faith was healing balm for his wounded soul and disrupted life. Richard felt truly grounded for the first time. Profoundly transformed, the other tempestuous man died, and a more introspective man emerged from a lifetime of often violent encounters and their tragic consequences.

Now he was on his way at last to resume the task set before him over two years before when an English Bible was placed in his hands on the shores of Sant Hoek Bay. With each stroke of the oars across below the Narrows, Richard's heart pounded harder, not from fear or exertion but from anticipation. Could he trust his own emotions? What would he feel and how would he respond when he met this young woman who had suffered not unlike his own wife? One of Director Kieft's conscripted soldiers at the fort, he returned home to her agonized screams as she was hacked to death. Scarcely a minute later and their infant and toddler would have been killed as well. He went crazy. He just didn't kill the intruder. He hated him. He mutilated him as the assailant had done to his beloved. Provoked by the bloody scene of his wife's murder, Richard's anger against his father, repressed for years, explosively burst through the fragile boundary between balance and madness.

Richard Stout's father thought his son's first true love beneath their status and rejected the love match. Passionately in love with the young lady and feeling betrayed, he left the home of his birth and joined the navy, not a good or necessary choice but the impetuous one of an angry young man. When his final voyage with a ship that accompanied a trading vessel stopped at Mannahatta, he received a small plot of land for tobacco near the Dutch fort if he joined other Englishmen conscripted for military defense. There he found love again, but all that was destroyed in less than one brutal minute. The only thing that saved him and others from any further acts of his crazed grief was the realization that he must now be father and mother to their precious sons, all that remained of the couple's affection for one another, and that they must have something better from him than what he received from his father. This time he would make a better choice and be the thoughtful, loving father than the one he never saw again.

Were the injuries of the young woman as serious as Sakima Popomora described to Patroon David Pietersz. de Vries? It's unfathomable that after a long ocean voyage she even survived the ship-wreck, terrifying massacre, and days alone in a strange new world, a wilderness, without clothing, food, or water. Would visions of his wife's horrific mangled body flash before him? Could he do as the patroon insisted that his heart must be quiet, composed, and reflect respect? During that first encounter, Popomora's silent pauses and body language revealed hesitancy to give the woman up. He apparently did not consider her a captive but rather regarded the remarkable young woman as a sacred trust believed by him to be protected by the Great White Stag.

Richard was grateful that the water was calmer than usual that day. As he paddled with all his strength to keep pace with the powerful, skilled rhythm of his Canarsee companions, he relaxed into a place that quieted his heart and stilled his racing mind. He was freed to think about his mission, the request the patroon and Lady Moody asked of him. There were other more educated men of status and vast experience in her colony. It was an honor to have been chosen, and it meant that she trusted him above the others with this sensitive matter. He would be in control of his emotions.

Dame Deborah with her unfailing insight perceived that even as Richard had been unable to save his wife, this time he might save another. The Englishman, however, reflected what he was saving this young woman from. *Saving* did not seem quite the right word anymore. It simply did not fit what he had been privileged to witness during his first visit with Patroon David de Vries. Richard saw in her Navesink rescuer a man of great dignity and integrity, one who, indeed, did talk straight, one who could be trusted, one who clearly was very powerful yet tenderly and competently cared for his pale daughter. Even though he could understand few words of the sakima's Wiltse during the first visit with the patroon, he immediately respected him in a way he did not often feel about other men while in the King's Navy, some of his fellow Englishmen at Gravesend, or many others he met since debarking from his last ship of service and lived near the fort at Mannahatta.

Something was going on here, something significant, and Richard was astonished to be in the middle of it all. He perceived the possibility now for that kind of mutual regard that is the basis for the cessation of conflict, the promise of peace, and a cleansing of the blood stained soil born not of retaliation but of redemption and renewal.

*****

When the treaty was signed and the news spread, Popomora knew the tall Englishman would return. Summer was almost over and the season of falling leaves would soon begin. Women were busy with the harvest, preserving berries and food from the sea while children gathered the last few wild grapes, but Popomora asked that his wife follow him to the shore and urged Woman Who Lives in Tree to join them. With little James tightly clasping her hand, she looked up from the foamy water and saw the dugout approaching. The Englishman was clearly with the Canarsee rowers. She began to tremble as she remembered the words of her Navesink healer. It was scary to leave this place and people she loved and who cared for her. She was conflicted about continuing on to Nieuw Amsterdam where the maps she and Dirck studied in her father's study had almost faded from the memory of her fast receding past, but she was curious about this Englishman. What would he really be like? Could she trust him to find kind people for her to live with? Would they speak English or Dutch or some other language, and what would they think of her and the scars?

Even as Woman Who Lives in Tree was accustomed to seeing many tall, well-built Navesink warriors, she was surprised to see how tall the Englishman was when he came ashore. He exuded strength and easy going confidence. Sakima Popomora was the first to greet him. She could not hear what they were saying with the aid of the Englishman's Canarsee hearer/speaker, but she saw the man glance her way a few times. Obviously, she stood out from the other women in her village. She had always been very fair and even with the summer sun did not appreciably darken. Her left arm was almost useless from the attack and unlike the other women her head covered. Although a few curls still tumbled about the nape of her neck, most of her hair, the locks her father loved so much, were gone from the partial scalping. What would this stranger think when he saw her up close? Surely her adopted father explained all about the attack on the shore.

The Englishman brought the many generous gifts that Lady Moody thoughtfully chose, some like the ever practical awls, duffel, shirts, knives, and several lengths of the always desirable and much expected Lange Eylandt zeewant, the most prized wampum. Unusual was the gift of her favorite beautiful comb, mirror, and brush for the sakima's wife, something only a woman of her large spirit would sacrifice to gain a life. Munsee women tended to grease their hair with bear fat rendering the brush useless, but the women would find a use for it with their little girls, and the mirror was special. Finally, after ceremonial exchange of words and more gifts, the remarkable leader motioned for his adopted daughter to join them, introduced her as *Woman Who Lives in Tree,* and left them alone.

Richard inquired about her Christian name with such quiet regard the moment seemed almost sacred. Except for herself, no one had said her name since her husband lay dying on the beach before the attack, but he warned her not to reveal her true identity to anyone believing she would yet make it to Nieuw Amsterdam. Dirck's family had longtime relationships with shipbuilders for the Dutch West-Indische Compagnie, and he was afraid that if his parents learned she was alive and pregnant with his child, especially if a son, they might force her to return. Her life, he worried, would never be her own and what was left of their dream lost forever. Of course, Sarah Elizabeth never knew the true nature of his departure from Amsterdam with all its attendant tragedy for his family and especially betrayal of his parents' trust. With Popomora and the Navesink, her life did seem to be her own even as she daily worked and chatted and laughed with them enjoying a remarkable bond of loving friendship.

Fortunately, the war with the Dutch never came across the bay to their village Ramesing although several warriors joined elsewhere in the fight. As was their way, many of the women's sons had already moved on and married into other clans where fighting was more immediate. Extended kinship groups stretched far and wide. Few escaped personal loss.

When she did not respond, he gently asked her again, "What is your name?"

It was as if his voice awakened her from a profound slumber induced by the dislocation of the shipwreck and trauma of her wounds from the attack. She was the Penelope who waited for the return of her husband Ulysses. It was she who was one of her father's steadfast Penelopes waiting for the men who might never return. Sarah Elizabeth Kent, bride of Dirck Hendricksz., died along with her husband on that blood-soaked shore strewn with shattered litter from the wreckage of the *Swol*—a memory that only gradually emerged from the darkness of those awful events. She was no longer the naive, overprotected little girl of Amsterdam. Bereft of everyone she knew and loved in that amazing city, she awoke in forested land where she was Woman Who Lives in Tree.

Finally, she called forth the courage to respond, "Please excuse me. Popomora wished to learn better Dutch. I have not spoken English since my husband and I were attacked after the shipwreck. My name is Penelope, Penelope van Prinsen, or as an Englishman, you can call me Penelope Prince." She dared not give Dirck's real name but rather the name of residence—as the Dutch were often wont to do—where her Uncle Willem was to buy a home on Prinsengracht, in English, Prince Canal. Her father and his study gone forever, there was no other home or family anymore as she had known it in old Amsterdam even if she did return.

"What is your name?"

"My name is Richard Stout. I was born in Nottinghamshire, England, and served seven years on a British man of war until I was discharged at Mannahatta five years ago when we accompanied a merchant ship from Barbados by way of Virginia trading at Nieuw Amsterdam on its return to England. We lived at Amersfoort during the war but are starting to return to Gravesend, our own new settlement of English families on the southwestern tip of Lange Eylandt just below the Narrows about seven miles from here.

"I was told what happened to you a day or two before your ship would have arrived had there not been a strong southeastern gale that forced your captain to seek shelter in Sant Hoek Bay. It is said the ship hit a sandbar and was shipwrecked. Popomora explained to the Dutch Patroon De Vries that you and the young man with you were savagely attacked, possibly by young hostile Raritan warriors who rejected Director Kieft's peace treaty. You probably have been told some account of the war that caused such anger and the sorrow it brought to the Navesinks, Raritans, downriver villages, and many others in the region including Lange Eylandt where I now live.

"Clearly you have recovered and appear to be quite at ease here among these people. They have been kind to you."

Penelope could not have explained even to herself how irresistibly she was drawn to the Englishman. Indeed, his eyes were honest, but they betrayed a deep sorrow of great loss. He too had suffered much. His voice, however, wrapped its magic around her heart. Was it because it had been so long since she heard the familiar tongue of her childhood home? Suddenly, Woman Who Lives in Tree ached for her father in a way that she had long since repressed after she fell unconscious into the strong arms of her gentle wilden protector and healer. Her bedtime stories to Aunt Alice's children were not fantasy but a life now that was very real.

Grown accustomed to the Wiltse dialect, it was the English words that almost were foreign to her ears, but it wasn't this man's words that spoke to her but his heart. It was how she and her Navesink father understood each other at first, the one universal human language, perhaps what we really mean when we say someone's words were truly heartfelt. This tall Englishman named Richard related to her not as a stranger but with an honest, open heart that spoke of common understanding and meaning. Popomora then motioned for her to leave.

Unspoken, Sakima Popomora and Richard Stout both knew captives would ultimately be exchanged as part of treaty provisions. They also understood that how Woman Who Lives in Tree departed from the Navesink shore and with whom mattered for her sake and theirs. With the first coming of the salty people in big boats, contagious, deadly diseases periodically reduced Algonquian numbers. Popomora sadly knew the implication of their weakened position with the Swannekens and English up and down the coast yet grasped that the right relationship could offer some advantage. Possibly this unusual Lady Moody the patroon spoke about, and who was generous with her gifts, might be trustworthy. De Vries was highly regarded by island and river people and others who lived close to him before his departure. The metewak had good instinct, as healers especially do, about the tall Englishman and were it otherwise, the patroon would not have chosen him. Since the war, he was angry and hostile toward Director Kieft, who coward that he was, seldom left the fort at Mannahatta. Although his Navesink villages and those of the Raritans fared better than many, he did not trust other salty people who came across the big water from faraway lands. Algonquians had traded with others longer than anyone knew, but with the trade goods of these pesky people came trouble—horrific disease, war, and loss of land. Perhaps there was cause for hope if Woman Who Lives in Tree became the means to bind their relationship for good purpose.

Richard asked if Popomora consented to her returning with him to Sewanhackey and Lady Moody. Her adopted father only replied,

"It is not for me to decide. She is under the protection of the Great White Stag and made promises to her pale father before he died. Woman Who Lives in Tree is of two hearts. It is she who must decide. The full moon appears soon. Wait again for one more. You may then return, and we will talk of such things."

As Richard turned to walk toward the dugout with the waiting men, he realized that Lady Deborah Moody, Sakima Popomora, and now this young mother, all extraordinary, were working their magic. They aroused in him a compelling sense of self-worth and purpose that was lacking growing up on his father's Nottingham estate and in the British Navy. They had that kind of integrity, decency, and compassion that lured you into a world that could be good, meaningful, and worthwhile.

Woman Who Lives in Tree realized that she must keep the promise she made to her father in Amsterdam. Her days with her beloved Real People father, his family, and his village were numbered. Her heart was pounding. The tall Englishman and she fully belonged to this wild new world in a way that likely would never have been an easy match for Dirck. Richard Stout fit in here, and so did she. They belonged to the islands and to the maine and the waters between and that flowed through them. She had a feeling that they would have a big family together, and her father would have his many grandchildren but so would the man who saved her life. He and the Englishman had tapped into a rare, unspoken bond. Only recently enemy combatants in a reckless war imposed on those charged with the fighting in defense of their homes and families, she perceived the miracle of innate trust between them, two men of vastly different worlds, yet bound as can only happen between those of common humanity and uncommon integrity. She would go with the tall Englishman after the two full moons, but she would also return one day to Sant Hoek with their children who would sit on their Navesink grandfather's lap and learn his stories.

CHAPTER 22

Between the Full Moons

Woman Who Lives in Tree received such tender care from her Navesink father Popomora, his family, and gentle, attentive female caretakers that after she recovered, she was remarkably serene in spite of everything that happened to Dirck and her. Even though all the tokens of family remembrance and thoughtful gifts to make their journey to Nieuw Amsterdam easier were at the bottom of the sea after the shipwreck of the *Swol*, her natural beauty mangled by her attackers, and her precious husband gone forever, somehow, strangely content, she still whispered her given Christian name, Sarah Elizabeth Kent, before falling asleep every night, the only English words she heard.

By the time she was fully recovered, Sarah was already used to Woman Who Lives in Tree and was honored that she was given a place among them with a wilden name. When her son James was born, she became more accustomed to their way of life. It wasn't exactly what she and her father talked about in his study before he died. None of them, not he, nor Aunt Alice, nor Uncle Willem could have imagined such an end to the bridal couple's journey, but she liked living among the Real People, as they referred to themselves and were recognized as the Ancient Ones by other Algonquian people. Woman Who Lives in Tree treasured the closeness they enjoyed that drew her into their circle of intimate and endearing companionship, and Popomora began to hint of suitors.

Once more, the stunning tulip season of her Dutch world was long over. The bulbs would have already thrust their sturdy stems and brilliant blooms through the slowly warming spring soil and then faded, folded, and disappeared by her parents' graves where they silently await their resurrection. Again time to plant new bulbs for the coming year, who would record them in her journal this year? Aunt Alice's Sara Lysbet? Here in such a wild place of dense forest wigwams and longhouses, it was the trees—red maple, walnut, hickory, and sycamores like the buttonwood trees—whose bright autumn leaves were feasts of color for the eyes. Woman Who Lives in Tree marveled at the abundance of this new world of surprising pleasures and belonged uniquely to those trees protected as she was in the womb of an ancient buttonwood and reborn to a life with the Navesink. She felt exquisitely alive, but the coming change of seasons and the tall Englishman's second visit since the treaty evoked new uncertainties, new conflicts. He must return again after the next full moon before the Grandfather winds fought each other, as Popomora explained, or wait until Grandmother wind returned again with warmer weather for the third time since the storm tossed ship ran aground on one of Sant Hoek's many dangerous sandbars, and the sturdy *Swol* succumbed to the turbulent sea.

On clear days, you could look across the bay from Sant Hoek and see the islands guarding the Narrows the tall Englishman pointed out—Staaten and Sewanhackey—and the approach to Mannahatta on her uncle's maps, the exquisitely and intricately detailed illustration of Dutch cartographers that so inspired the three of them in her father's study. James Kent called the fascinating shapes inundated by rivers, inlets, and bays "another water world" like Holland but not below the sea. It was amazing how many ships passed through the Narrows to that harbor although it certainly was nothing like the Zuyder Zee of a thousand ships, a forest of masts, colorful flags, and the ever busy and crowded, raucous quays of Old Amsterdam, definitely not like the skyline of the city she and Dirck left behind that fateful day. Would she really like Nieuw Amsterdam after all?

Her only familiar home now was among people she loved and who cherished her and appreciated how she and her infant son

thrived. Truly Sarah Elizabeth Kent Hendricksz. was no more. But
the question was then whether she was Woman Who Lives in Tree or
Penelope van Prinsen. Did she dare leave this place and this people
for still another unknown world that may be more alien to her than
what surprisingly was now familiar and dear?

Once before, Woman Who Lives in Tree ventured into the
unknown. Could she do it again? Would their lives get better and
better as Aunt Alice always said about the Kent family in Amsterdam?
Yes, when her father died, Sarah Elizabeth Kent imagined the void
would be filled by striking out for the New World with her strong,
bright husband at her side. They were young, healthy, and well
educated with many skills. Surely they would succeed and make a
way of it no matter how hard, but after they sailed away from the
delightfully bustling city of Amsterdam, their world began to unravel
almost at once, and suddenly the outcome was ominously uncertain.
Perhaps Aunt Alice and Uncle Willem were right after all, and for
the first time she questioned her father's judgment. What had been a
youthful, idealistic even foolish adventure abruptly descended into a
dark, inescapable vortex of indescribable anxiety and calamity.

Every night, the young mother passed in and out of more strange
dreams and increasingly vivid and violent night terrors revealing
more details until in her waking hours, she finally recognized that the
nightmares, the awful, awful nightmares were real. She remembered.
Dirck never really got over being sick and near the end must have
suffered from ship fever or other ailment that killed many passengers,
his fevered mind unable to respond to her family's stories. Even the
vast forests meeting the shoreline failed to spark enthusiasm. After
weeks and weeks at sea, with their destination in sight a day or two
away, Dirck struggled to stay alive for his young wife's sake.

They could not have imagined that the worst and the worst
again were yet to come when their ship crashed onto a sandbar
during a sudden gale. The last full measure of Dirck's will to live and
protective instincts pushed Sarah Elizabeth and a seaman away from
a projectile of loose rigging that slammed against his right foot. The
grateful man got them into the scarcely intact boat that ten weeks
earlier had carried them from the Amsterdam quay to the waiting

Swol where its impatient captain, seemingly irritated by the departure of the wealthy couple and the subsequent delay, was anxious to embark. Alas, there was a more sinister reason for his agitation. They would find out all too soon.

He urged those who made it ashore to move quickly, but Woman Who Lives in Tree remembered being left behind by the others, her husband too weakened and injured to walk. Hearing what she thought might be screams reassured herself that it was her own fatigue and fear and just the cold, salty wind of the retreating storm ringing in her ears. She tried to comfort Dirck, but he was dying and thought only of her rescue and safety in Nieuw Amsterdam. Surely, he said help would come in time to save her, but in his delirium and pain it was a blessing he could not have known how really dire their predicament was. Sarah's body draped over her beloved to keep him warm, the attack came so quickly that she heard more than saw it coming—screams, searing startling pain, blackness all in a single terrifying instant.

A few days ago, she awoke in a sweat. Those wonderful, calloused hands of the master craftsman's youngest son, that lovingly slipped her mother's ring onto her finger and clasped her hand when they became as one and that apparently secured their passage on the *Swol*, lay severed in the blood-soaked sand. It was her last nightmare. She didn't want to know if it was real.

How could she now leave the comforting love of family again and the firm yet tender embrace of her Navesink father? What new terrors would she have to endure? Even her father's steady, always reassuring voice in Old Amsterdam was silenced. Why did he have to die? Why could she not have had her family there with him reading to his grandchildren piled onto his lap? Isn't that what Aunt Alice wanted too? If it were not for the immediacy of her toddler nestled against her at night, his cute ways, giggles of delight, and daily small victories she would have gone mad when the nightmares began that ruptured the protective membrane between forgetting and remembering.

Which world belonged to her? Certainly not that of Sarah Elizabeth Kent Hendricksz. in Old Amsterdam to which she could never return. Too much had changed, her father, his study, and Dirck gone forever, but what about Woman Who Lives in Tree here among the Navesink? This world was now familiar, certain, reassuring. Dared she then become Penelope van Prinsen in still another strange world and forsake these people who had been so good to her? No matter what, she would endure it all for the sake of this child of her dead husband and grandson of her dead parents. She alone would have to do this for all of them, and she could only pray that God would provide the strength and wisdom for her to make the right choice for everyone she loved and who loved her. While the men fished and collected clams and enormous oysters for the last time, she and her little tyke took pleasure from the damp, cool sand at the water's foamy edge of Sant Hoek Bay. These were the thoughts she struggled with as she had every day since she learned of the two men's visit and the first time she met the tall Englishman, searched his eyes, and heard his voice.

Her father twice lost the women he loved. He knew what it was like to live for years without the sweet caresses and companionship of a beloved spouse. James Kent always had such compassion for the women who waited and watched from the Schreierstoren, yearning to wrap their arms around their sea weathered husbands, brothers, boyfriends, fathers, and called the waiting, anxious women *Penelopes*. Now bereft of her husband, Woman Who Lives in Tree was one of the Penelopes, waiting endlessly for loved ones who would never return. Her eyes scanned the waters of Sant Hoek Bay as she had done when they left the shores of Amsterdam and finally passed through Texel Channel of the Zuyder Zee, and as she had done all alone after briefly regaining consciousness from the merciless attack when she was forced to take stock of her painful and precarious predicament—the mangled body of her beloved husband and herself soaked in blood—at a place not all that far away.

That remembrance did not serve her and their little James well. Woman Who Lives in Tree fought within to push the awful, awful away, and for their son's sake she must remember the image of the young handsome scholar in her father's study and must keep the promises she made long ago to her father, the only sure stepping stones to their future in such an uncertain world.

Suddenly a wind came up and swept the surface of the water. Was it Ruach upon the waters of a new creation, the Spirit of God, her father spoke about? What did it mean? Her eyes searched the vast blue expanse of undulating waves for the man whose voice wrapped around her heart. Was it because it was the first time she heard the English accent of her father and Aunt Alice in over two years or was it something else? Was he married? Did he have children? If not, could he love her in spite of the scars? What wounds did he carry behind those deep sad eyes? Why was she even thinking of such things? What tricks were the dreams and nightmares playing with her imagination?

And so the days between the full moons passed, disrupted by the inner turmoil of painful memories that evoked endless, exacting questions until finally the second full moon shone brightly above the tip of Sant Hoek pointing its long, scraggly finger toward the island water world beyond. Would the tall Englishman return once more?

Penelope's Song

PART 6

Gravesend, Nieuw Amsterdam, and England, 1646–1650

To everything there is a season, and a time
to every purpose under heaven:
A time to be born, and a time to die;
a time to plant, and a time to pluck up that which is planted;
A time to kill, and a time to heal;
a time to break down and a time to build up;
A time to weep, and a time to laugh;
A time to mourn, and a time to dance;
A time to cast away stones, and a time to gather stones together;
A time to embrace, and a time to refrain from embracing;
A time to get, and a time to lose;
a time to keep, and a time to cast away;
A time to rend, and a time to sew;
a time to keep silence, and a time to speak;
A time to love, and a time to hate;
a time of war, and a time of peace.

—Ecclesiastes 3:1–8
King James Version of the Bible, 1611

CHAPTER 23

Pearl of Great Price

Lady Deborah Dunch Moody and her people were returning to Gravesend to begin anew. The unique circumstance and status they were to enjoy with the Dutch offered more flexibility, freedom, and autonomy than even the most distinguished and respected among them ever enjoyed in any of the Bay Colony towns. With the hope that her son, Sir Henry Moody, Baronet, sailed soon from England, she ensured he would be among the thirty-nine granted village and plantation lots. They were joined by Ensign George Baxter, who only a few months earlier was appointed by Willem Kieft to translate documents in Dutch and English. He, James Grover, James Hubbard, the Tiltons, and the William Bowne family, like Deborah, were previously from Salem and Lynn. Lieutenant Hubbard, a surveyor by trade laid out the plots according to Lady Moody's marvelously designed town plan. Richard Ussell, the Walter Walls, and Thomas Whitlock, possibly influenced by Lady Moody, were also of Wiltshire. Richard Gibbons and his wife were from Oyster Bay and Thomas Spicer's family from Rhode Island. Richard Stout was already settled near the fort where he grew tobacco.

Lady Deborah Dunch Moody, including her private concern for Henry still fighting in England, definitely had her dark days at Amersfoort—as did all the Gravesenders, some of whom did not return—days of delay and disappointment, two years of waning hope and deferred dream. However, Richard Stout, like so many of the men, came to admire the lady's resiliency, vision, and remarkable leadership skills, always the preeminent diplomat. During her short stay at Nieuw Amsterdam when they first arrived at the fort and also the final days of Patroon David Pieterzs. de Vries following the destruction of his own property during Kieft's war, she had already begun to assess and learn quickly how to get what she wanted from the volatile, arrogant, and impulsive Director General Willem Kieft. There, and during the longer residency at Nieuw Amersfoort, she could observe and grasp the obvious and the subtleties of being English Nonconformists alongside the established official Dutch Reformed Church of Nieuw Nederland, valuable insight to lead her newly acquired village.

Two years earlier when Patroon De Vries approached Lady Moody at Gravesend, she immediately recognized how significant the young woman could be to her fledging community, hopefully a liaison with the wilden across the Narrows and their kinsmen on Lange Eylandt, the Canarsees. It would seem that during the time she lived with Popomora's people that she would have acquired some fluency with their Algonquian Navesink Wiltse dialect. The English Bible indicated she was English and if from Holland, as supposed, perhaps also fluent in Dutch. She could use such an ally, another female with fresh insight and influence.

Richard's report after he and the patroon met with Sakima Popomora and then alone with her under the metewak's watchful eye two years later was reason for hope. All that remained was the outcome of his visit after the two full moons. Until then they could not be sure of Popomora's full cooperation. Hopefully, the sakima would discern some advantage if Woman Who Lives in Tree was willing to leave the only people she knew in this vast Atlantic world thousands of miles from England and Holland to live among strangers under entirely different circumstance. Would the fact of shared English language with Richard Stout instill confidence in her to return with him, or would her obligation to the wilden who cared for her and saved her life and that of her child prevail?

Although everyone in Lady Moody's new village survived the war with all the regional wilden, Nieuw Amsterdam itself was reduced to about one hundred colonists. Other settlements and out-lying farms were just about wiped out. Those who stayed despite the havoc and horror were fully preoccupied dealing with their own fear and rebuilding homes and farms. It would seem likely no one was waiting for the young woman's arrival or even knew of her captivity as the Navesink were on the periphery of the conflict and Dutch inhabitants restricted from entering Sant Hoek Bay. So long as Lady Deborah and Richard Stout said nothing now that peace was con-cluded, no one could take advantage of the mother and her infant during a formal exchange of prisoners.

Yes, Richard Stout had the right qualities for the challenge De Vries requested, but from the first the thoughtful woman had a more personal objective in mind. Both he and the young woman had suffered horrific loss and had little boys, but she pondered would they be a good match for all the right reasons that outweighed mere necessity? They would soon know. Richard secured rowers from the Canarsees and left right after the second full moon. For now she could only hope and pray, and turned to The Gospel of Matthew, chapter 13, verses 45 to 46:

"Again, the kingdom of heaven is like unto a merchant man seeking goodly pearls who when he had found one pearl of great price went and sold all that he had and bought it."

From the very first and without hesitancy, Deborah committed to give not what merely was of customary ceremonial significance between the Dutch and the wilden. She would give more. She would give what was most precious to her in a land so far from her ancestral home. A pearl of great price exacted that from those with heart to understand.

CHAPTER 24

Penelope

When the final treaty was signed August 30, almost two years after the October attacks on their new settlement and before they even returned to Gravesend, Richard Stout threw caution aside and left immediately to venture out again to Sant Hoek Bay. He was different when he returned, and Lady Moody suspected an attraction between him and Penelope during those very first moments alone together. When the Navesink sakima required that he wait and return again after two full moons with more weeks of waiting, Richard worked harder than ever to avoid a solitary moment without something to keep himself busy. After they all left Nieuw Amersfoort for Gravesend to start anew and Penelope finally with them, he seemed hesitant to approach her in any way that she might regard as personal interest. From the way he behaved, how was anyone to know that the very reserved man could scarcely bear to live without her?

Likewise, Lady Moody observed that the transition from Woman Who Lives in Tree among the Navesink of Ramesing at Sant Hoek Bay to Penelope Prince of Gravesend, Lange Eylandt was not quite what she hoped nor anticipated. The young mother was much in demand by the women who appreciated her midwifery skills acquired from wilden women to ease the pangs of labor, and she seemed most cheerful when helping with their newborns, obviously experienced. Penelope was generous and kind where help was needed whether among the new mothers or Dame Deborah. She had also acquired the Real People's skills with native herbs and local foods. Occasionally Lady Moody and others were treated to Dutch specialties from her growing up days in Old Amsterdam. The singular joy from which she drew her strength, however, was her devotion to little James. Recently, whenever Penelope could steal time from endless chores they all faced every day, she retreated to the seashore of their water world. It was as if she had withdrawn into the world of Woman Who Lives in Tree.

More to the mystery of it all, the young woman, although scarred, was still quite attractive, bright, and gracious, but she did not respond to any of the younger single men's advances, of which there were many, either at Gravesend, or when they took the ferry to Nieuw Amsterdam on market day. It was obvious to Lady Moody, however, that Penelope and Richard were smitten that day waves lapped the sand where they looked into each other's eyes for the first time and exchanged names, but they had become star-crossed lovers each trapped in their private worlds of doubt. It was getting to be too much—two distracted, seemingly lost individuals both valiantly struggling to parent without the companionship, love, and help of a spouse. Finally, Lady Moody had an idea. Motivated to share her insight, she approached Richard.

"Richard, I think Penelope misses her Navesink friends very much. She told me when she first arrived that after the shipwreck and awful attack it was as if she woke out of a deep, troubled sleep to find herself surrounded by a loving family. Her predicament was of such concern to them before she ever regained consciousness that they felt personally responsible. Wafting in and out of sleep and painful awareness, helpless and totally dependent while her wounds healed and her baby safely delivered, Penelope told me she came to appreciate their goodness in spite of everything that was different about them and their way of life from her family back in Amsterdam.

"Richard, I'm a single older woman. That is without question. I cannot be an entire family for her and most especially replace her loved ones in Old Amsterdam or at Sant Hoek. This is why she is so distressed. She lingers down by the bay gazing out to sea as if waiting for someone, perhaps what she lost a second time in her young life—

family, and I don't think she has found it again here. Yet, we knew that if Kieft or the magistrates learned of a Dutch woman with the Navesink, Popomora would have to give her up during any exchange of captives following the war. She would be taken to the fort. With no relatives there and owning nothing, she and her son would be indebted to the WIC and considered a burden.

"Even if she wasn't discovered then and given how fair she is, eventually someone would learn of her presence there. You noticed how relaxed and happy she was when you first met her. The longer she stayed, the more emotionally horrific for her to leave people who apparently cared for her. She might even have married a devoted Navesink husband who fathered their children making a later separation more painful. For these reasons I do believe we did the right thing, but I'm sad that she finds it hard to embrace her new life with us except for her little James who gives her such comfort and purpose. Being welcome and appreciated is simply not enough. Yet I suspect she doesn't want to appear ungrateful and is most private with her thoughts."

"Meladie, your words mean more to me than I can express. I too have wondered about her and now know with certainty what to do, but it means that I must leave for a few days, perhaps more. I will need to leave my two sons with you and your servants."

"Of course, Richard. When you return, her little James can join them—a handful to be sure, but my servants are very helpful and caring. Everyone else has so many little ones."

Lady Moody's insight kindled new hope, and Richard pondered if what he felt from the beginning for Penelope and what he thought was evident in her eyes was real after all. When he returned from Sant Hoek and left Penelope with Lady Moody, it seemed beyond reason or belief that such an attraction in such unusual circumstance really happened and that it could be more than infatuation. Back to his farm and community among stolid Puritans, that moment vanished, a mere mirage, both sun and moon eclipsed, and any romantic intent renounced.

Suddenly, he understood. That Penelope avoided any other romantic possibilities had something to do with him after all.

Attempting to do the honorable thing, he had convinced himself it was only right that she married a man who was her age. The years between them was considerable. She was an innocent. Burdened with guilt and regret and out of genuine love for her, he had not yielded to the passion that burned within for the sake of what seemed best for a much younger, deserving woman. Apparently, however in Gravesend, she must have felt abandoned again in a world not of her choice, and she wanted more from him than he had dared to offer. He would take bold, decisive steps. He would not waver this time.

Lady Moody, Richard, and the other patentees knew that it was prohibited to go ashore at Sant Hoek. From the Dutch point of view the land was part of their territory by right of discovery and first settlement at Mannahatta, but it was still under control of the Navesinks and the nearby Raritans. It would not do for Englishmen at Gravesend or even Dutch colonists elsewhere in Nieuw Nederland to presume arrangements of any kind and certainly not now in the immediate aftermath of the war. Governor Kieft had few soldiers to spare for any kind of protection and was too grudging with gifts. He could not under any circumstance authorize or approve further settlement or visits below Staten Eylandt or south across the Narrows from Lange Eylandt.

Richard, well supplied with zeewant, would seek out the new Canarsee leader Tackapousha, nephew of the deceased Penhowitz who was wary but respectful of Patroon De Vries, and request his Canarsee rowers. Now much tanned by work in the fields, he would strip down as he had done previously to avoid detection across the seven miles to the opposite shore and there talk with Sakima Popomora. What he was about to do had never been done before but neither had his earlier trips had any precedent. It would either go badly or very well, but Richard had already waited too long to weigh the downside and was more than ready to take the risk. He was desperate to resolve his future with the young mother and her child.

Five days later, he returned and reported to Lady Moody. Together they confirmed their plans for the three little boys should his plan work. Unbeknownst to Richard, Gravesend's female town planner, as usual, was very well prepared and had subtly worked her way with Penelope sending her on an errand to the shore that morning. She alerted Richard. The net was cast!

He was always mystified by the many layers of clothing women wore—baffling and complicated to men—but here was this young woman down by the shore, her shift scarcely covered by the outer garment and not even an apron. The summer breeze lightly stirred her clothing as the foamy water gently caressed her bare feet as it had the first time they met. Richard was captivated. Certainly Gravesend men and women from Puritan Massachusetts would have found her watery caper opposite Conyne Eylandt all very shocking. How odd, he mused, thus lightly clad was actually more practical for such a hot summer day. Fortunately, he thought, none of them saw her with Popomora at Sant Hoek scantily covered like the Navesink women except for her makeshift head covering. Having lived with the wilden for two years, where apparently she was quite happy, how constrained she must now feel. How often he had chafed under the written and unwritten dress codes of the time. Even the well-appointed Lady Deborah resisted the sumptuary laws of Puritan Massachusetts that so ordered a woman's dress sleeves less than twenty-two and a half inches a crime. Fascinating.

"Good morning, Woman Who Lives in Tree, may I join you?"

"Richard, this is a surprise and strange you addressed me with my Navesink name."

"Well, wasn't that your name the first time we met? You struggled to say Penelope Prince. Indeed, you seemed reluctant to say it. Woman Who Lives in Tree better suits you."

Ignoring the comment, she changed the subject. "Richard, when we left Sakima Popomora and his people, I expected to visit them again soon. Even though you, Lady Moody, and others have been generous and kind, I've missed my Navesink father and the others very much."

"So I thought. Do you trust me enough for us to talk alone here?"

"Yes, I do. You were gentle and considerate from the very first time we met, and clearly you took great risk. I often wondered about that, but you seem to have avoided me after I was settled in at Lady

Moody's. Please forgive my impertinence. Did my scars remind you too much about what happened to your wife?"

"Woman Who Lives in Tree, time is a great healer. After Patroon David Pietersz. de Vries and I approached Sakima Popomora the first time, two years passed before the final treaty made it possible to return for you. For the sake of my sons, I had to look to a future that could not include my murdered wife and can now be at peace with that even as you have also had to do so without your husband. No, your scars are not a reminder and not the reason I avoided you, and I cannot use the ever present, demanding hard work an excuse any longer. Please forgive me."

"Richard, there is nothing to forgive. I, too, have been rather aloof—often even withdrawn. I'm pleased but puzzled that today you continue to use the name Popomora gave to me when everyone now calls me Penelope."

"I say it today, after all this time, because I want to tell you that from the very first time we met I fell in love with that young woman on the Sant Hoek shore but feared you may have married a Navesink warrior in the meanwhile or that when you came here, you would seek someone your age. Every time you go to the market place, I fear that some dashing young Dutchman newly arrived from Amsterdam would sweep you up and sail back to Holland with you. I thought myself too old or not well-educated like your father or husband. Once I knew this about them, it did not seem right or fair for me to encourage your affection nor did I want you to see me only as the man who came for you and feel obligated."

"My dear, dear Richard. May I so address you? Free your mind of obligation on my part. I was content with the Navesink and owed my very life and healthy little boy to them, but your voice penetrated to the center of my being, and I could not forget you. After the second full moon when you came for me with the Canarsee rowers, we were not alone and could not talk, but my heart was a twisted rope tangled by the loss of those who cared for me yet the miracle of being found by you. I nearly fainted from the wonder of it all that you might love me as I was immediately drawn to you. After a few weeks here, I was embarrassed that I so fully embraced an illusion, humbled that I assumed too much. I began to doubt and think it was just another fantasy. What is it? My husband and I saw each other for three years in my father's study with seldom a word between us, but crisis in our lives evoked his feeling for me and me for him. I had begun to think I have an impetuous streak that perhaps is not worthy of mature love."

"I should hardly think you unworthy or incapable of mature love."

"Here, I'm surrounded by Englishmen, likely the kind of Englishmen my parents left behind when they fled to Holland and my aunt fell in love with a Dutchman, yet I don't seem to belong. Unlike Popomora's people, we speak the same language, yet it was his loving family that opened my heart, and I belonged. I am lost and find myself in a strange land comforted only by the soothing Wiltshire lilt of Lady Deborah and chatter of my little James."

"I feel the same way, Woman Who Lives in Tree. Could we not bring comfort and love to one another and be mother and father to our sons? I love you. You captured my heart the day we met, but I felt unworthy of your pure goodness that Popomora praised. Is it really possible that you would honor my desire to marry you?"

"Yes, Richard, I would so honor you as you honor me. I love you with my whole heart, and I'm very fond of your sons John and Richard and want us to be family, truly I do. You say you are not educated enough, but you have that kind of knowledge about life that is worthy of profound regard, and I do see that people here have great respect for you. You harshly judge yourself not good enough, but Lady Moody and others say you are the most honest man in Gravesend. People trust you. Popomora trusts you as no other man from across the seas. My father would have been proud to have you marry me, and I do not care one wit about the age difference."

"It would seem we both waited longer than we needed to."

"It has been hard, bewildering, lonely, but as my father always used to say, 'In God's good time.'"

"Yes, in God's good time. Woman Who Lives in Tree, this is a very good time!"

"Richard, I am not so innocent as you seem to think and must tell you then about the truth of my identity, but it must not be shared with others. I presume that your sons were named after your father and you. My son was named after my father at the urging of my dying husband rather than his father or himself. He was concerned that if his parents, who had strong connections with the shipping trade, learned that I survived him with a child, especially a son, they would do everything in their power to force my return. This land here was our dream, my father's dream. Dirck knew I would never return to the place where both my parents died because I was the only one left to plant our seed and my father's vision in the New World.

"My real name before marriage was Sarah Elizabeth Kent, and I want to name our daughters after my mother Mary who died when I was little, grandmother Sarah, and aunt Alice who raised me. I promised my father, God willing, I would bear him many grand-children, the grandchildren he always wanted to hold on his lap. Without realizing it, I slipped into a frightening chasm of my own making because of fears the dream was false, presumptuous, perhaps even vain. Instead, I now know it was a powerful dream biding its time, our time, and our readiness to receive and embrace it. Richard, it is real then?"

"Yes, I declare it is so, but how did you come to be called Penelope Prince or as you said Penelope van Prinsen?"

"My father called the steadfast women *Penelopes* who waited near the quays of Amsterdam Harbor for the men in their lives. They would be gone a long time like Homer's Ulysses, Penelope's husband of old, or never return. My aunt's family planned to move to a new, larger home along Prinsengracht or Prince Canal. As you know, the Dutch often use the place from where they come for a name, and Dutch women most often keep their birth name. It seemed to me that Sarah Elizabeth Kent died that day along with her husband. It was a miracle I awoke from the scalping and blow to my head, slashed abdomen and arm with scarcely enough sense or strength to find a temporary place of safety in a hollow buttonwood tree where Sakima Popomora, a healer, later found me. They say he carried me over his shoulder all the way back to his village where I remained unconscious for several days. When I first became truly aware, I remembered nothing of my past and was to learn that I was Woman Who Lives in Tree."

"Woman Who Lives in Tree, I asked if you could trust me. Lady Moody will ensure your James is in good care while I share a special place with you. Just beyond Gravesend and a few inlets, there is a small, beautiful cove. It's where Patroon De Vries directed me to meet him when we left for Sant Hoek. It has become a place where I find great peace and want to share it with you now. My canoe is close by, and we can be there in less than an hour. Will you take my hand and come with me so that you will know why I called you Woman Who Lives in Tree today?"

"Yes, Richard, I do want to know why. 'Tis a strange thing, and I want to know more. Although others would disapprove, I deem it a small thing to go with you in your canoe to your special place. I once spontaneously responded to the very sudden prompting to leave Amsterdam in an overcrowded ship and sail across a vast ocean to this very water world that no map not even the Dutch or imagination could fully reveal. The dream is real—endless forests unlike Holland that depends on Baltic lumber, the colorful wilden, invigorating breeze, islands and salt marshes, bays and rivers, and now your inlets and nearby cove. Today you complete in me what Father, Dirck, and Sakima Popomora began. I knew that the day we met, but somehow I became lost on the way to this moment. At long last we belong each to the other fully alive and whole. Would you hold me, Richard?"

"Yes, you complete me too. How much I have yearned to hold you close, too close, I fear. We are to be alone, and I dare not make either of us vulnerable to unrestrained passion. I must not betray your trust, not now. I assure you, my dearest Woman Who Lives in Tree, your request would be my greatest pleasure, and it will be soon…as your father said, 'In God's good time.' So be it. Shall we get started?"

"I have never been in a canoe before, even with the Navesink until you came for me in the Canarsee dugout. Richard, will you teach me the way of it?"

"I will teach you how to paddle but today just watch. You should learn and may have need of the skill someday, but in the ocean currents it requires great strength. The real capability comes from understanding those currents and how they can help or hinder one's progress.

"When we left Popomora and his people behind us, I could not see you and dared not look back. Today, I want you all to myself. I want your beautiful smile and amazing eyes that brighten my day and pierce my heart in the dark of night when I cannot bear to be without you. We can talk or we can be silent. Either way, we are together at last, truly together."

The time went too fast for both of them as it does with two people, love freely declared and alone for the first time when all that matters is to be close. As they neared the shore by the inlet that led to Richard's secret cove, Woman Who Lives in Tree noticed empty dugouts.

"Richard, are we safe? Who is here, the Canarsee or others? Do all of the warriors in every village still honor the treaty? The ones who attacked Dirck and I did not. I'm afraid."

"I assure you, there is nothing to fear. Remember, although very different men, Sakima Popomora and the Canarsee Sakima Penhowitz were kinsmen. Your Navesink father is measured, reflective, generous while Penhowitz was crafty and bitter. Neither of them had affection or trust in the Dutch, the English, or any who came across the Atlantic Ocean. There has been too much treachery, disease, and loss of their land. Their way of life is changing against their will, but their peoples cannot risk the loss of more lives. Tackapousha respects Popomora and also grasps it is to their benefit to now attempt a good relation, if at all possible, and with at least the few they can trust. Our association with Patroon De Vries before he left provides some measure of that, and you are a rare exception, protected by Popomora's Great White Stag. You are Woman Who Lives in Tree, adopted daughter. You are safe. You will be among friends.

"I want to show you something. Lady Moody gave me this precious brooch inherited from her mother and grandmother to include in our gifts to Popomora's people when we first visited him. The sakima did not disperse it with the other gifts to his village. He knew it could only cause jealously but also knew it represented something more precious than how Europeans would deem such an object. The patroon's Canarsee hearer/speaker explained that it was passed in each generation from mother to daughter but this time it was given in gratitude for a life that was saved. No other salty person had given up something of such personal meaning among the more practical gifts and much desired lengths of zeewant. He knew then the woman called Lady Moody was different, generous, reaching out, and willing to sacrifice something very dear and personal for another life. To a metewak, a healer who understands the language of symbolism, this was significant. The jewels on the brooch meant nothing to him. What it represented did."

"Then how is it that you have it now to return to Lady Moody?"

"A few days ago, I visited Sakima Popomora. He wanted our Lady Deborah to wear it again close to her heart. He knew what he needed to understand about her character. She and we had made our honest, heartfelt, genuine intentions known. We could be trusted.

"Someone is waiting for you, Woman Who Lives in Tree, someone who has missed you as much as you missed him."

"Father Popomora is here, now? How can that be? I was beginning to think I might never see him or his family again."

"He is here. Woman Who Lives in Tree, I appreciate this is sudden, even presumptuous. Will you marry me today? There is no one to give their blessing at Gravesend. We have no minister, and Lady Moody prefers we not seek a Dutch Reformed *Dominie* as that might open the way to ministerial interference that is not allowed in our charter, and we dare not invite it. This is the best way we can safeguard our own freedom of religion. When we return, our magistrates can record our decision to marry in the town book. That is all that is required. We will be the first couple married at Gravesend and so no English laws are yet in place, and we are not under the legal jurisdiction of the Dutch. We do not have to post banns."

"Are you saying, Richard, you brought me here today because you then seek Popomora's approval and blessing for us? You never cease to amaze me. How is it that everything in my life goes about in its daily way, and then suddenly, it all gets rearranged in an instant filled with astonishing miracles? You are certain? Tell me, Richard, you are certain?"

"Dearest darling, can I call you that now? Dearest darling, yes, I am very certain."

"Clearly, you do understand that once the sakima gives his blessing, it is expected that we consummate the marriage right away?"

"I spent two days with Popomora while he explained their customs. I shared that under Kieft's orders, we could not visit him at Sant Hoek but that you never ceased to love him as a devoted daughter would her father, his family your only family here, and that his approval mattered to you as it does to me. He suggested we meet him here. We must always be true to this man. I perceive he does us great honor, indeed, unique honor. You have had little time to think this over. Before we go ashore, I want to be very sure you are the one who is certain. If you wish to return to Gravesend, I understand and will take you there immediately."

The pent up passion in each of them imprisoned by time, circumstance, and their own doubts was freed at last.

"Richard, I waited by the sea. Father said to go there if I felt alone and uncertain. It's where my Father said one might best feel the wind upon the water, a reminder of the Spirit of God. It is where so many wait for their loved ones to return home. Father Popomora is here now. My loved one is here now. You are here. My heart pounds, freed, and no longer a twisted rope. Two lives are one. What joy to call each other darling at long last. This very day, then, you and I will be husband and wife, Richard and Penelope Stout, and I will not leave you now or ever. We will live a long time and have many children. My father believed in that for me, but I became lost and afraid, as adrift at sea but now *my inward parts move with joy*. Now I know the dream was fulfilled in God's good time. I trust you, Richard. I love you, my sweet beloved, my dearest darling."

"I love you, precious Penelope, with all my heart and will endlessly hold you in my arms, protect, and provide for you and our many children. Now, I believe it too!"

CHAPTER 25

The Fall of Oxford

The year 1646 was the best of times for Gravesend, Lange Eylandt. The Peace Treaty with regional wilden of August 30, 1645 was secured for all of Nieuw Nederland and the formal charter for Gravesend signed, sealed, and delivered December 19 that same year having been approved by the High Mightinesses Staten Generaal at the Hague. Behind the aspiring English Gravesenders were the desperately uncertain and unsettling two years that severely tested the mettle of patentees and leadership of Lady Deborah Moody. She had a way of inspiring confidence with integrity and can do vision. It wasn't about the impossible or even the improbable. It was about what already was full-term pregnancy—new life gasping it first breath of air and freedom, potential and being. Indeed, 1646 promised a very good year in that place so far away from the turmoil of their motherland, but not all that far away in the maternal heart of the ever steadfast woman.

The year 1646 was the worst of times for King Charles at the exiled court and capital in the university city of ancient Oxford, already more than four hundred years old set high on a bed of gravel, surrounded by water, and well-fortified. Sixty miles west of London and most easily reached by Thames River boats and barges, it was the very place where two decades earlier the adolescent Henry Moody earned his bachelor's degree at Oxford's prestigious Magdalen College. In 1642, His Majesty, bereft of funds or any other awards, granted advanced degrees to him and other Cavaliers who heroically risked their lives during the disastrous military mayhem at Edgehill that set the country on its course to civil war. Those degrees, although controversial among academics, did bestow numerous benefits and privileges at Oxford where most university faculty and students were loyal to the Crown and its cause.

Many of the townsfolk, of different sympathies, would have preferred quick closure to the conflict. The daily lives of all were radically inconvenienced and displaced by the needs and number of the king's administrators, courtiers, refugee nobles and gentry with their families and servants, craftsmen, thousands of soldiers and their military arsenal, horses, and hospitals. Just sixty miles west of London, English monarchs had traditionally visited Oxford for generations, and Woodstock a few miles further boasted an often enjoyed royal residence.

Unfortunately for the Royalists, however, 1645 was a disastrous year after Parliament authorized Oliver Cromwell to replace increasingly ineffective main field armies on the verge of collapse after the 1644 Second Battle of Newbury. The Army, Newly Modelled of fourteen thousand men weren't ordinary mercenary soldiers previously trained for defensive warfare. They were disciplined and highly motivated professionals religiously driven by Cromwell in the belief that their cause was righteous. No longer were they to be led by high ranking elites but by officers promoted for their courage and military competence with newly acquired tactics. Recently promoted, Generals Cromwell and Sir Thomas Fairfax struck a major offensive that resulted in numerous defeats for the Crown including nearby Bletchingdon House.

The Royalists were taken by surprise and ill-prepared for this new military fighting machine that decimated the king's seasoned troops and best officers during the Battle of Naseby, the most significant and historical turning point in the war. Lady Moody had every reason to be anxious for her Cavalier son as reports of the war's direction increasingly dashed all hope the King's forces could recover and win the day. Ironically Oliver Cromwell, the victorious commander increasing in prominence and power, was her kinsman. The Royalist defeat at Stow-on-the-Wold in March of 1646 and surrender of Lord Hopton's army in the West was the beginning of the end for King Charles and his Cavaliers.

The fall of remaining garrisons a scant few miles away including the fortified Woodstock meant that it was a matter of time when these well-manned, well-trained, and well-supplied troops of horse and foot by The Army, Newly Modelled surrounded Oxford itself led by Fairfax. Although housing close to five thousand of the King's men, protected by rivers and fortifications, and believed still defensible by some, the King's Privy Council, Oxford Governor Glenham, and others with the King's approval sought to avoid wreck and ruin to the ancient city, its people, and the university with its irreplaceable Bodleian Library. Lieutenant General Fairfax, once an Oxford scholar himself, was committed to its surrender without more bloodshed and destruction. Victory for the Parliamentary Cause was secure.

After much negotiation by all parties, the matter was finally settled. Ancient rights of Oxford would be respected and the city left undisturbed. Royalist troops, three thousand of them, would be ensured their safety and peacefully marched out of Oxford June 24. James, the King's brother and Duke of York, would join the royal couple's younger children in London while the eldest, Prince Charles, escaped the victors' ire. King Charles was beyond their reach as well. Princes Rupert and Maurice, nephews of His Majesty through his sister's marriage to Frederick V, King of Bohemia and Palatine Elector, served valiantly during the war. Although Royalist commanders, they were also royal foreigners and allowed to leave with three hundred gentlemen. Their passes, however, strictly forbid them to enter London and required them to leave the country by the end of the year.

Passes were also granted for officers and ladies to leave the country or return home to friends or family. Many must go to Goldsmith's Hall in London to compound for their sequestered estates within six months, at best to recover a portion of what once was theirs, or they too must leave at any port to go beyond the seas, among them Sir Henry Moody who served in the King's Life Guard at Naseby. He appeared November 6 in London but was ascertained to have worth of less than three hundred pounds. Alas, he had neither family, wealth, nor estate to return to in England but mysteriously did not depart. Could or would he ever leave to join the mother at Gravesend who desperately wanted to know her son was safe? Would he one day arrive there in time to permanently secure his patent awarded that nineteenth day in December 1645?

At last in early 1647, a brief note arrived at her home on the edge of Lange Eylandt. For Dame Deborah, it, too, promised to be a very good year.

"Fear not, Good Lady, your son is alive and unharmed." HC

CHAPTER 26

Petrus

Long Island Sound was busier that May day in 1647 than it had been since before the Puritan migration from England abated to the Massachusetts Bay Colony, New Haven, and the English settlements of Eastern Lange Eylandt during the English Civil War. English merchant ships to their Atlantic coastal settlements were much reduced by the conflict. Trading ships laden with tobacco from Virginia and Maryland, despite official word from their motherland's parliament to desist, continued to pass through the Dutch harbor of Mannahatta toward the Massachusetts Bay Colony and east to Europe. Tobacco was their growing cash crop that increasingly necessitated slave labor from the Dutch West-Indische Compagnie, and they weren't about to give up that relationship and such a means of lucrative income.

That warm day, something different was happening. Crowds were displacing the usual quay side activity. The Breukelen Ferry between Lange Eylandt and Mannahatta couldn't make the crossings fast enough to suit the many impatient would-be passengers packing the shoreline. Canoes and dugouts with river peoples in their colorful feathers descended on the harbor from the upper Noordt Rivier, even beyond the vast patroonship of Rensselaerswijck and their villages east and west. Yachts, sloops, schooners, and other small trading vessels of island coastline villagers competed for space among the larger merchant vessels trading from the two colonies to the south, perhaps even as far as the West Indisches including the impressive fleet of

Dutch ships with the new director general aboard the *Groote Gerret* seen sailing through the Narrows and approaching the Upper Bay the day before.

It wasn't market day or a sale of newly arrived slaves from Africa or mostly Creoles by way of the West Indisches or Rhode Island, but everyone who could, and dressed in their very finest, pressed tightly against each other along the Nieuw Amsterdam shore and the nearby fort waiting expectantly for a glimpse and to hear the address of the new governor from Curaçao, Bonaire, and Aruba on the Spanish Main. All were there to assess the measure of the man for signs of how he might direct their lives, and all was at the ready when Petrus Stuyvesant made his first appearance as Director General charged with putting the beleaguered outpost in order after the disastrous policies and practices of Willem Kieft.

In order it needed to be—too many intrusive pigs, too much street rubbish and filth, and way too many taverns. Sober, commanding soldier, he was clearly the man to do it. In time, residents from very diverse European understandings and expectations would be confronted and unprepared for this very austere man, son of a strict Dutch Reformed Church pastor in Friesland, and in every way so unlike the merchants of Amsterdam and that cosmopolitan city through which they had passed. Such a place and manner of religious plurality was alien to him convinced as he was that the God of the Dutch Reformed Church was the only true divinity.

Neither by reputation, temperament, or sense of duty nor would he be a leader to hide within the safety of the fort as did his predecessor. Decked out in breastplate, sword at his side, and surrounded by soldiers, there was no doubt Stuyvesant was already in command. The lines of his face did nothing to suggest a man given to familiarity or pleasantries while the firm, somber tone of his brief message conveyed he would demand obedience and knew how to use authority without hesitancy to achieve that end. He seemed to see everyone at once but not personally with an abiding indifference that conveyed to the anxious residents of the West-Indische Compagnie town that he could be a leader of consequential severity.

It was less than six months since the signing of the formal charter for Lady Deborah Moody's Gravesend English settlement. She was grateful that in so little time they secured their town lots within a well-constructed palisade, roads and fences now well maintained. As stipulated, magistrates were duly sworn, and monthly town meetings required of every patentee were carefully recorded by her longtime friend John Tilton, first clerk of Gravesend. Given Stuyvesant's austere presence, she and fellow patentees without need for discussion would come to the same conclusion. All must be in good order for his first visit and review.

While those around Lady Deborah could not avoid a glance at least once directed to the spot where his right leg should have been and now replaced by the silver banded polished wood substitute, she appraised the stately lady clearly with child at his side. Was it out of consideration for her pregnancy and the fatigue and discomfort she would have endured on the long Atlantic voyage from the West-Indisches that he kept his remarks brief and all too soon directed her toward their new home as quickly as possible? Lady Moody pondered their relationship, possibly the one endearing soft spot in the new Governor's otherwise hardened demeanor, a chink in his breastplate. She was keen to learn more about his attractive wife. Was it true, as rumored, that she was an educated, French-speaking Walloon and that they met when she nursed him back to health upon his return to Holland after the horrific battlefield injury that took his leg? They were a remarkable couple of striking contrast, but she would soon visit the woman and Stuyvesant's sister, a widow. She would cultivate their friendship despite the man's hardened military bearing and deliberate uncompromising presence. She would find the soft underbelly.

Even as the crowd was breaking up and gossiping among themselves, the strategic yet genuine lady of good will was already checking off her long list of to-do to ensure that kind of hospitality which once made Wiltshire Garsdon Manor a delightful respite for their guests. Lady Moody and her servants would attend to every comfort for Stuyvesant, his wife and widowed sister, provide tasty dishes from the nearby coastal shore and delicious fresh vegetables and herbs from her newly established kitchen garden. Certainly Penelope would gladly prepare irresistible Dutch sweets fit for a king. Her new home would be their refined retreat from daily duty and distraction at the dreary fort. She was the *"Grand Dame of Gravesend"*.

CHAPTER 27

Regicide

The news was disturbing, shocking, inconceivable. King Charles of England was hastily tried, escorted to the scaffold near the Tower of London, and executed, his head raised high above the stunned and hushed crowd. Such was the appalling announcement that just started to trickle into the Dutch colony.

"Meladie, John Tilton and Richard Stout are at the door."

"Please bring them in at once. Good afternoon, gentlemen. Do sit down and make yourselves comfortable. I'll ask my servant to provide some drink and refreshment. You seem troubled. What brings you here?"

"Thank you, meladie, we would prefer to stand for a moment, but do please sit down yourself. We have information we fear distressing for you especially."

"Do please tell me. Is it Henry?"

"No, meladie. King Charles was executed January 30."

"What? How can that be, how can that possibly be?"

"The news was delivered to the Director General at the fort, but word spread quickly when crew and passengers from Holland debarked. Wherever you go in Nieuw Amsterdam, everyone is talking about the matter. All too soon it will be the subject in our more secluded, quiet village and contested between supporters of the Crown, who are few, and those who followed the progress of Cromwell's New Model Army."

"Gentlemen, do please sit down. We knew His Majesty was confined, escaped, captured again, and taken to London. Prince Charles evaded capture on more than one occasion, his sister Mary in Holland, and Queen Henrietta Maria and others in France. We heard nothing of a trial. By whose authority was this done? I hope he didn't suffer. How was he killed?"

"Meladie, we tried to get as much information as possible before taking the Breukelen Ferry but came in haste. We wanted you to hear this first from us rather than from others unaware of how personally worrisome this would be for you," Richard gently responded.

John Tilton continued, "The decision to execute the King was made by a much reduced Parliament, if you could even call it that after Pride's Purge. In early December, Colonel Thomas Pride prevented members from entering the Commons. They restrained nearly half, mostly known sympathetic to the King, from entering Westminster Hall and over forty imprisoned, all MPs he believed would oppose submitting the King to trial. The House of Lords, known in the majority to be more favorable to the king in their sentiments, were disturbed by this action but also denied entrance and excluded from any further proceedings. What was left was a small group, the Rump Parliament, no longer representative of the country, to establish a biased High Court of Justice, unheard of and without precedent in English law.

"Despite His Majesty's challenge to the legitimacy of the court they would not even allow reasonable defense to the charges that he warred against his own people and thus guilty of treason. Parliament's role in the conflict that escalated into full scale civil war was not recognized, ignored. Denied consideration from those who were shut out of the proceedings, Charles was declared guilty by a vote of sixty-eight to sixty-seven of the much reduced Parliament. The matter was handled hurriedly so as to prevent a reaction in London before the King was taken to the scaffold and beheaded on a makeshift platform extended from a Banqueting House balcony of Whitehall Palace on January 30. It is said he submitted with calm dignity. The stunned and grief-stricken crowd was quickly dispersed by troop of horse."

The men, keenly aware that Lady Moody's son was a Cavalier and that she would be all the more anxious for Sir Henry, wished to prepare her for the talk that would follow even in the sanctuary of her secluded Gravesend home. The mother's heart could only agonize, was he in prison? Alive? Wounded? Dead?

"What else can you tell me? Were others executed?"

"All we know is that some of those commanding officers who served the King's cause, among them the highly regarded Lord Capell, were confined in the Tower as well. We have not heard yet what fate befell them. As you noted, some members of the Royal family were already abroad," added John.

The men knew that Oliver Cromwell was a kinsman of Deborah Moody. The influence and consequences of his leadership were already a source of distress to her. Rare letters that reached her from the few relatives and friends she left back in England disclosed that the conflict had already brought ruination to their loved ones and their fortunes.

"I've heard little from or about my son for so long that I fear what we may yet learn despite the confidence of his friend Hugh Casswell, the more to comfort me I think when he came to visit at Swampscott. Neither he nor Henry could have foreseen such a long, bleak war."

"Meladie, would you like Penelope to visit with you? There were so many hopeless moments in her young life as you well know, but here she is in our midst, happy and comforted by family and friends. May that also be for you and Sir Henry soon."

"Mary would be more than happy to join you as well. Their female companionship is a gift they can offer you until we hear more. Please do think about it. We want you to know you are surrounded by loving friends. You are not alone."

"Thank you, Richard, and thank you, John. If I had to hear this alarming news, it was best to first hear it privately from the two of you. Of course, Mary and Penelope are always welcome. Please tell them to bring the youngest children, a welcome distraction. Perhaps playing my harp will quiet them for a nap and free us for some time together."

CHAPTER 28

The Long-Awaited Letter

"Meladie Moody, a messenger from Nieuw Amsterdam just delivered this letter. The chief officer for one of Isaac Allerton's trading ships ordered him to deliver it to you as soon as they docked and debarked."

"Thank you."

*****

August 4, 1650
Dearest Mother,

At last I can write to you with certainty that we shall soon be reunited. I can't believe it's been ten years since you sailed for Massachusetts Bay Colony. Our ship just arrived in New Haven from England. We will stop over here for a few days to reprovision and trade and then to Nieuw Amsterdam to report our presence before sailing to Gravesend. One of merchant Allerton's vessels that trades between New England, Long Island Sound towns, and the harbor at Mannahatta was about to weigh anchor. His Chief Officer obliged my request to have an assistant deliver this letter.

He knew of you and was very gracious to grant my earnest wish.

May 6, the Council of State approved Colonel Francis Lovelace and I to go beyond the seas, he to Virginia by way of Long Island, and I was released to join you at Gravesend. It was my good fortune that your cousin Sir Harry Vane was elected to the Council a few months before my case to leave England was considered. Whether his influence was significant I do not know, and certainly our differences during the war, now behind us, were many and great.

We should arrive at your home in about two weeks from the date of this letter. With us is the sister of the colonel, widow of Reverend John Gorsuch, and their five children. It would be a great favor to provide for their comfort during a very brief stay until their ship catches a favorable wind for Virginia. You will find that he is a very fine man and will enjoy his poetry and that of his brother Richard, a much esteemed poet. The children seem well behaved in spite of the long voyage, but their mother is weary as they all suffered much from the Civil War.

How I long to hold you in my arms at long last, dearest Mother.

Your devoted son,
Henry

*****

Alas, Sir Henry's patent at Gravesend had expired. To avoid idle land speculation and long absent patentees unable to make improvements and maintain their property, the town council, as recorded by Clerk John Tilton, mandated that all patentees must reside within three years of acquiring their lots. By 1650, the founder's son was no longer included among patentees and residents of the town she envisioned and formally chartered in December of 1645, that terrible year for His Majesty Charles I of England that ultimately led to his final demise.

CHAPTER 29

Travails of the Cavaliers

"Henry, it was so thoughtful of you and Colonel Lovelace to purchase Anne Bradstreet's poetry book for his sister Anne and myself. I've never heard of such a thing, the first English woman to publish a book of poems."

"Yes, quite remarkable. I knew you would treasure it, and she is also the first published poet in the Atlantic colonies, quite a distinction. Apparently, her brother took her poems with him when he returned to England and published them in London where they were well received. The Colonel accompanied me to Hugh Casswell's former bookstore to revisit fond memories before we left London for the last time. We were fortunate to secure a copy for each of you."

"Would that more of the men here possessed the excellent character of Colonel Francis Lovelace. I regret their ship's captain was pressed to leave so soon. Time with our guests was too short. Aside from Director General Stuyvesant's wife Judith, there are few literary conversations of note here, and certainly his sister Anne would have benefitted from a longer stay."

"I agree, Mother, and certainly Gravesend is no London."

"When the Parliamentary Council of State finally issued our passes in May for safe conduct beyond the seas, the master of our ship was authorized to carry Francis and his family to Virginia by way of Long Island solely to deliver me here at Gravesend possibly as a favor to you given your kinship to Cromwell and Sir Harry Vane.

Had the winds and current not been so favorable, they would have had reason to linger with us yet a little while, as was our hope.

"Indeed, Colonel Lovelace and his family were held in high regard, noted for their sacrifice and leadership even before the war. Francis, his four brothers, and sister suffered much for the Royalist Cause, but they never wavered in their devotion to the King and his family. Colonel Lovelace was governor of Carmarthen Castle in Wales until it was forced to surrender to Parliamentary forces in 1645 and where one brother was killed in battle. Francis would like to join two brothers supporting Charles II in exile and will strive to see him restored to the throne but was permitted to leave England only for Virginia, the sole crown colony loyal to the King during the war. When news of the execution arrived, the Virginia councilors and burgesses immediately voted to recognize the Prince as their rightful monarch, and on the death of his father dated their documents beginning with the first year of his reign. That is where I believe Cromwell will make a move when he knows he has sufficient power and resources to do so. In his view, their position is traitorous, and he will seek to bring them to heel I'm sure."

"I'm grateful then that my home provided Colonel Lovelace and his family a reprieve, if even much too brief. The poems *To Althea from Prison* composed by his older brother Richard touched me deeply. His family has suffered much."

"Mother, Richard Lovelace, was among the most excellent of poets in the king's court. He could entrance his audience as no other with his moving and melodic verse of chivalric love and fidelity. Yet, at the same time he did what few of us could do through his potent poetry. He strove to better advise King Charles. We understood that Parliamentarian critics were able to evoke controversy and thus rebellion by their focus on Henrietta Maria as Catholic and her foreign birth and ancestry. They loved to use the word *popish* for stronger off-putting effect keenly aware of the hatred for the pope's worldly power and history of persecution. Richard was one of the few who knew how to address this tender, sensitive issue to the king. As with so many of the court poets, playwrights, actors, dancers, and musi-

213

cians he responded to the conflict armed with both word and sword. Twice he suffered terribly in prison losing his love and his fortune."

"I shall cherish his poems all the more then and am very grateful they were printed last year so Colonel Lovelace could bring a few copies. We do not get such Cavalier literature here although Puritan pamphlets, newspapers, and books can easily be acquired from Massachusetts. It's a wonder he was able to get through port security. Hugh Casswell told me of the problems anyone connected with the Royalist Cause faced at Parliamentarian check points."

"Mother, one can always find a way with some forethought. Apparently, you are a fine example of that. I was gratified to learn that Hugh arrived safely in New England and was able to fulfill my request of him. When I learned of your conflict with the elder John Winthrop and his magistrates and ministers, I could not imagine you would back down and confess what you do not believe. It seems that with some forethought you found a way, and here you are with your own colony! My goodness, you were only a little girl when your father died. Even if he passed when you were a grown woman, in his wildest imagination he could never have envisioned that his daughter would lead a group of men and families to found a town in a Dutch land beyond the seas at the far western extension of their empire."

"Henry, yes, the Tiltons, I, and the others who joined us sought a way through our crisis with the Puritans, but it was God's grace to ensure the circumstance of our escape from such spiritual confinement, to not only spare our lives but to enrich and provide this promised land. What more of your companions at Court, Henry?"

"Mother, it was comfort to me that you did not witness nor hear of their demise and my most grievous loss during the Civil Wars. With the King's remove from Whitehall and the Banqueting Hall, the cultivation of the arts under his Royal Patronage was devastated. Many of the talented courtiers schooled from childhood in music, art, and poetry, and actors trained to perform had not the mettle nor natural capacity for fighting. When Parliament closed the theaters and prohibited plays wherever they could find them, these individuals lost all means of income. Some, if still alive, after the First

Civil War or the Second were destitute and rarely able to return to their beloved performances with fellow artists."

"We did learn that the Puritans thought it quite a noble, even sacred act to close the theaters in the face of wartime suffering. Certainly, for those that did not follow the King into battle, that act with the force of law would have deprived them of fulfilling their God-given talent and denied the satisfaction of their earnest effort and means of support for their loved ones."

"That was true. Those who were able followed our beleaguered King through battle after battle. Alas, the dearest and most gifted William Lawes, a member of the King's "Lutes and Voices," was killed near Chester. His Majesty tried to restrain him from battle, but William would have none of it. Although he was assigned a position in the King's Life Guard and thus thought to be safe from most of the worst fighting, he was killed by a stray bullet. Tragically, the soft lead bullets inflicted terrible wounds. Even as Lord Bernard Stuart, the King's cousin, only twenty-three, was killed during that battle, he was most profoundly saddened by the loss of William, first his childhood friend with whom he played viol consorts and then his personal musician at court. When he received news of his death, he sorrowfully declared, *"Will 'Lawes' was slain by such whose wills were laws."* He so loved the man and admired his gifts of song that delighted, inspired, and consoled us that William was thereafter to be called the *'Father of Musik.'*

"Mother, there was no greater loss to me than the reality he and his viol were silenced forever. I would have suffered a thousand wounds for his life just to be in the presence once more of all that he was, the finest composer in all of England."

"How it does seem so much beauty is sacrificed on the altar of war. Perhaps we have talked enough for one day, Henry. You are so dear to me, and I still can't take this all in, that you are here, that I can hold my beloved son in my arms at last. I hear you talk much about your fellow courtiers and Cavaliers with no mention of what you yourself endured."

CAROL J. DeMARS

"Mother, you credit me too much, my heart is full of sorrow for those I could not prevent from frightful wounds and for those lost forever. If you have not tired, there is more I must say.

"The execution of our King and his most loyal of servants, Lord Arthur Capell, weigh heavily upon my soul, a terrible burden."

"How can that be, Henry? How could they be your burden?"

"Lord Capell was a Member of Parliament in 1640, the year you settled in Salem. He was a strong supporter of Parliamentarians at that time in their criticism of the King's view of Royal prerogative, his poor understanding of how to better govern, and naivete of how serious was the religious intractability between Puritans, High Church of England, and the Queen's extreme outward display of Catholicism. When it became clear to my Lord Capell that these men were more intent on destroying His Majesty and Queen Henrietta, who the King dearly loved, than finding common ground, he pledged his allegiance to Charles.

"From the time the Court fled to York and Oxford, the Lord was ceaseless in his support, almost always in the field fighting or raising money and troops for the King and impeached by Parliament in absentia for treason. At one point Capell secured a supply of guns for a thousand men at tremendous expense to himself and thought safely hidden at his family's Hadham Hall. It was a great loss to our cause when the Duke of Bedford learned of the weaponry. His troop of horse successfully ransacked the estate and confiscated all of it.

"Mother, Lord Arthur Capell was the finest, most honorable man I've ever known and was privileged to serve. Colonel Lovelace was an adjutant to him for the Council of War, and we talked much of him during our voyage from England. In that and other positions Lord Capell was also one of those profoundly responsible to the King for the safety of the Prince, difficult as that situation was after His Majesty surrendered to the Scots in May 1646, presumably for protection, and Oxford was surrendered to Parliamentary forces. Lord Capell was free for the time to return home to his beloved wife and children.

"Even if we had retained all of our properties after Father's death, we would have lost all. You would have been in grave danger.

216

Wiltshire was continually contested by both Parliamentary forces and our own. Malmesbury was always situated in a strategic location between Bristol and London, none more so than during the war. It would grieve you to see the abbey riddled with bullet holes. The estates of almost all Royalists were sequestered and became property of Parliament then awarded to their favorites who might therefore collect rent from tenants and proceeds from the crops to pay a portion to support the Parliamentary Cause. We were called delinquents and when apprehended required to fight for them, return home with an oath never to fight again for the King, or travel to London to appear at Goldsmith's Hall before the Committee for Compounding. After our sale to Lawrence Washington, who later died a Royalist in 1643, the remaining small portion that was left to you and I was sequestered and fines levied with compounded interest. By 1646, scarcely 300 pounds in value remained. I was discharged and free with a pass in late November with no further expense but only after I took the despised National Covenant, then required of every English male over eighteen, and the Negative Oath that I would not take up arms against their Cause. Mother, I come to you a pauper."

"A pauper perhaps of pounds sterling but a man rich in courage, devotion, and integrity. You, my dear son, are rich in what matters most. Others high and low have always recognized that in you. On my account, you carry no burden but at long last lighten my load that was the dread of losing you forever."

"Thank you, Mother. One of the most devastating sorrows of the war was the guilt carried that you would receive only fragments of reassurance never certain of my life or death."

"Henry, thankfully we are both now relieved of that anxiety."

"There is more that I must share. I never forsake the Oath of Fealty to King Charles witnessed by you after Father died when knighted by him, but that is not the end of it. As you know, I did not leave England after the fall of Oxford and ordered to Goldsmith's Hall. When the Scots failed to keep their promise of protection to King Charles and turned him over to Parliament in 1647, the Duke of Hamilton, however, resumed fighting with Royalists in Wales, Kent, and other counties. Valiant men in Kent lost their lives at Maidstone while those still able to fight joined Capell and his Cavaliers when he raised more troops again in Essex. We occupied Colchester but after several weeks of siege when they were forced to surrender, a terrible time. Lord Capell and officers were promised quarter by Sir Thomas Fairfax. Alas, the most prominent instead were taken captive to London and the Tower for trial.

"During his six months in prison, my Lord did everything in his power to write almost everyone of eminence and influence he knew to secure the King's release and urged others to come forth in His Majesty's defense. Especially after Pride's Purge of Parliament and the monstrous charges levied against the King, it became clear that neither would be granted fair, measured consideration. My Lord Capell then secretly urged others to rescue him from the Tower to help him save King Charles Stuart on the way to the scaffold.

"I was enlisted for that plan. At midnight Lord Capell was to let himself down from the window of his Tower room with a rope that was hidden for him in his chamber by a trusted servant and swim or wade through the Tower ditch to meet his secret rescuer at the river stairs. When he was much delayed in arriving, we feared the failure of his and our efforts and were frantic over what happened to him. Finally, he appeared covered with mud and exhausted. We were astonished to learn that the ditch was so nearly filled with mud and slush that he could scarcely drag himself through it. As it came up to his chin had he not been such a tall, powerful man, surely he would have suffocated and drowned. It was thought the water spies missed Lord Capell's rescue when the secret hiding space of the Inner Temple was reached without discovery. We made haste to ensure he had warm water to bathe, dry clothes, and time for food and rest. Other Cavaliers, at great risk, and myself were gathered to aid in the rescue of the King. We who were once practiced in the theater arts would disguise our Lord and ourselves as was done for his rescue, and we were prepared to rush the guards escorting His Majesty to the scaffold.

"The next night, January 28, Lord Capell, myself, and one other—whom I shall not name—left in a boat from the Temple stairs to cross over toward Sir Thomas Cotton's house where it was thought the King was then kept. As we pulled away, Captain Rolfe of the Parliamentary Cause seemed to notice us, but he made no move. Well disguised we thought ourselves safe and that we then made it to the house in Lambeth Marsh where I hid earlier and thought our Lord Capell well concealed and secure once again.

"Others looked to his needs while I hid everything we used for our disguises and took some rest. Shortly before dawn, soldiers from Whitehall broke into the house and with great stealth quickly seized our most honorable, loyal councilor and protector to King and Prince before we knew of it. That day it was announced in the House of Commons that a Thames waterman who had tracked us was paid forty pounds sterling for colluding with Captain Rolfe. Lord Capell was taken again to the Tower under much stricter guard and the window where he escaped repaired. To make matters worse, unknown to us, the King was moved before the attempted escape so that the plan as originally conceived would not have achieved its desired end. That I and the others escaped from the search for all those involved with his rescue was a miracle. Most certainly because of our disguises we were not identified. Without question their primary attention was to the execution of His Majesty Charles Stuart and maneuvered with such quick dispatch that to my knowledge no one was ever tortured to reveal our names. It was only a matter of time and procedure that Lord Capell and two others, the Duke of Hamilton and the Earl of Holland, would follow their King to the scaffold."

"Henry, all of this is so startling and unimaginable…risking your all, my problems here pale and vanish by comparison. I am very proud of you and humbled by your devotion and courage but do not see how all this is to be considered your burden."

"Mother, alas, while engaged in quiet conversation so as to appear normal and not secretive, the other man and myself, accustomed as we were to pay him homage, inadvertently addressed him as "My Lord." In the dark, quiet hours of the night, sound along the Thames can easily be heard. It haunts me that his title was perchance picked up by the waterman, Captain Rolfe, or some unseen water spy and thus the true nature of our task revealed. I blame myself for his capture, return to the Tower, and even death."

"My dear Henry, you sacrificed everything in filial service of your King and in the end for Lord Capell. That the final effort failed is not your fault. Too many other circumstances were as snares before his escape was even attempted it seems to me. You cannot know with certainty that your address to him in the manner to which you were accustomed or that of your companion was at cause even partially or the only cause. Did anyone ever approach you about such remark? If not, then you must remove all blame from yourself and so free your heart and soul of this terrible weight. Of certain, it is disheartening and disconcerting that you did not achieve your goal and success-fully fulfill your final act of devotion to those you served and highly esteemed. It goes without saying the tragic loss of those you hold dear—your precious companions at Court and war and these men of honor—is a void that will never be filled. Only the passage of time will relieve the intensity of your pain and remembrance."

"Would that it be so."

"God understands our deepest points of sorrow, loss, fear, pain, guilt, humiliation, discouragement, and terror. The way in which we approach adversity becomes a sacred listening to the power of God's Grace through the way we direct our lives. You did remain true to your conscience, duty, and dream during the most troubling and demanding times any man could face. You must be kinder to yourself."

"Just being able to share this with you, Mother, has lightened the burden, but my grief for the loss of everything and everyone held dear for many years is great. Were it not for the company of Colonel Lovelace during the voyage and the joy of your presence in my life again, I would be lost indeed. It's doubtful this Dutch colony could ever be home without my brothers in arms so long as Charles II lives, and I find solace that I may be reunited sometime in the future with those who made it to Virginia."

"Henry, Anne confided in me that Colonel Lovelace told her the King himself honored you for your heroism at Oxford after the Battle of Edgehill. For now you are much desired and needed here, but I foresee, indeed, that you will find your way to those like your-self who sacrificed much in this cruel conflict that yet is to be fully resolved. The Dutch here and in Holland consider the Netherlands a republic and dislike monarchies. They looked to the English Puritans as fellow Calvinists but now refuse to regard such a Commonwealth whose members of Parliament sought to strengthen and vindicate their cause with the execution of the King. I was told the High Mightinesses Staten Generaal met at The Hague in special session and authorized an embassy to England seeking to influence a different outcome, but their earnest discussion with Cromwell and Fairfax was clearly to no avail.

"Let's rest now, Henry. We shall have a very good night's sleep at long last. I love you, my dear son."

"I love you, Mother, and missed your wise and loving counsel ever so much."

For Henry, sleep was not to be. The long conversation evoked too many traumatic memories he would never share with his mother. The only consolation was to hear the heavenly melodies of that most dear composer and his viol and to see once again that courtly face and bearing of the valiant Cavalier yet sensitive poet who even in his most difficult hours could write unforgettable poems inspired by the muse of unconstrained mind and heart pulsating with genuine, unfettered liberty of conscience,

Stone walls doe not a prison make,
Nor iron bars a cage;
Mindes innocent and quiet take
That for an hermitage;
If I have freedome in my love,
And in my soule am free,
Angels alone that soar above
Enjoy such libertie.

"To Althea From Prison," Richard Lovelace, 1642

Penelope's Song

PART 7

Gravesend and Nieuw Amsterdam, Holland,
England, and at Sea, 1651–1659

*It is incredible how much one unquiet perverse
disposition distempers the peace,
prosperity, and unity of a whole family or
society. For they seldom stand alone;
the matter, if they did so, were not great. But they having begun, then
partaking and contrarieties arise; and the contagion spreads like a strong
herb in pottage, every man's mess savours of it.*

—Lord Capell's Meditations CLXXXI
as recorded by Lady Theresa Lewis
*Lives of the Friends and Contemporaries
of Lord Chancellor Clarendo,* 1852

CHAPTER 30

Dear Aunt Alice

Gravesend, Lange Eylandt
Nieuw Nederland
September 20, 1651
Dearest Aunt Alice,

Please forgive me. That our vision of great adventure and purpose would cause you sorrow was a weight upon my soul that was almost unbearable after we left Amsterdam, but it was Father's and our earnest dream. When Uncle Willem would have learned from the West-Indische Compagnie of the *Swol's* shipwreck one day's journey from our final destination and everyone presumed dead, your worst fears were realized. The loss of our companionship and then another Kent death must have been terrible for you and your family.

Truly precious aunt, how I longed to write and console you, but, alas, could not. When it was finally possible, I feared that what must be said would not be a cause for joy but only trouble you further. It seemed a kindness to remain forever silent. Now at long last, I can share that I am alive and well, that my father has the grandchildren he so passionately yearned for, and we now have a little Alice born just one month ago who we affectionately call "Alsie" as did your Willem of you. Your namesake brings me great comfort and remembrance of your enduring kindness to Father and me.

My life did get better and better here after all, but first what I must now tell you is hard, very hard, perhaps only less painful because it happened long ago. Only now can I confidently convey to you that the most awful of circumstances, "in God's good time" as Father would say, became even for good. Father's vision did prove true and fulfilled while the worries of you and Uncle Willem were bound to our future as well. How strange.

Dirck became very ill while we were at sea, but the krank-besoeker who might have consoled us died of ship fever. Early to be sure but hoping to lift Dirck's spirit and keep him alive, I shared the news that I was with child when the harbor of Nieuw Amsterdam was in sight. He was so happy, and I believed and prayed with all my heart that with our destination just a day's sail away he would get better. Alas, there was a sudden, powerful storm, and our ship hit a sandbar in Sant Hoek Bay the captain sought for protection. Although Dirck was weak and unsteady, he managed to push a seaman and myself out of harm's way when rigging split apart and crashed about us. The grateful man struggled to put us into the only small boat not fully destroyed and got us ashore safely. Some passengers already died during the voyage, and the wreck took more lives. On shore, we thought ourselves fortunate to have survived.

It was then that the captain alarmed everyone that he learned the night before our ship was to leave Amsterdam that there was war between the Dutch and surrounding wilden people. He urged us to flee on foot as quickly as possible to reach a place of greater safety. I suspect now that only the wealthy couple that departed at the last minute was told this information. Despite concerns he might have had for crew, passengers, and himself, he was under contract to embark without further delay.

The cold, violent storm, shipwreck, and Dirck's effort to save our lives sapped the very last of what sustained him. He was unable to walk, and I could not bear to leave him behind and alone. The captain reassured me that if they made good time, we could expect help in a few days and that with some luck, a few barrels of food and water may wash ashore. We were in a sorry state with what was left of our wet clothes. Father's books and manuscripts, Dirck's tools, the tulip bulbs you gave us and all of your thoughtful and generous gifts—everything we owned— remain at the bottom of the sea. Poor Dirck, he tried so hard to be brave, but we both knew that he was dying. He urged me to name our child if a boy after Father rather than himself or his father.

Before I could think, we were brutally attacked. It all happened so fast, dear Aunt, and a blow to my head knocked me unconscious. Apparently, we were left for dead. When I regained consciousness, my dear, sweet, brilliant husband had departed forever, and I was forced to seek some kind of shelter in a hollowed out tree in the forest beyond the shoreline. I passed in and out of consciousness with only sap from the tree for sustenance.

Was it hours or days before help came? Overcome with pain, loss of blood, and the shock of my predicament, I hardly knew. A kind wilden hunter discovered my hide out and carried me to his nearby village where it happened he was a skilled healer. He treated the wounds to my head, arm, and abdomen as capably as your brother-in-law or any Amsterdam doctor might have done, even the revered Dr. Tulp! It was many weeks before I could get up and begin to walk about, and the little gift of life that was inside me, all that remained of my precious husband, miraculously survived too. James looks more like his father every day.

Dear Auntie, for two years Baby James and I lived with these wilden who call themselves Navesink of the Real People and took such good care of us in every way that a family could. I came to love them and their way of life very much. Popomora, who is a highly regarded leader and the caring man who saved my life, named me Woman Who Lives in Tree and wanted me to stay and marry one of their young men. In many ways he is much like Father, generous, open, wise, and compassionate. They would have derived much delight from each other's gift of intellect and spirit like Father and Dr. Blake.

While the conflict between the Dutch and the warring villages continued in and around Mannahatta, it was unsafe for them to attempt any contact with the Dutch or expose information about my presence. Finally, a treaty was signed, and this loving and remarkable protector allowed me to leave with Richard Stout, an Englishman living on Lange Eylandt, who heard rumors that a white woman from the shipwreck was living with them. The two men have since come to trust and respect each other, astonishing given the unjust and merciless war Director Kieft incited.

Richard lost his wife and was left with little John and baby Richard. We are deeply in love and very happily married with our ever expanding brood. In addition to the three boys, we are blessed with little Mary, after my mother of course, then Jonathan, and now Baby Alsie.

The Dutch do not allow its citizens to visit Navesink land, but Popomora and others from his village sometimes cross the water to visit the Canarsees near us. Richard piles the family in his canoe and rows us to his favorite cove where the little ones climb on Popomora's lap. He tells them stories like I once did with your children. In a peculiar way it is also the spirit of Father who embraces them and finally holds his grandchildren on his lap. Except for the promise I made to Father that, God willing, he would have his many grandchildren and they would carry the names from our family Bible, I would never have left the Real People. They were the only family and friends I knew in the world except for you, Willem, and your dear children so very far away.

We have a town lot and a large productive, outlying farm at Gravesend, Lange Eylandt, next to the amazing Lady Deborah Moody who founded the village. Imagine that! Her husband was Sir Henry Moody, a baronet. His grandfather saved the life of King Henry the Eighth and was awarded vast farmland and manors that the king took from the Catholic Church. Sir Henry died suddenly in 1629 in London where he served in Parliament.

While her son, Henry, did what he could to preserve some of their wealth, and given the circumstance of their lives, she sailed to Massachusetts Bay Colony where she knew Governor John Winthrop and other Puritans in Boston. Lady Moody and many others found them to be as intolerant and cruel as the Church of England under Archbishop Laud. When she was condemned for not supporting infant baptism, a group of Anabaptists like herself joined Lady Moody where they sought the protection of the Dutch. Governor Kieft granted them land and the right to establish an English village here under her visionary leadership.

Peter Stuyvesant, now the Governor, and his wife Judith Bayard, a French-speaking Walloon, and Lady Moody became close friends. The Stuyvesants do not speak English, and she does not understand Dutch, but together they enjoy each other's company. Lady Moody and the Governor, who prefers the Latin name Petrus, converse in Latin and the two ladies in French. He seeks out her advice as did Willem Kieft. Judith sings beautifully accompanied by Lady Deborah and her harp who sometimes treats our children to her angelic music. They think she is an angel!

It seemed as if Sarah Elizabeth Kent also died that awful day on the shore with my beloved Dirck and came to see myself as one of Father's "Penelopes." Thus, I am now Penelope Stout, but I shall forever be your Sarah Elizabeth and love you so much. My faithful, loving husband and father captured my heart the day we met beside Popomora. I did not want to return to Holland. I wanted to stay here once again surrounded by love.

Please do write and tell me about the children. They must be quite grown by now. I miss them so.

Your devoted and grateful,
Sarah Elizabeth

CHAPTER 31

Sara Lysbet's Letter

Amsterdam, Noordt Holland
February 4, 1652
Dear Sarah Elizabeth,

You're alive! We could scarcely believe your words. I was close to our front door when your letter arrived and fortunate that it was delivered for Father. Very perplexed, I took it immediately upstairs to our loft where he receives and inspects merchandise hoisted directly from barges on Prinsengracht that carry goods from the ships. The wealthiest merchants can afford this convenience of their own *koopmanshuisen*, and Father has done quite well since you left.

Your news was stunning and Father emotionally shaken. Tears streamed down his face. When your father died just before you and Dirck embarked, he was then your guardian and legally could have prevented your departure. I understood for the first time the burden of blame he shouldered all these years that he did not stop you...My dearest sister, oh, how we missed you! How can this be?

Father insisted we calm our emotions before sharing your letter with Mother. He was very concerned about her response to your description of the wilden attack along the shore and living with them for two years. He knew there had to be an extraordinary reason for such a sudden return to shore by an official of the WIC, and it troubled him. When Father found out the truth of the matter, he shared only that the *Swol* was shipwrecked with no known survivors and said nothing to any of us about the Dutch and local wilden villages being at war. Withdrawn from grief, the rest of us were out of touch with school and marketplace gossip. After your letter, my brothers told me they heard rumors.

When we told Mother that a miraculous, good news letter from you arrived after all these years and that you were alive and well, she wept for joy. Although a chilly day, she opened the window to better read it, but when she came to that part of your letter about the attack, she fainted into Father's arms. He gently laid Mother down in the parlor until we could safely take her upstairs to bed. A few hours later, I read only the more cheerful portions of your letter to her. Hearing about your dear little Mary and Baby Alsie…and, oh, all those boys revived her considerably, but she fell asleep again. It was three days before she was rested and strong enough to come downstairs. Mother asked that I write this letter to you from all of us since she is so emotional her hand shakes when she tries to reply.

She said you were the striking likeness of her sister the day you married Dirck and never stopped believing you were alive. We planted yellow tulips, your favorite color, between your

233

parents' graves in memory of you, but as the years went by, it became such a strain that of necessity, Father urged her to accept the finality of our loss. Yesterday, the entire family went to their gravesite where Mother told your parents about your new life and their many grandchildren in a far distant land. The boys named your sons, and we girls named your daughters. Then we each lifted some of the bulbs that should arrive with this letter. Mother had a surprise pregnancy she did not expect at her age, and we too now have a little Mary!

My brothers are no longer boys. Wilm wants to be a merchant like Father, and they go to the Bourse together on business since he is now a young man. Christiaan plans to be a professor of medicine at the Leyden University like our uncle and is well into his studies. He is fascinated about your wilden healer's knowledge of wild herbs. My little sisters are not so little anymore except for baby Mary so we still sing the little ditty you ended our story time in Dutch and English every night:

Trip a trop a troenje
De varken en de boenjen,
De koejen en de klaver,
De paardje en de haver,
De kalfje en de langen gras,
De eenjen en de vater-plas;
So groet myn klynen pappetje vas.

Up and down on a little throne;
The pigs are in the beans,
The cows are in the clover,
The colts are in the stable,

The calf is in the long grass,
The ducks are in the pond;
So big my little baby was.

Please write and tell us about all the animals
where you live like the beaver with all the fur and
big floppy tail. Have you seen one? We can make
up new lines.

Mother thought your marriage to Dirck and
securing passage on a ship to Nieuw Nederland
was improbable, impossible, but that did happen. When the news of the shipwreck arrived
and others then said your survival was impossible, she trusted you were alive because your
father believed so firmly in what was best for
his only daughter that it had to be so "in God's
good time," even if a very long time. The dream
revealed to him alone turned out to be true, and
our family is together again although far apart.
Mother was finally able to read the rest of your
letter because you are alive, and you are well with
lots of children. Uncle James and Aunt Mary
then live on too. She is finally at peace.

Father made a remarkable statement at dinner. He said that he must always weigh many
considerations before granting approval to all
trading arrangements, rationally and with a clear
head. Knowing that lives are always at stake with
possible loss of ship and merchandise as you
found out the hard way is a serious matter and
always financial risk for the sake of future profit.
Your father, he said, had a different kind of truth
that guided many of his decisions. Like you said
they were both right, but Uncle James, who
Father always highly regarded, knew and lived a
reality far more profound. The important thing,

Father explained, is to know which one to trust in our lives according to what is required of us in each moment of decision. We do not know the future, but there are knowable facts and deep understanding that comes from within. The wisest person examines and values both.

There is much distrust of Cromwell since the regicide of King Charles, whom most Hollanders now consider a Christlike martyr, and many Royalists came here to live. Trade has already been severely disrupted by England's Navigation Act. The Dutch deem it a betrayal of our longtime relationship with the English and free trade grounded in international law since the time of Rome and further refined and established by our Hugo Grotius. We have already lost many ships, and fears are great that we will soon be at war. Father tries to hide his anxiety, but we all know time-honored trade between our two countries on the high seas and along shore is already compromised. Father says I must get the bulbs and letter off to you right away as the threat is now most grave. Alas, my letter may not even reach you.

You will always be the beautiful bride we will never forget. We love you, we love you!

> Your devoted sister, cous-
> ins, yes, but sisters always,
> Sara Lysbet

CHAPTER 32

Maritime Mayhem

One at a time the five men—Lieutenant Nicholas Stillwell, Gravesend Clerk John Tilton, Richard Stout, William Bowne, and Thomas Spicer arrived at the home of Lady Moody in response to her request the previous day. Living with his mother, Sir Henry was already present.

"Good morning, gentlemen. You are probably wondering why I called you here and asked that you not mention my invitation. There are other capable men, but I prefer a small group whose integrity and opinions I've come to respect. John will not record our conversation since this is neither a town meeting nor intended to be official in any way.

"It goes without saying that the recently proclaimed English Navigation Act radically changes the presumed good will but never perfect relationship between England and the United Provinces. As you know, Cromwell supported an unsuccessful diplomatic attempt to form an alliance between his Commonwealth and the High Mightinesses Staten Generaal. It was no surprise to any of us that the Dutch did not trust their intention and rejected the proposal. Not soon after that, news of the Navigation Act spread quickly to all the Atlantic shore colonies. Although countries were not specifically stated, we all know it was aimed at the Dutch as do they. What we have here is very serious potential for a trade war that will ultimately affect all of us. William, will you review key specifics so we are all exactly clear what the act demands and its potential for conflict?"

"Certainly, meladie. The news is very recent. The Act limits trade from anywhere in the world with all English colonies in America, and that means from Plymouth south to the West Indies unless all goods arrive at their ports in English bottoms. Dutch commerce and economy has relied heavily on their carrying trade of salt, fish, and fish oil, Baltic grain and lumber, and other trade goods which would be severely affected.

"Trade with Holland and Atlantic intercolonial trade has been our lifeblood with an especially lucrative connection between the West Indies, Nieuw Amsterdam, and Virginia that was much expanded during the Civil Wars. We have established legal and financial reciprocity, and many family networks are spread throughout all the colonies, regardless of religion and nationality. Even inland and river trade with wilden peoples could be disrupted. Our homeland explicitly forbids such trade with Virginia and Barbados, both of those having remained loyal to Charles I. Their very solid trade with Holland and Mannahatta is too valuable to lose. Maryland too has had mutually profitable trade with the Dutch for years."

"Thank you, William. Captain Stillwell, would you further elaborate on what you know about the situation in Virginia? We know that you served there after leading the defense of Gravesend during the war with the wilden."

"Your son and I privately discussed their predicament. They did remain fully loyal to the Stuart family under the leadership of Governor Berkeley and the Assembly, and they are staunch advocates of free trade between the colonies of the Atlantic world regardless of countries of origin—Dutch, English, Portuguese, and since 1648, the Spanish. We increasingly profited from each other especially when few ships arrived from England due to the war. Of course, Cromwell and Parliament are not pleased because their economy derives little profit from our trade.

"If a trade war breaks out, Virginia will pursue intercolonial relationships as they have in the past. They believe most of the conflict will be on the high seas and closer to the European Continent and England. Cromwell and Parliament are still engaged in war with the Scots, now nine years since the Battle of Edgehill. As much as they may want to bring Virginia and Barbados to heel, it is believed they do not yet have the focus, finances, manpower, and ships to wage war here. It's doubtful that from such a distance they can threaten us directly. Critical for the Dutch, the English will be able to prevent them from reaching the North Sea for life sustaining Baltic grain and lumber for ships. Unable to sail south through the English Channel to the coastline of southern Europe and the Mediterranean, the economy of the Netherlands would be decimated and indirectly have very serious implications for its Nieuw Nederland colonies.

"Thank you. Richard, please tell us what you learned a few days ago."

"My wife Penelope has family in Amsterdam, and she recently received a letter from her cousin whose father is a VOC merchant. It seems the English navy that was greatly reinforced during the Civil Wars and English privateers have already seized over one hundred Dutch ships. Merchants face grave financial risk. Apparently, her uncle is anxious that war between the two countries is imminent and very worried about future commerce for VOC and WIC sailing ships and independent Amsterdam merchants. Having grown up in the heart of the United Provinces and near the harbor of a thousand masts, she was surprised how many ships that sail the open seas and smaller coastal vessels pass through the Narrows. We want to keep it that way."

"Thank you, Richard. We have a dilemma, gentlemen. When Director General Stuyvesant's leadership was under assault by a hostile faction in Nieuw Amsterdam who sent representatives to the Staten Generaal, our magistrates quickly prepared correspondence that emphatically stated our full support for the Director and recorded by John Tilton. It was well received at the Hague and so averted a change in leadership. We have enjoyed the profound gratitude of Stuyvesant ever since. If there is war between the Dutch Provinces and our former homeland, the loyalties of everyone in Gravesend will be difficult to sort out and potential cause for much conflict. Every patentee was required to sign a loyalty oath to the West-Indische Compagnie and the High Mightinesses Staten Generaal, but I wonder where loyalties will be when war begins. Henry, would you comment on that?"

"Yes, Mother. I believe everyone in Gravesend now was already in Plymouth, Rhode Island, or Bay Colony town and a few in Mannahatta when the Civil Wars began in England. Although many, if not most of you, had relatives, friends, and business associates there during the conflict, you know something of the hard choices to be made and lived, but you and your families here escaped the up close and personal, ugly mayhem. Citizens in Gravesend, you manage your town in the manner of the English but own property, raise your families, and prosper at the largess of the States General, nor need you fear imprisonment or death for beliefs you hold dear. You have not had to choose sides but merely live out your lives in peace, but the English Civil Wars forced people to choose for King or Parliament, moderation no longer an option. It hardened once flexible positions into bloody, battle bound commitment. Should the Navigation Act lead to war, loyalties will be tested, choices made, and the open, mutually supportive community you and my mother sought here and enjoy very possibly at risk."

"What you are saying then, Sir Henry, is that we could find ourselves in a predicament where no middle way would be possible."

"Yes, Thomas, that was the way of it in England, hopefully not here."

"Meladie, what then is the purpose of our meeting and what do you wish of us?

"Thank you, William. What I seek is for calmer heads and hearts to prevail, to listen and observe, not to spy on anyone, but with good spirit strive to understand and appreciate the fears so that if differences arise, and they will, to mediate and avert intense emotions and actions that escalate to the detriment of all. Hopefully, our lives will not be seriously altered by war should it get to that and our status within the Dutch Republic remain secure.

"I am not asking any of you to do anything you are not already accustomed. The six of you were invited because you are known to be thoughtful, steady, considerate individuals, honest, fair, and wise. You are all respected in Gravesend and Nieuw Amsterdam, and so I would not tell you what to do but only to be who you already are, capable of dealing with difficult situations and relationships and especially now should the need come to pass. '*To whom much is given, much is required.*'

"Gentlemen, thank you for coming and for your patience. If anyone would like to speak to me in private, I am always available and open to your insight and suggestions."

"Meladie, we thank you for your trust and regard."

Unspoken but certainly on the minds of everyone present was the fear of storm clouds on the Atlantic horizon. The Portuguese, the Spanish and French, the Dutch and English, even the Swedes were players in world trade and empire. One could not naively ignore that the country across the Channel from the Netherlands just took a very aggressive step to become the dominant presence and power on the high seas.

CHAPTER 33

Contrarieties Arise

Things went from bad to worse. Trade Wars are like that, and the Anglo-Dutch War of 1652–54 was no exception. The bellicose energies of war bode ill for the human predicament and psyche. *Contrarieties arise. Contagion spreads,* national, societal, and personal relationships upended. What was once a good relationship between Director General Petrus Stuyvesant and the English at Gravesend was becoming a contentious "*everyman's mess.*" Essentially a loyal employee of the West-Indische Compagnie and its policies, Stuyvesant was dogmatic and authoritarian by nature, upbringing, and experience. Many Dutch citizens and especially the English throughout the colony and who knows who at Gravesend were increasingly disaffected with the way he governed. That frustration, exacerbated by the Navigation Act and the Anglo-Dutch War, prompted many to examine their loyalties and imagine that England would one day prevail over the poorly defended and less populated Nieuw Nederland colony situated by the deep harbor. Besides, England had always asserted their claim to the entire North Atlantic coast since the voyage of John Cabot despite Dutch rights of discovery and settlement east and south of the Noordt Rivier. The English would take it in a minute provided the right opportunity.

Clearly, since the meeting at her home four years earlier, Lady Moody and her confidants became increasingly wary of tension arising among their fellow patentees. She was indeed worried, even distraught, but not prepared for what came next when there was a knock at the door that early spring day in 1655.

A bit unnerved when she saw the look on their faces, her son and Lieutenant Stillwell had not arrived with good news.

"Mother, please sit down. We came as soon as we learned disturbing information at the fort."

"Lieutenant Stillwell, please tell me quickly."

"Meladie, early this morning Ensign George Baxter, Sergeant James Hubbard, and James Grover raised the English flag here on Gravesend soil and claimed all of Long Island for the Republic of England."

"What, what are you saying? How can this be the ultimate betrayal?"

Apparently, Baxter was said to have declared,

"*We, as individuals of the English nation, here present, do for divers reasons and motives, claim and assume to ourselves, as freeborn English subjects, the laws of our nation, the Republic of England, over the place as to our persons and property, in love and harmony, according to the general peace between the two states in this country. God Almighty preserve the Republic of England, the Lord Protector, and also the continuance of peace between the two countries. Amen.*"

"I'm speechless. This is treason."

"Mother, Lieutenant Stillwell and I were near the fort on other business when they were brought in by the *schout* and taken into custody. Indeed, their act is treason, and we have every reason to believe it will go badly for them, as it should."

"Their action reflects poorly on the fidelity of our town, and we will now be distrusted and closely watched. Dominie Megapolensis already rails against us for being disorderly and godless because we have no Dutch Reformed Church. Now this? These men were originally from Lynn prior to my departure. John Tilton and I knew of some criticism there toward James Hubbard and George Baxter. James Grover was younger and apprentice to Hubbard. When Director Kieft offered all three patents, we had reservations, but we lacked the required thirty-nine patentees without them, and they are very competent men."

"Clearly, meladie, Sergeant James Hubbard has provided valuable service to us—town surveys, governance, and defense—and

243

Ensign Baxter, hired for his fluent Dutch and English, was much needed for communication with English residents like ourselves and governors of Atlantic colonies. Given he was paid a salary all these years, accorded the honor and all the advantages of an original patentee at Gravesend, and in recent years had the confidential trust of Governor Stuyvesant for important matters of state and privy to every imaginable document, he of all people had reason to be loyal and honest. There were some who questioned whether Baxter best served Dutch or English interests, potentially unworthy for a man in his position of trust, during the settlement of boundaries at the Hartford Convention by the *Versche Rivier* Connecticut presumed to claim. Both men have repeatedly been nominated and elected by our town and approved as Gravesend magistrates by Kieft and Stuyvesant."

"As you so state, Lieutenant Stillwell, this is inconceivable. One wonders how long they have had these plans for rebellion all the while holding significant offices. It's unthinkable. John Tilton will be most upset but not completely surprised."

"Mother, I know this matter puts you and Gravesend in a very awkward situation with Stuyvesant who is furious, but he has always known and appreciated your full support and constancy and will so continue. I'm sure of it."

"The original patentees know how bad our plight was under Director Kieft, but those who later acquired some of the original allotments after Stuyvesant arrived cannot fully appreciate what was required of the man to restore order, security, and progress. A few of us, meladie, remember well before you and your friends arrived what it was like to have our homes attacked and destroyed by wilden in response to that man's despicable and ill-considered aggression. I named my settlement Hopton after my first wife's family. Sister to Sir Ralph Hopton, a Royalist commander and an honorable man, Sir Henry knew him well during the Civil Wars. Their family suffered much in England, and my dreams with my Dutch wife here after much work was burned to the ground. I still have other family in England loyal to the Parliamentary Cause so I look to renewed friendship between both countries for everyone's sake, but the Dutch were good to my brothers when we fled from England to Holland and then with my family here. To the best of my ability, I will always be their faithful and dutiful subject."

"I know you have so done and will continue to do, Lieutenant. You are an example of honorable ways to serve, but what happened this morning lacks integrity and reflects looking out for one's selfish interests and shifting loyalties in ways we cannot respect. These three men were accorded every opportunity on this Dutch soil ever since they arrived from Lynn over twelve years ago. Though they may not like the way matters are run in Nieuw Amsterdam now and so protested, as magistrates in Gravesend they have had much power. It's hard to fathom that they have sown seeds of malcontent that once having become invasive vines will be hard to uproot.

"Indeed, we have all noticed gradual, subtle, and not so subtle changes in behavior and personal regard that indicated this growing tension. Of course, the initial enthusiasm with which we began our own unique town with equal respect for all of its members was bound to dissipate as we went about developing farms and raising families with endless work. We had to get down to the daily business of life, but it is abundantly clear now that at least three and likely more have been inciting dissension toward the Nieuw Amsterdam government and undermining goodwill within our community for some time. I can accept that I'm not a young woman anymore and that regard for me and our once common vision would shift with time. What I cannot accept is that kind of individual who abandons the common good of community building and decency to forward their own ambitions that betray the trust placed in them. Many English found safety and prosperity in Holland, and all of us here at the invitation of the Staten Generaal of the United Provinces responded with our oaths of loyalty. Because of this reciprocity grounded in mutual respect, honor, and obligation, we have enjoyed many pleasures and privileges, no villages in Nieuw Nederland more so than Gravesend. That should mean something. That should certainly mean more than what happened here today. It is an *"unquiet perverse disposition"* that has made a *'mess'* of the unity of this once-blessed village."

CHAPTER 34

Word from Amsterdam

Amsterdam, Noordt Holland
April 2, 1655
Dear Penelope,

My dearest sister, I still can't get used to your name. You will always be Sarah Elizabeth, the two of us with matching names, cousins yet truly sisters. How I loved that.

Father says I must be brief. He just learned a ship will leave shortly for Nieuw Amsterdam. I have two marvelous pieces of good news to share with you. I'm to be married soon! His name is Maarten. The first banns will be posted this week, and so we must wait patiently for only a short time now. You met Dirck in your father's study, and I met Maarten in my father's koopminshuisen, the son of another VOC merchant who came by to discuss business. I answered the door, and my cheeks must have blushed something terribly when Maarten appeared for the first time. I took them both upstairs to see Father and tried valiantly to remain composed when he permitted me to stay. He has been teaching me skills to assist in the business. I think all the more so since Maarten and I met. Of course, Father took much time before approving the match to stress its importance, but Mother was quite pleased, so he could not avoid the inevitable. You know how your Aunt Alice is.

Briefly mentioned in my last letter, we were all stunned here by the execution of King Charles, but you can't believe what a Christian martyr he has become, practically a hallowed saint and the object of much poetry and the theater. We even saw one of the dramas. Your father would have been shocked as were we that the King is practically compared to Christ and his sacrificial death. The proliferation of adoring literature and etchings is extreme to say the least.

Father believes the Navigation Acts enforced by Cromwell and the war which so interrupted our trade that cost lives and ships only intensified the reaction in the United Provinces, especially here in Holland. It is clear the English intend to fully compete against us on the high seas and eliminate the Dutch carrying trade we have had for decades. Their most aggressive attacks were on our main trade routes through the Danish Sound into the Baltic Sea that destroyed our herring fleet and blockaded our coast. Our economy collapsed. People starved because shipments of Baltic wheat and rye were severely reduced. Fighting in the English Channel to prevent our trade with France, Spain, the Mediterranean, and the Indisches—East and West—was to the extreme as well. We at least defeated them in the Mediterranean. Clearly, they want to dominate all trade.

WIC merchants say Virginia still chafes under their homeland's navigation laws, were not supportive of the war, and persist in trading with Nieuw Nederland. For how long? Who can say? Our shared heritage of Calvin, what was thought to be a common bond with the Puritan Parliament and Oliver Cromwell, was severed. We are told that Cromwell became much distressed with such conflict between our two Protestant nations, but it was a costly catastrophe he started. King Charles may have favored his Queen's Catholicism, but the Lord Protector Cromwell, who ought to have been a true friend of our provinces, has become far more unpopular. Certainly, you and your friends must also share our anxiety about the future now.

The Anglo-Dutch War behind us and Father, deeply troubled and more frugal than usual, astonished me with a splendid idea but certain to cost many guilders. While recently in Delft, a friend introduced him to a young painter, Johannes Vermeer. He is not yet well known, especially compared to Jan Steen or Rembrandt van Rijn, the master, but Father was much taken by his portraits and commissioned him to do one of mother reading your letter again by an open window—hopefully not fainting this time. Apparently, Vermeer is a very slow, deliberate painter and working on another portrait so it will be some time before Father can take her to his studio in Delft. He mentioned that the painter had a peculiar object called a camera obscura that aided his study of light for his work. Apparently, near the time you left Amsterdam, Peter Mundy, a very curious English merchant, visited Vermeer to see how he used it. Father was fascinated.

Right now, it is our big secret shared only with me today to include in my letter to you. He wanted you to know. The finished portrait will hang by our window, an ever present reminder of the day we learned you were alive and mother of your parents' many grandchildren, of which I assume there are now still more. Somehow I think this is as much to help my father heal from the many years he thought he failed the Kent family to prevent what happened to you. He's too hard on himself because he loved your father as a brother and felt impelled to honor his wishes.

So much more to share, but Father says I must close now.

Your devoted and proud Sara Lysbet

CHAPTER 35

Nieuw Amsterdam Is No Amsterdam

It was one of those beautifully clear autumn days when the worst heat of summer was gone, the winter chill yet to come, and the breeze scarcely a whisper against the cheeks of the women approaching Lady Moody's home. They were a special group, some of whom left their Wiltshire homes with their families to brave the vast Atlantic with her in search of religious freedom and like the woman who inspired them again to leave when they were profoundly disappointed in the Massachusetts Bay Colony. From Wiltshire were Ann Wall and her husband Walter, Thomas and Suzanna Whitlock. The Walls and of course the Tiltons, like Lady Moody, lived in Lynn prior to their departure as did John Ruckman and his wife Elizabeth who had since died leaving behind a single son. William Thorne and Susanna moved from Gravesend shortly after the formal 1645 patent to live in Flushing. His wife arrived ahead of the others delighted to spend a few days alone with Deborah. The Bownes, William and Anne, who she met in Salem, soon joined the group sailing from Lynn. Thomas and Michall Spicer followed Lady Moody from Newport, Rhode Island. Richard and Elizabeth Gibbons were also original patentees of Gravesend. Of course, Penelope Stout was invited and other women unable to attend.

The men met once a month for town council meetings where their attendance was required, but for the women scattered throughout the seven thousand acres of Gravesend encumbered by the ever-demanding responsibilities of child rearing, household and garden chores, meeting with so many other women was an unusual treat. So they could enjoy plenty of time to reminisce and chat about things common among mothers, it was suggested that only nursing babies accompany them leaving older children to care for their younger siblings.

"I am so pleased that all of you would honor my invitation and honor each other by responding so enthusiastically. Opening my home to many longtime, dear friends is very special and something we've never been able to do before, isolated as we often are from each other. Please feel free to help yourselves to the many dishes provided by my servants before we get started, and they will serve whatever you wish to drink. I want you to be comfortable, and well satisfied with food you did not have to prepare, all the more to enjoy each other's company before I share why you were invited today."

There had been nothing like this before in Gravesend. The women fully enjoyed themselves. It was a happy time. The gracious, generous hostess resisted as long as was possible to interrupt their much animated, amiable conversation, but the days were getting shorter, and they would need adequate time to get home before dark. Some of the men and older sons had offered to ensure they all arrived safely home.

"It is such a joy to be together. You left troubled pasts behind to participate together in our pursuit of liberty of conscience, to freely seek our own path and relationship to God. It has not been easy. Some of us from Wiltshire sailed together, others at different times from England. Kindred spirits all, many became acquainted in Salem and Lynn, or you joined us in Gravesend for this grand experiment, an English town in a Dutch world, and I am grateful.

"Newcomers and visitors have questioned why we do not have a public church in Gravesend. From the beginning we were different from motherland and New England villages. Given our experience there, some of us valued Roger Williams who defined religious liberty, or what he called '*soul liberty*' as that space established for many faiths to exist harmoniously together. We thought we could achieve that when Gravesend was offered to us with the understanding that we not build our own public church, nor by our charter could they compel us to be subject to Dutch Reformed dominies, and we agreed to their terms. We were also told that we would not be molested in any way for beliefs we held privately in our homes. All of us knew this from the beginning, and we cherished this blessing.

"For years we understood this arrangement, but many are disgruntled now. For the last five years, there have been many grievances against the Director General and the West-Indische Compagnie and Staten Generaal which he must obey. We thought the Dutch reputation for acceptance of different religious sects more open than we here experience. Five years ago a group of Lutherans took it upon themselves to call a Lutheran minister to form their own church in Nieuw Amsterdam, given the Swedes along the South River were so permitted. They assumed that their effort would be looked upon with favor in Amsterdam because a public Lutheran Church has been there for decades. There is a Scottish and English church, a French Protestant church, even an Anabaptist church, and Jewish Synagogues according to Penelope whose family fled there from England. Her aunt married a Dutch merchant who warned, however, that Nieuw Amsterdam was no Amsterdam.

"Stuyvesant is no Roger Williams. Viewing diversity disorderly like the Puritans, he has become increasingly harsh toward those he despises especially Catholics, then the unfortunate Jews fleeing the threat of Inquisition with the Portuguese takeover of Dutch Recife in Brazil, most of all Lutherans, and now Quakers. The unusually harsh treatment of Quaker Robert Hodgson never witnessed here before was justified in Stuyvesant's mind. Supposedly it was not for the man's beliefs. Hodgson's refusal to defer to those in authority, his bold public preaching, and refusal to pay fines were all a public nuisance and breach of law and custom to the Director General. Increasingly the Dominies Megapolensis and Drisius are voicing hostility to us here but can do nothing because the High Mightinesses won't allow violation of our charter.

"The Governor and his council recently issued an ordinance and the only one that has ever been legally imposed against any religious group. Anyone who hosts a Quaker in his home is subject to a fine of fifty pounds sterling. Apparently, they got the idea from Plymouth and Connecticut. John Tilton was arrested, jailed for a short time and given a reduced fine of twelve guilders. Perhaps that he has been our clerk from the beginning and responsible citizen, the fine was more lenient. John and Mary are dear friends to us all. I also hosted a small number of Quakers here, nothing less than good old-fashioned Wiltshire hospitality. I know there are others among you who share this sentiment, and I've always believed diplomacy and good will is far better than anything else even with people who may disappoint us or with whom we disagree.

"My longtime friend Susanna Thorne, whose husband was an original patentee during those awful days of Kieft's War, was gracious to travel here from Flushing where that town's Remonstrance in response to such persecution was signed at the end of last year. Most of the signers were non-Quakers like her husband and son. Some of you have seen the Flushing Remonstrance in its entirety, but I asked her to read the last paragraph:

> *Therefore if any of these said persons come in love unto us, we cannot in conscience lay violent hands upon them, but give them free egresse and regresse unto our Town, and houses, as God shall persuade our consciences, for we are bounde by the law of God and man to doe good unto all men and evil to noe man, and this is according to the patent and charter of our Towne, given unto us in the name of the States General, which we are not willing to infringe, and violate, but shall holde to our patent and shall remaine, your humble subjects, the inhabitants of Vlishing.*

It seems to me that just as the Puritans found the influence of Roger Williams and Anne Hutchinson troubling so it seems is the response of our Director General to the Quakers. It is fearful to those in authority when others believe the presence of God is in every person and that God might speak directly to the inmost understandings of our hearts and so do not find reliance on clergy of established churches a necessity for guidance and edification. This relationship to our inner light is of more account and may emanate from women as well as men. That both may trust and speak this truth is a fearful thing to others who rely on outward authority of men and all of their trappings. Quakers seek to publish the truth that sets people free to any who will listen and cannot help but be empowered to share beyond the confines of their own homes, apparently now even in our own Gravesend village the cause for the recent civil disturbance.

"My dear friends, we need to stay strong together as we have always done in the past. It's been fifteen years since our first harvest here when Kieft's War forced us to flee to Nieuw Amersfoort. I was not young then and the years have taken their toll. My strength much diminished, I longed to embrace all of you one last time and ask that you extend my blessing to other women who could not come today and to your husbands and children. I will honor the Flushing Remonstrance here until I die, but I will also do so with all the grace, diplomacy, and good will this circumstance will allow me to effect with Director General Stuyvesant. We do believe along with Roger Williams that it is possible to live together harmoniously. Each in our own way will advance that notion one day at a time, the dream we share. This will be so when it is understood that one can fully enjoy liberty of conscience and honor one's own beliefs without imposing them on others and so deny them such liberty. We are most free when all are free.

"Thank you for listening kindly and patiently. Penelope taught me a Dutch hymn composed after their long struggle against Spanish oppression, her family's favorite hymn in Amsterdam. We sing it often here and what we can have in common with our Dutch Reformed neighbors. I'll play the tune on my harp while she sings it. Please join in as you desire."

CHAPTER 36

Healer, Dreamer, Lover, Believer

A dark, heavy veil descended over Gravesend, birds silent, waves timid at shore's edge. Lady Deborah Moody was Gravesend, the guiding spirit who willed it into being, her bold, brilliant light finally snuffed out by the endless struggle of tumultuous times in which she lived.

Sir Henry, somber but deliberate, turned to Richard and Penelope. They embraced each other enveloped by unspeakable grief. Certain that his mother's servants were about the business of preparing refreshments for other mourners who would soon arrive, he led the couple to her private place of sanctuary and cautiously closed the door.

"Richard, you and Penelope gave my mother something no one else was entrusted to provide. You gave her family again. My sister succumbed to delicate health before she was fully grown. When my father died after a brief but tragic illness, a part of Mother died too, and we would have to make many changes in the lives we were accustomed. After much discussion, it was decided that we would sell our interest in Garsdon Manor and other holdings to Sir Lawrence Washington, and I would remain in England to further manage our affairs. She would seek more religious freedom in New England than was possible at the time in England and persuade others to follow her to John Winthrop's Massachusetts Bay Colony. You know the rest of the sorry disappointment there and decision to accept Kieft's offer to begin anew at Gravesend.

"The Dutch Colony here has never been home for me the way it was for her, and I will leave for Virginia soon to serve as their liaison with Nieuw Amsterdam and Director General Stuyvesant. We found great comfort that although many esteemed my dear mother, she trusted few. Richard, many sought her counsel, but she sought yours and the gift of your confidential silence. Penelope, you were the daughter she lost long ago, and for you she was the mother you scarcely remembered…and then all those boys and darling daughters! How she loved them. Gravesend would, indeed, have been a lonely place without their company."

"Sir Henry, it was our honor and our good fortune to have been so favored by your endearing and remarkable mother. She was a great lady who earned our profound respect and to our children an angel with a harp, unequaled in these parts."

"She knew that you, Penelope, were especially eager to live near Sant Hoek and how much you looked forward when some of your Navesink friends had reason to occasionally travel here when they met with their Canarsee kinsmen and allies. Although a few others unsuccessfully sought land south of the Narrows below Staaten Eylandt, it's clear that the Dutch and Director Stuyvesant have not been in a position to see if an agreement is possible with the Navesink, but we know that all of the wilden in this region have struggled against the ravages of disease. Their population, severely diminished, will not be able to withstand the rapid migration from England and New England colonies when that time comes. Your many children when fully grown will have limited opportunities here in Gravesend for their families.

"Many have thought since the Navigation Act and Anglo-Dutch War, as did the men who raised the English flag at Gravesend, that England will eventually succeed in taking this colony. The West-Indische Compagnie never invested sufficiently to defend its claim here, and everyone knows it. The latest news since Cromwell's death is that his son Richard who succeeded him is totally incompetent. Soon Parliament will have no choice but to recall Charles II to fill the void in leadership that now threatens the stability of our homeland."

"Perhaps it's best, Sir Henry, that your Mother did not live to see the coming changes. We talked about that once, and as much as Stuyvesant is arrogant and stubborn, he worked tirelessly and did much to improve conditions. As hard as he was on most, he always respected her and treated her accordingly. The rights and privileges granted to her, a woman, may be denied with a change in colonial oversight."

"Perhaps you are right, Richard. The Tiltons will be here soon, but I must first tell you that Mother set aside some things when she was ill and made sure they were in a safe place with instructions that they be given to you during her last days. Little of her estate in Gravesend will be left after I take care of all her debts, but now I can talk of the trunk that was delivered to you one week ago, to remain locked until now. Penelope, she left you her favorite cloak and shawls and the brooch passed down from her mother. There are blankets and fabric for your growing family, some drapes, and special gifts for your daughters as well as her china."

"Sir Henry, really this is too much. Your mother's memory fills us completely. How can we thank her now? How can we thank you?"

"Penelope, you have thanked her. You captured my mother's heart completely from the moment Richard brought you here. The connection was very special and healed you both I think. Today, there is one more thing. She asked that I give you this."

"Sir Henry, my father's Bible. Where did she get it?"

"Richard recalls that it was given to Patroon David Pieterszoon de Vries when they visited the village where you were cared for by Sakima Popomora. He gave it as proof that you were with them. It most certainly saved your life. Opened wide and tightly bound across your abdomen when the ship crashed, it apparently kept the knife from cutting deeper when you were attacked, but it was so water soaked that your family names were washed away, and your blood damaged it further. All that they could make out was that it was an English Bible. De Vries gave it to Richard, and he gave it to my mother. It was then that she knew it was meant for you to eventually come here."

"I don't know what to say. My father bequeathed it to me on my wedding day after our vows. I thought it was lost at sea during the wreck. There is little I remember from that moment. Why did she keep it?

"Penelope, at first she felt the trauma might be too great as did Popomora before her, and then she resolved to learn more about your family so that their names could be recorded again."

"But, Sir Henry, I do not see them here."

"That is because she recorded them in her own Bible. Your father's Bible was too fragile and beyond repair. She remembered the story you told her of how your father repeated the family names, and you traced your little fingers over them before he read you a Bible story on his lap. Now, you and Richard can do that for your children in remembrance of their grandfather, Reverend Dr. James Kent, and your mother, Mary."

"Your mother and father's Bible should be yours, Sir Henry."

"Penelope, my father also gave me a Bible to take with me to Oxford when I left home, and I shall not be having any children. Like Richard Lovelace, the much favored court poet, I too lost my love during the Civil War and any hope of grandchildren for my mother. Our line will be gone with my last breath."

"Sir Henry, we know so little of how much you suffered, how great your loss during that terrible time. I'm sorry to hear."

"Thank you, Penelope. It was another lifetime ago. Mother wanted you and Richard to recall all your days with your father and mother and with your Lady Deborah here at Gravesend, Grandmother Deborah, if your children will so honor her."

"Oh, they will, we all will. This is the most miraculous gift beyond all imaginings, as if she returned my family of so long ago to us. Even in death, she is larger than life, the most honorable, beloved, esteemed Lady Moody."

"Richard, my mother left a letter for you and John Tilton, her most trusted confidants. You saved her in ways you never have considered, and you saved our Penelope for all of us. Your family was our family, the only family we have known so far in time and place from those happy days with our precious loved ones."

"Alas, as soon as my mother's affairs are in order, I must leave for Virginia, and I know that one day, in 'God's good time,' as you say, Penelope, you will sail across the Narrows to Sant Hoek. I believe your Navesink villagers will welcome your family and friends to your benefit and theirs but not the Dutch. Perhaps I shall return and see you again before that happens, but should that not be the case, I shall remember you both and your very lively brood with great affection as did Mother. Now we must join our other guests."

*****

How it seems that the vision is most vibrant and alive before the destination of our dream is reached. Perhaps that is the way of it. Manifestation of our most passionate aspirations do not live up to the ideal, the utopia of our imaginative soul vanishing even as we seek rainbow's end. We do catch a glimpse now and then of what the world can be and ought never cease to strive. Gravesend protected private devotion born of profound seeking and understanding, but intent and circumstance impeded the religious institutions that provide structure and guidance that help shape our conduct in community beyond home and hearth. Where both are free of coercion, liberty of conscience prevails. This is our human task, never complete but always beckoning. Reach deep inside, for it is we who are the healers, the dreamers, the lovers, believers.

Penelope's Song

PART 8

Crown Colony of Virginia, 1660–1662

They were no men of credit, bankrupts born,
Fit to be trusted with no stock but scorn.
You have more wisely credited to such,
That though they cannot pay, can value much.
I am your debtor too, but, to my shame,
Repay you nothing back but your own fame…

—Sir Henry Moody
Commendatory Poem for Philip
Massinger's *New Way to Pay Old Debts*
London, 1633

CHAPTER 37

Tell Mee Noe More...

The sale of his mother's home and land had not gone well for Sir Henry Moody. The buyer took up residence but failed to pay as promised and refused to leave without prolonged legal action, a very messy and disappointing delay. Henry was forced to lodge with Daniel Litschoe, a Nieuw Amsterdam innkeeper near the Breukelen Ferry. Determined to rejoin his former Cavalier companions in Virginia and much in need of funds from the sale for travel and living expense, he was unable to cover the charges for his stay at the inn except to leave his vast collection of more than fifty books as collateral. They reflected Sir Henry's mastery of Latin, English, and Italian, and included his father's important state papers in service of the king all long ago entrusted to friend Hugh Casswell in London for his mother.

Many Royalists and Cavaliers fled to Virginia during the Civil War or were given permission to leave England after compounding their estates to go beyond the seas and made their way during the years that immediately followed the First and Second Civil Wars, as did Colonel Francis Lovelace who sailed with Sir Henry. Unlike New England, Virginia remained loyal to King Charles during the conflict and to his namesake son after His Majesty's execution. Governor Berkeley and the General Assembly declared the first day in the reign of Charles II with the date of his father's death although in England not legal for another twelve years.

During the summer of 1659, it was already known that Oliver Cromwell's son Richard, who succeeded him, was incompetent and of necessity did indeed give up the office of Lord Protector thus restoring the power of the Commonwealth Parliament. By January 1660 when Sir Henry Moody landed in Virginia, Royalists already sensed that Charles II would soon be called to England from his last place of exile in the Netherlands. In March of 1660, intelligence confirmed the restoration of Charles II. The words *King* or *Majesty* referring to him by those titles could now be used in public proclamations and acts. In May, he landed at Dover and then onto a wildly ecstatic reception in London.

The timing of Sir Henry's arrival could not have been better, the dawn of a new era. Indeed, at last it seemed that his star was rising. Among brothers in arms, who risked everything in support of Charles I and survived, they alone without words shared uncommon sacrifice and loss. Among these Royalists and former Cavalier companions, yet on good and familiar terms with Director General Peter Stuyvesant, who could not help but positively regard a fellow battle hardened combatant, and the residents of his Dutch colony, Lady Moody's son was appointed Ambassador to Nieuw Amsterdam in 1660. He was received with full diplomatic honors. Charged to exchange ratifications of a treaty to regulate commerce between the two colonies, his credentials were signed by the Speaker of the Assembly Theodore Bland and Governor William Berkeley.

The same age as Henry, the governor also attended Oxford and like him was knighted by King Charles I. His play, *The Lost Lady* performed in 1639 for the king and queen, was indicative of their shared interest in the theater. Descended from a far more ancient aristocratic family than the Moodys, Berkeley was appointed to the King's Privy Council and then Governor of Virginia in 1641 before the onset of hostilities. In response to the governor's enduring loyalty to the Crown and refusal to enforce the Navigation Act of 1651, Cromwell's Commonwealth and Protectorate governments forced him to leave that position from 1652–1659. The Virginia Assembly, however, perceived the imminent restoration of the Stuart monarch and in March 1660 restored Berkeley to his former position as the governor.

In gratitude for their loyalty, the newly crowned king awarded the Virginia Colony a new seal, making it the fifth dominion alongside England, France, Ireland and Scotland and since called the Old Dominion. Among those King Charles II honored were Sir Henry Chicheley, a lieutenant colonel who plotted against Parliament, was captured and taken to the Tower until released in 1650 and given leave to go beyond the seas to Virginia. Thomas Whitgreave saved the young life of the later restored king at the Battle of Worchester. Anthony Langston served in Prince Maurice's regiment, and Lieutenant Colonel Guy Molesworth was said to have sustained twenty-five wounds in the service of the King. Alexander Culpeper, like the others, lost his fortune and estates in England for the cause and also permitted to leave for Virginia in 1650. The sister of the three Moryson brothers, who gave their all, was the widow of Lucius Cary, Lord Falkland, killed in battle. Most were destitute or severely reduced until the Restoration and were rewarded with large swaths of land in Virginia. Others saw their positions, titles and estates restored in England or passed to the heirs of those who lost their lives as was granted the son of the executed Lord Arthur Capell.

Another, recent to Virginia and honored posthumously, was Sir Henry Moody, likely a victim of the much feared seasonal disease. A man in his early fifties without an heir, his last days were at the home of Colonel Francis Moryson who served as Acting Governor when William Berkeley was called to England by the newly crowned king.

Courtiers such as Lady Moody's son were perhaps accounted trivial, superficial, self-indulgent by Puritan Roundheads who understood little of their devotion to Sovereign, their spiritual and artistic ideals, and each other. Spontaneous, romantic, over-the-top exuberance, elegant dress, and lavish banquets and dramatic masques for the king and queen's courtiers were certainly expressive of *carpe diem* to seize the day with its immediate pleasures and little regard for the future. Perhaps that great body of Cavalier drama, music and poetry, a genre of its own—chivalrous, metaphorical, and unique to its time—would have been otherwise had they known what the morrow would bring and when called to arms ready to serve naive as to its future horror seemingly without end.

Richard Lovelace, the gifted poet, who was much adored for his courtly grace, unaffected charisma, and uncommon handsome features committed all that he was by person and fortune for the King's sake and cause. Often restrained in prison for his courageous words and action, he tragically died a weakened and impoverished man, destitute, and alone. Colonel Francis Lovelace, who left Virginia in 1652 for the continent later returned to England to support an aborted uprising to restore Charles to the throne. He was captured and imprisoned in the Tower during the waning months before the King arrived in London and so unable to console his brother. William Lawes, the King's *Musik*, was gone longtime passing but not before he unknowingly immortalized Henry's poetic gift among his prolific works of sacred and Cavalier music.

Tell mee noe more her eyes are like
two rivall Sunns that wonder strike
for if twere soe how could it bee?
they should bee thus Ecclipst to mee...

Thus, it is we glimpse what remained of the life of Lady Deborah Moody and the son of that Grand Dame of Gravesend, Sir Henry Moody, Baronet, Ambassador, Cavalier poet and knight, who endured to the end of the great and awful conflict that consumed an entire generation of all persuasions in its terrible wreck and ruin.

Penelope's Song

PART 9

New York Harbor and Jersey Coast, 1663–1667

Whosoever commands the trade of the world commands the riches of the world and consequently the world itself.

—Sir Walter Raleigh, c. 1600

CHAPTER 38

Return to Sant Hoek

It wasn't the first time the Navesink and Raritan people who controlled Sant Hoek and Raritan Bays were approached to sell their land. Augustin Heerman, a Bohemian with the Dutch, had travelled widely from Nieuw Nederland through Maryland by canoe and inland trails and personally met with a powerful leader, Mattano. He successfully signed two deeds for a vast area of the southern shore in 1651. However, Governor Stuyvesant later revoked the deed. That same year, the Dutch issued a patent to Cornelis van Werckhoven for a large swath of land in the area that began in Sant Hoek then west and north toward the Noordt Rivier. Baron Hendrick van der Capellen signed a deed with another Navesink chief, but later it too became another disputed and failed acquisition of land motivated by speculation for personal enrichment. Dutch policy and practice hindered further progress. Aspirations of concluding any land treaty for settlement or speculation was put completely to rest during the devastating Peach Tree War of 1655 and its aftermath. From then on, official policy opposed contact with the region and its people as it had during the previous decades.

This time, December 3, 1663, a group of twenty men, mostly from Gravesend and led by John Bowne, the son of William Bowne who was Lady Moody's longtime friend from Lynn, set out one brisk morning in a sloop across the Narrows south toward the bay shore of Navesink land without permission from the Dutch. Bowne was well-connected to English sources that provided covert information about imminent English plans for the Dutch region's future. Since the imposition of the English Navigation Act, the Anglo-Dutch War, and the vast population spread of encroaching English settlement, it was increasingly apparent the United Provinces could not hold onto Nieuw Nederland indefinitely and likely sooner than later would lose it.

Ensign George Baxter, Sergeant James Hubbard, and James Grover did not reciprocate the open door to them in Mannahatta twenty years earlier in a very reasonable or considerate way. In fact, their actions eventually resulted in imprisonment on charges of treason but were released one year later upon Lady Moody and Sir Henry's intervention. Their further activities necessitated escape or exile. In 1656, Baxter and Hubbard sent Grover to England by way of Boston to take a memorial to Lord Protector Oliver Cromwell and returned in 1657 with a letter from him addressed to the English inhabitants of Long Island, including Gravesend. Their leaders wisely declined to open it. Grover then left territory controlled by the Dutch.

Contrarieties aside, they were astute men and did correctly read the approaching shift in power between the Golden Age of Dutch Empire and the rise of emerging English Empire with its determined intent to control trade. They did accurately read the frustration of their fellow Englishmen at Gravesend and Nieuw Nederland residents of diverse nationalities toward their authoritarian Director General Peter Stuyvesant. His grit, harsh efficiency, and persistence had served the colony well in the aftermath of the Kieft debacle, but it was not in him to shift to an understanding of the increasingly pervasive mindset epitomized by the Gravesend inhabitants in revolt seeking the improved rights of Englishmen and improved religious toleration since the two Civil Wars in their motherland.

On the continent of Europe, the Thirty Years War ended in 1648. There and in England, the long human journey from the Renaissance's humanism and awakening to new connections, turmoil of ever shifting Reformation; and all extended and deepened by movable type that produced a proliferation of affordable literature, newspapers and pamphlets, the ever growing trade across the globe, and battle fatigue of continuous warfare gave way to that kind of individualism that resists what was and embraces what can be. The European world was changing and with it new opportunities across social and economic classes. Stuyvesant's military model of leadership simply did not match the new spirit and reality of the age and was never well supported financially by a West-Indische Compagnie that was in slow economic decline for two decades.

Nor could the rigid director, who devoutly believed in the Dutch Reformed Church of his fatherland, end his determination to target and restrict Lutherans, Anabaptists, Quakers, and the twenty-three once well-to-do Jewish exiles whose ship of escape from the impending Inquisition in Brazil to Holland, repeatedly pirated, left them destitute on their unanticipated arrival at quayside Mannahatta. They who had served important mercantile roles in Holland and beyond its seas were in need, but the Director General had no intention of providing respite and renewal. In spite of reprimands from his homeland that he had gone too far in these relationships, Stuyvesant was seldom fully checked. After the death of Lady Moody and the departure of her son, tensions, anxiety, and repression worsened. Her good friends the Spicers and Tiltons were arrested again for having attended Quaker meetings, released with threat of banishment, and arrested once more after they attended and hosted Quakers in their homes. The Lutherans made little progress, the dominies escalated their vitriolic attacks against the Gravesend Anabaptists, and the new Jewish exiles granted only a few of the concessions with the insistence from Amsterdam. The merchants there partly had their way, economic pragmatists that they were. Enough was enough.

The restoration of Charles II to the throne in 1660 further shifted the dynamic between the Dutch and English Empires. The English at Gravesend easily grasped where this was going, and their tea leaves did not lie. As the years raced by, they looked beyond the confines of their town and farm lots. By 1663, the race was on to take possession of Navesink lands facing the Atlantic, Staaten Eylandt, and lower harbor. Gravesend men with well thought-out plans were well prepared and backed by an association of wealthy financial backers at Newport, Rhode Island, and on that December day they were in the thick of it.

Stuyvesant had sent out Captain Martin Crigier in a boat with Covert Lockermans, Jacques Cortelyou and twelve soldiers. When they reached the mouth of the Raritan River, they encountered another Dutch sloop with Jacob Couwenhoven and Peter Lawrenson who informed them that Englishmen were meeting with Navesink and Raritans upriver. Strong winds, however, prevented Dutchmen from pursuing them so they had to wait it out in the bay. When the Englishmen returned to shore, the Dutch bellowed harsh words at them, but the Gravesend leader briefly responded in denial, ignored the rebukes, and sailed toward Sant Hoek until they rested at nearby Many Mind Creek. When the Dutch reached them, angry words again ensued but without resolve. Stuyvesant was going to be furious when he received the Dutch account of the matter.

His plan was to secure a land purchase with Mattano, a powerful leader with whom they had dealings before. They managed an understanding for a yet to be agreed upon price for a large slice of Navesink land before they thought the Gravesenders could respond and assumed the deal was in their favor and soon to be consummated. What the Dutch did not realize was how much they were disliked by the Raritan and Navesink people. With support of other leaders, Mattano had tricked them when on December 20, he set a price of four thousand guilders, high to the extreme. Stuyvesant then thought to bully the bay area Algonquians with soldiers but a confrontation in the Hudson Valley required his attention and his men. Mattano's involvement had been a deliberate ploy to bide for time until the influential Navesink Popomora and his brother Mishacoing could gather other sakimas—sachems—and cross the Narrows to Gravesend, a town that had always been on good terms with the nearby Canarsee.

The Canarsee, Raritan, and Navesink were keenly aware of the contest for land between the Dutch and the English. After ugly, brutal wars with the Dutch, and appraising the reality of their own much reduced people, their leaders shrewdly decided to make the best arrangement they could with Englishmen already trusted at Gravesend before other intruders were inevitably forced on their people and land. January 25, 1664, Sakima Popomora and his brother signed the first deed for Navesink lands near Sant Hoek to John Bowne, William Goulding, James Hubbard, Samuel Spicer, Richard Stout, and John Tilton Jr. all of Gravesend. A second purchase, dated April 7, 1665, was approved by Taplawappamund, Mattamahickanick, Yawpochaminund, Kackenham, Mattanoh (Mattano), Norchon and Qurrmeck to the same men and Richard Gibbons. A third and final purchase was dated June 5, 1665, by Manavendo, Emmerdesolsee, Poppomermeen (Popomora), and Macca to the same men and the *rest of the company.*

Meanwhile in March of 1664, King Charles II made a gift of a vast stretch of Atlantic North America including Nieuw Nederland to his brother James, Duke of York. The die was cast. Richard Nicolls was a royalist who stayed at the King's side when he was a young prince and aided his daring escape from England to the continent. The newly established Duke of York assigned him command of four gunships with four hundred and fifty men. Sailing into Boston that summer, Nicolls alerted New England governors what was about to take place and sailed through Long Island Sound where his ships and men came to rest in the deep water harbor of Mannahatta and near Gravesend. September 8, Director General Peter Stuyvesant was forced to surrender without a shot fired and Nieuw Amsterdam renamed New York. Dutch village names were changed to English even as John Bowne, Richard Gibbons, James Grover, and Richard Stout were already building homes for their families at Middletown near the Navesink village of Chaquasitt and not all that far from where one of the women, Penelope Stout, years before was attacked and her life saved.

April 8, 1665, the new Royal Governor, Colonel Richard Nicholls, formally granted the Monmouth Patent for their purchase agreements with the sachems to the men already settled and their associates, twelve in all.

> *In all Territories of his Royal Highness Liberty of Conscience is allowed, provided such Liberty is not converted to Licentiousness, or the Disturbance of others in the Exercise of the Protestant Religion...*

Given under my hand and seal at Fort James in New York on Manhattan Island the 8th day of April in the seventeenth year of the reign of our sovereign Lord, Charles the Second, by the Grace of God, of England, Scotland, France and Ireland, King and defender of the faith in the year of our Lord, 1665.

By the end of 1665, the one hundred families required by the Patent to settle within three years had already arrived. Many were friends and relatives of Gravesenders, or from the Newport investors' families. Penelope's husband Richard was appointed one of the Custodians of the moneys for the three townships formed by 1667 including Middletown where they had already settled, Portland Poynt, and Shrewsbury. Before that year was over, patentees from these townships had already formed the first legislature held in New Jersey...and that spit of land that pointed its scraggly finger toward Mannahatta has since been called Sandy Hook.

Penelope's Song

PART 10

Middletown, New Jersey, 1710

We gather together to ask the Lord's blessing;
He chastens and hastens his will to make known;
The wicked oppressing now cease from distressing;
Sing praises to his name he forgets not his own.

Beside us to guide us, our God with us joining,
Ordaining, maintaining his kingdom divine;
So from the beginning the fight we were winning;
Thou, Lord, was at our side all glory be thine.

—Unknown Netherlander
and published in 1626

CHAPTER 39

Long Time Passing

Where the numerous Navesink Original People claimed the shore-line, coastal streams, and estuaries of Sandy Hook Bay well supplied with ever abundant oysters, clams and fish including spring runs of shad, trading and fishing vessels of strangers to their land from England, the Netherlands, their colonies, and Scotland took the place of Algonquian canoes and dugouts at the once pristine shore now dotted with docks. Gone forever from their beloved shore-line encampments and villages near Sandy Hook, absence of the Ancient Ones would have been inconceivable to Italian Giovanni da Verrazzano who explored the Atlantic coastline of North America in 1524 and even more so to the people who gazed in wonder at his ship. Their origin shrouded in the mysterious mist of time, inhabi-tants for millennia of the Atlantic coastal woodlands, they could not have imagined their once vast numbers would have been decimated in one horrific century.

Already into her tenth year of a new century, five years after the death of her husband Richard, Penelope Stout pondered her Navesink friends longtime passing, "How could everything have changed so much in a few decades?" The Ancient People had every-thing they needed for tools and weapons to catch and utilize plentiful wildlife—deer, rabbits, raccoons, and waterfowl—for food, clothing and decorative feathers, including clay beds for pottery. The beyond-shore soil was rich for spring planting and fall harvest of corn, beans, and squash. The fertile earth readily yielded wild plums, grapes, berries, nuts, and herbs for healing. In 1664, when she and Richard moved with a few other families to Middletown near the Chaquasitt village within Popomora's broad swath of influence and not that far from Ramesing, where he first carried her from the shelter of the buttonwood tree, they were still vibrant villages.

The aging leader, however, painfully realized the days of his people were waning. Where once his Algonquian brothers beyond the bay were many, they were now few, overcome by the endless comings and goings, goings and comings of Swannekens and English to the shores and lands of the sakima's neighbors. Wilden were trading people long before they exchanged goods with these endless visitors, but such exchanges with them for decades meant that highly contagious and deadly diseases carried by these intruders spread quickly from village to village. The skills of Popomora and other wilden metewaks were unable to prevent measles, typhus, influenza, and respiratory diseases from destroying their people, land, and way of life. Smallpox returned every five years, each time taking far too many. When it abated for fifteen years providing a much needed reprieve, it then struck with a vengeance. Few had immunity from previous epidemics especially the young and almost their entire generation all but wiped out. Most of those with vast leadership experience gained over many decades had died leaving much younger men and women to guide their people and manage their affairs in the face of overwhelming adversity within and without, difficult transitions that required shrewd insight.

Penelope recalled that by 1686, most of the surviving Munsees from much reduced Eastern villages regrouped among themselves to compensate for lost land and lost members but of necessity forced to move westward. A distant chief at Minnepenasson in the wilderness of West Jersey learned of the Stout family and requested help. The older James and younger brothers David and Jonathan responded and followed the Minisink Path and the Raritan River to his village. Jonathan, who grew up closest to Popomora when the family moved to Middletown, would spend a long time at Minnepenasson. He and David became first settlers of nearby Hopewell and Amwell followed by other descendants of Richard and Penelope. How she missed them, her large family, and their many offspring spread near and far.

Lost in such thoughts, Penelope appreciated the faint touch of the distant sea breeze, a tender murmur of remembrance. Ruach, the Spirit of God birthing life in the wind that chased the fatal storm away and hovered above the waters when the earth was formed, beckoned to her. Recalling her father's words the day before her wedding to Dirck, indeed, it infused the soul of her being. The gray haired Lutheran her father talked about in Old Amsterdam was right. *"God is smaller than anything small, bigger than anything big, shorter than anything broad, slimmer than anything slim...everywhere present within and without."* Except for the Quakers, the Dutch and English didn't talk that way, but her Navesink metewak and his people lived it every day, and Penelope Stout yearned to embrace them one more time. She asked her great grandson, Johnny, to come to her aid and help her mount his horse that they might catch a better glimpse of the water at the bay shore's edge one more time.

"Johnny, I need your help. They are calling to me, and I need to go down to the Zuyder Zee to meet them."

"Grandmother Penelope, what are you talking about? There is no Zuyder Zee here, only the Raritan and Sandy Hook Bays, and who is calling you? I don't hear anyone."

"Johnny, please help me get up on your horse. You know I can't do it alone anymore. We have to go now and can just take the old Navesink trail to the Atlantic Highlands, not even all the way but just far enough to see the water. I hear them calling. We must not tarry."

"Oh, Grandmother, I will do what you say because you asked for my help, but I am worried for you and fear what father will say if you get hurt. You know what he thinks of even our outings closer to home."

"Now, Johnny, haven't we always talked about trusting that still small voice inside each one of us? This is one of those times. We must go now, and I need you to trust that we will both be fine. Reach inside the pocket of my skirt and feel the scars from when my first husband and I were attacked during Kieft's War. I want you to see the scars on my arm too. Didn't I survive with the help of others and live a long life?"

"Yes, Grandmother."

"Well, that's exactly what I need now, your help. We both will survive a mere horse ride until we can at least get through the clearing as I have done for years. Now, Johnny, don't be shy, feel the ridge right here where the scars are worst, and I'm going to take off my head covering. Do not be afraid or embarrassed for me because you must know that there will be dark, scary times in your life, but for certain you will get through them. You may need the help of others as I once did from my Navesink father when he took tender care of me and healed my terrible wounds, or you may need to provide help to others just as I need your help now. Nothing is ever as bad as we think it is at the moment, Johnny, and even the worst can be for good. My father believed that, and I want you to believe that too. That is what believers do. That is what dreamers and those who love others do, and what is good to do. It is what makes the toughest times good. It is what matters. Do you understand that?"

"Yes, Grandmother."

"It's all about relationships. None of us is an island. We are all a part of the maine. See every person you meet, no matter who they are, with innocent eyes and know that we all want to discover the purpose of our lives, my father said. We all want our children to be well and grow up and have children of their own. People want to be free to find their own way in life. The metewak taught that we must feel that love for all the creatures of our world and treat them with respect and gratitude. I love you, Johnny. Will you remember this and do it?"

"Yes, Grandmother Penelope, I promise."

"Okay, then, get me up on this ol' horse, and let's get moving while the weather is fine. Today, I feel exquisitely alive. I will soon be going home."

"My," Johnny mused to himself, "Grandmother is very wise, but she is very old and saying and doing some strange things today, but I will remember because she loves me, and I love her. There is no one else quite like her. If she says so, it must be so, but this is very peculiar."

"You know, Johnny, I've had a very long and good life, indeed, an amazing life and the many children my parents who had only one child could not imagine. Just think of it, ten children, and so many grandchildren and even great and great-great grandchildren that I lost count long ago."

"My mother had to stuff a whole stack of extra pages in our family Bible. Grandpa insisted she keep a record. Just think of it, Great Grandmother, you and Great Grandpa Stout have almost five hundred descendants, and Mother said there are more on the way. Gosh, almost everyone in Middletown and Hopewell are related to us Stouts. It's really quite a miracle, don't you think?"

"Yes, Johnny. My Aunt Alice thought my coming to this part of the world was so improbable even impossible, but that is what a miracle is. The very most improbable something you don't think could possibly happen does and even a blessing beyond one's wildest imagination. You may be one in five hundred, but I love you as much as if you were my only great grandchild, my only grandchild, my only child. You have your whole life ahead with surprises that today may seem impossible, but they will happen. Believe it. Believe in the wonder of it all."

"Oh, Grandmother, if you say so, I will believe!"

"Johnny, I hear their voices. We must hurry. They are calling to me. I see Father. He is wearing the cloak Mother made for him. I was so little when Mother died, but that must be her. She is so beautiful just like her sister. Father has his arm around her, and she is chatting with Aunt Alice and Uncle Willem. That handsome man beside my cousin Sara Lysbet must be Maarten. Oh, I must tell Dirck that the English families at Gravesend would have been so thrilled for him to tutor their children. The one the Dutch sent to Nieuw Amsterdam was terrible, and we English managed our children's education on our own. Dirck, we did have a baby, a little boy I named James just like you asked. You can't believe that he is a strong, grown man with children and grandchildren of his own, and there is my wonderful Richard and the Navesink chief who saved my life and the remarkable Lady Moody with her son Sir Henry. You know, Johnny, he was once a courtier and Cavalier in the Life Guard of King Charles I."

"Grandmother, that must have been a long time ago."

"It was, but I see them out there now, Johnny, just beyond the shore of the Zuyder Zee. I know they are calling for me to come, but I don't know the way, and I hear them singing the old Dutch hymn I taught you. Can you hear it?"

"Grandmother, let's go home before you get too tired. It will take us longer to get back. Drink some of the water I brought, and I'll help you get back on the horse."

"You're right, Johnny, I don't want your parents to worry, and I can't see my loved ones from long ago anymore, but I did hear them calling to me and singing. Did you see them? We must find more time together very soon so I can tell you about all of them because they are waiting for me. Did you see my dear, dear English father, the Reverend Dr. James Kent, and my Navesink father, the wisest men I ever knew?"

Johnny struggled to find the right words. Grandmother was talking crazy. "Grandmother, I think only you were meant to see them. They wanted to talk to you. They must have missed you very much."

"You know, Johnny, my Aunt Alice and Father always said that except for my mother dying so young our lives in Amsterdam just kept getting better and better. From my very first moments in this strange, new world, I learned early what it was like to lose everyone I once loved and who loved me, to lose everything I once owned and treasured, and even my own well-being. I was helpless and fearfully alone. So many times, there was disappointment, pain, and tragedy, but my life and our lives here did get better and better. Alas, too many others lost their all, the Ancient Ones who were born, lived, and died in this beautiful land. We must remember them because we who came from other lands possess what they once earnestly believed was given to them by their Creator, for them to use and responsibly take care. That obligation gave purpose to their lives and what mattered most to their conscience, what they believed to be most true. It grieved them profoundly when that liberty was taken from them long time passing.

"Let's go home, Johnny, let's go home. I love you."

ACKNOWLEDGMENTS

The serendipitous discovery of Covenant Books in Murrells Inlet, South Carolina, led to a delightful journey through the realm of book publishing. I was fortunate. Kasha Voret, Vice President of Acquisitions, was professional and personable from the very beginning. Clearly, my first book would be in good hands. My publication assistant, Tina Collins, was always prompt and patient providing clarity to the publication process and deftly facilitating my concerns and changes with those of the editors. The entire team at Covenant Books was just amazing from first contact to my finished market ready novel, and I am very grateful.

Since 1974, Dr. Charles Gehring, whose doctorate was seventeenth-century Dutch, has translated thousands of pages related to the colonization of Nieuw Nederland. Director of *The New Netherland Project*, he pursued this task with unrivaled dedication at the New York Public Library where he brought to light a vibrant and more accurate history of a poorly understood, previously underrepresented, and short but consequential era in our colonial history. His work is the foundation for a treasure trove of recent books and vast repository of digital resources, many of which provided valuable insight for the development of *Penelope's Song*.

My father, Les Jones, provided family history records that introduced me to Penelope Stout while my husband Donald, ever beside me, supported my research and writing until his death in 2017. I vividly remember the night long ago when we first chatted about the Tulip Bubble, and each of us searched the Web for fields and fields of tulips. Entranced by their extraordinary beauty, we went at it for hours. Our friendship that led to marriage began while corresponding when he traveled in Europe. We both loved Dutch art and given the story line and our own letters to each other, Vermeer's *Girl Reading a Letter by a Window* was an obvious choice for my husband's cover design. How I miss his loving presence.

With the loss of their father, our daughters Genevieve and Fabienne, the lights of our lives, managed almost everything and facilitated my move to Georgia reuniting the three of us and their families. They provided a lovely new cottage home with writer's sanctuary for all my books and research to resume crafting *Penelope's Song*. Their facility and familiarity with the digital world we now inhabit was invaluable.

My sister and avid reader Jeanie Johnson, Shirley DeMars Ericson, and Victoria DeMars Moseid; friends Carole Derrick, Jane Fellman, and Elaine Paletz; and Cal Lutheran University classmates David and Janet Andersen, Joanne Cornelius, Linda Gunn, and Marty Schwalm called, texted, emailed, and sent cards relentlessly prodding me to finish *Penelope's Song*. They revived the muse within that was silent for months, and I credit them and daughters Genevieve and Fabienne that we reached the finish line together.

Early on, Susan Murphy, manuscript and archive specialist, provided hands on research of archival documents at the Brooklyn Historical Society Library. Librarian and Doctoral Candidate Yvonne Wilber, Head of Undergraduate Instruction and Outreach at California Lutheran University Pearson Library, provided valuable material for my search of the illusive Sir Henry Moody. Jenny R. Baez-Rojas, Administrative Assistant at the Center for Adventist Research sent me all the installments: "The World of Deborah Moody," from *Liberty: A Magazine of Religious Freedom* authored by Victor Cooper who resided in Berkshire, England. Monica Gormley, of AAA Middletown Travel Center and life time local resident, helped with the lay of the land from Middletown to Sandy Hook shore. Cathy Medeiros, *Words on the Go, Etc.* and Scott Hammond, *Drive Rescue*, in Southern California, ensured that my digital files were secure during the move to Georgia and provided other technical advice. Scott generously provided the Dell laptop that became my go to computer. All were gracious, eager to help, and professional.

Long time passing was Dr. Herbert Ravetch, an English professor I met during my freshman year and by far the most unforgettable educator. He grounded me in a love for a liberal education that bridged disciplines, cultures, and our respective faith traditions to ponder the deeper meaning of our lives. He knew we were all part of the *maine*, none of us an island, and so related to all of his students. I was grateful to be one of them and years later honored to speak at the retirement banquet celebrating his presidency at the local college where we first met.

Through the dreams and stories of who we seek to be, Rabbi Ted Falcon PhD, awakens us to these divine lifelines that God extends to all and intended for profound purpose and good. Since 9/11, he and his companions, the *Interfaith Faith Amigos*, have guided others to find common ground through love, compassion, and peace, from which this novel drew inspiration.

My approach to *Penelope's Song* was also much influenced by the Graduate Humanities Program at California State University, Northridge, with special appreciation to Professor Ronald A. Davidson, PhD. He introduced me to the field of cultural geography that informed the relationship of my characters and their times to the water world of the Atlantic Ocean and its shores. The power point lectures of Dr. Abel Franco, Associate Professor of Philosophy, left indelible impressions of seventeenth century arts, literature, science, philosophy, and theology worthy of inclusion in this novel.

Author's Notes

Place and personal names in historical documents and contemporary narratives were subject to multiple transliterations of Dutch, English and Algonquian words from several dialects. Even what we call Manhattan today had numerous pronunciations and spellings before and during Dutch control and changed again under the English. In so far as reasonable, I utilized spellings reflective of the times and the people, for example, *Leyden* instead of contemporary *Leiden*. To call the *Noordt Rivier* the *Hudson* prior to the English takeover in 1664 does not do justice to the Dutch origins of the area but may risk confusion to the modern reader. An exception was English *Gravesend* rather than Dutch *'s-Gravensande*. Under Dutch jurisdiction, it was granted exclusively to Lady Moody and other English patentees. Town meetings and records were recorded in English. Gravesend characters in the book interchangeably use English and Dutch identifiers. Also contributing to the multiplicity of spellings is that capitalization and spelling were not yet standardized during the seventeenth century.

Every effort was made to accurately place well-known historical figures and lesser known individuals by time and location. However, *Penelope's Song* is a work of fiction. Story line, dialogue, action, and character development was substantially derived from the imagination of the author although generally in the context of known historical events. Quotations in italics, however, were the actual words of persons recorded in reliable, public domain documents. The following are totally fictional:

The Reverend Dr. James Kent family including Sarah Elizabeth are imaginary, but Penelope Stout truly lived. She was my ancestral grandmother, and her legend was the original inspiration for this novel. Well-known in New Jersey with its many versions, it is easily accessed on the Internet although my discovery began with our personal family histories and now public domain local history editions before they were digitized. Generations of Stout family researchers have failed to locate any records in Amsterdam or elsewhere in Holland—marriage, ship manifests, or otherwise—that identify the actual names of either Penelope's father, previously thought to be a minister, or that of her supposed first husband both presumed to have lived in Amsterdam. Fictional Kent family names, were based on naming patterns of the Stout children. Although possible, there is no proof that she migrated from Amsterdam to the Dutch colony of Nieuw Nederland, hence repeated allusion to *improbable* and *impossible* given existing laws. However, I relied on Amsterdam as a starting point because it was indeed the European mother city of what is now New York and often neglected in our teaching of colonial America with its emphasis on English origins.

A Peneloppey Prince, with no hint of how she came to be there, appears in a 1648 Gravesend court case five years after her story begins in *Penelope's Song*. Absent evidence that Richard Stout was previously married, it is traditionally assumed that together they had ten children, more likely after 1648 than 1643, who grew to adulthood and that Mary may have been one of the oldest.

Aunt Alice and the Willem Pauw family are imaginary.

Dr. Robert Blake and his wives are imaginary.

Philippe Rapalie is fictitious, but Joris Rapalie and Catalina Trico, who married at a young age prior to their voyage with other actual original Walloon settlers, were the very first colonists and for the Dutch equivalent in importance to passengers of *The Mayflower*.

Hugh Casswell, his family, and narrative related to him is fictional.

Special notes below relate to real individuals or items worthy of further mention.

Sir Henry Moody, Baronet, was the only son of Lady Deborah Dunch Moody. He was inadequately and inaccurately represented for more than 350 years in the few references to him in histories of Massachusetts and New York, yet he turned out to be the most fascinating of all the characters. There is no record of any adult transactions for him when his mother arrived in Massachusetts about 1639–1640, so Henry was sometimes described as her young son, but he would have been about thirty-three. In 1643, and again in 1645, he is listed as a patentee of Gravesend, the second after his mother, suggesting he lived there and so assumed by local historians and others, but that turns out to be unsupported. Under Roman-influenced Dutch law, women had considerable legal and financial rights, and Lady Deborah Moody may have been accorded power of attorney for her overseas son or as founder permitted to include him. There are no other citations in Gravesend town records or elsewhere that he was in colonial North America prior to late 1650.

At least two early historical documents, however, state he was a courtier of King Charles I and "*suffered severely*" due to the English Civil Wars. Curious about that statement, I uncovered several very short but significant "Sir Henry Moody" sightings in England prior to 1650. Taken together they revealed a vastly more developed figure than had credited him prior to that year. Single sentence entries or a few sentences are most frequent. Nonetheless, such references are very notable and confirm that he was more engaged with life in London, courtiers and Cavaliers, and the events that changed all their lives during the English Civil Wars. Sir Henry's part in the escape of Lord Capell from prison to rescue King Charles was based on George Hatton Comb's book, *For King and Kent*, later published in 1882 by London's Remington & Co. It was discovery of this previously undisclosed information to colonial historians on this side of the pond that impacted and reframed the trajectory of *Penelope's Song* and so intertwined the parallel wars of England, its colonies, and the Dutch world.

Sir Henry's commendatory poems during the 1630s appear in their entirety in several historical and contemporary literary works. His "Beauty in Eclipsia," set to music by William Lawes and found elsewhere, came to life again three hundred and fifty years later when the words, "*Of Ruine or Some Blazing Starre*," were taken from that poem for David Tibet's 1993 album title in England.

It was not until May of 1650 that Sir Henry was allowed to "*Go beyond the seas to Gravesend where his mother lives*." He is not listed as a resident of Gravesend in an early 1650 survey before his arrival. Events in the decade that follows in Nieuw Nederland does establish his presence there. Recorded visits to New England included the sale of his mother's Massachusetts homes in Salem and Lynn. A request to Sir Henry in 1652 to determine if a Thomas Adams in Stamford, Connecticut, was the exiled Charles II suggest that some colonists were aware of his familiarity with the deposed royal family. Although similar in appearance, Moody verified that Adams was not a son of King Charles I. Sir Henry's royal papers and large collection of books in Latin, English, and Italian were documented by a notary in Mannahatta. Official Virginia Colony documents placed Lady Moody's son there and in Virginia after her death and during 1660–62, as do Nieuw Amsterdam records.

David Pieterszoon de Vries left extensive journals of his travels around the world. After his settlement at Staaten Eylandt was destroyed during the first phase of Kieft's War, he stayed frequently at the fort when Lady Moody and some of her friends arrived in spring of 1643. The narrative of his visit to Gravesend and Sant Hoek in the chapter, "The Summons," is imaginary.

Popomora was an actual and influential sakima (chief) of the Sant Hoek Navesink, one of those who signed the Monmouth purchase of which Richard Stout was a patentee. Various versions of his name appear on about sixteen separate treaty documents during the time of *Penelope's Song*. However, the name of the metewak (healer) who saved Penelope's life is uncertain, possibly because it was forbidden to speak an Algonquian's name after death. Penelope may have respected that custom out of regard and gratitude. Sadly, the true identity of the extraordinary man who saved my ancestral grandmother's life is lost in the sands of time, but because of him this descendant and hundreds of thousands are alive today to tell the story!

In the final chapter, Johnny was indeed a descendant of Richard and Penelope, and the account of her showing him the scars to prove she was mangled during an attack is also family history. When Penelope is very old, the narrative that she sees and hears family members and the old Dutch hymn by the Zuyder Zee is fictional. The literary device was derived from Lewy body dementia that includes symptoms of visual and auditory hallucinations.

Many more Gravesenders and others from Rhode Island investors followed the first five families to the area of the Monmouth Patent becoming prominent families in New Jersey for generations. More than half were Baptists and formed an unofficial Baptist church by 1668 in Richard and Penelope's home, possibly the first in New Jersey.

Colonel Francis Lovelace was appointed Governor of New York by King Charles II in 1668.

Poet Anne Bradstreet's husband Simon became Governor of Massachusetts in 1679.

The Rivington Free Grammar School founded by Lady Moody's maternal grandfather, Bishop Pilkington, exists to this very day.

The *Swol* did sail from Amsterdam for the West Indies in Spring of 1643 and later appeared in Nieuw Amsterdam after it was purchased by Peter Stuyvesant who later sold it.

The Great White Stag or deer is a motif in many legends, particularly in European and Celtic mythology but also found in some North American tribes. As portrayed, the narrative of the great white stag, a literary device, is solely from the author's imagination derived from the presence of a deer in some Penelope legends.

Among the twenty-three Jewish refugees who arrived in the pirated ship, the St. Charles, in 1654, there were enough men to form a minyan, the beginning of the first synagogue in North America, Congregation Shearith Israel and still thriving today. Fifteen other ships from Recife made it safely to other destinations.

About the Author

Carol DeMars graduated from California Lutheran University in Thousand Oaks. A sociology major interested in social change, she also studied the Bible, European church history, and the growth of American churches during colonial and pioneer periods. She earned a teaching credential at California State University, Northridge, and taught English and United States history for several years. Then choosing to pursue research as an independent scholar, she returned to CSUN for further graduate studies and qualified for membership in *Phi Kappa Phi,* the prestigious national scholastic honor society. *Penelope's Song: A Seventeenth Century Tale for a Twenty-First Century World* is her first book. Carol now resides in Georgia.

CPSIA information can be obtained
at www.ICGtesting.com
Printed in the USA
LVHW111325081119
636778LV00001B/15/P